MAMA'S GIRLS

MAMA'S GIRLS

Janette McCarthy Louard

sepia

★BET

BOOKS

BET Publications, LLC

SEPIA BOOKS are published by

BET Publications, LLC
c/o BET BOOKS
One BET Plaza
1900 W Place NE
Washington, DC 20018-1211

ISBN: 0-7394-2805-5

Printed in the United States of America

All honor and glory be to God, from whom all blessings flow.

This novel is dedicated to:

My husband and best friend, Ken, for his steadfast support and unwavering belief that my long-held dream of becoming a writer would one day be realized. Thank you for teaching me to appreciate the importance of taking chances, the excitement of new beginnings, and for showing me, yet again, that true love is not just for books, but for real life. "You're all I need to get by. . . ."

My amazing parents, Voldie and Brenda, for their love, guidance, sacrifice, and encouragement, and for always providing me with the safety net that is called family. I knew that with you both there to support me, I would never fall!

My beloved son Jamaal. Words cannot adequately express how much joy and laughter you have brought into my life. I love you, my darling, and whatever you do in life, wherever you go, always know that your mother's love goes with you!

ACKNOWLEDGMENTS

There are many people whose kindness and support have helped me in this journey, and while I am not able to list you all, I do thank you from all that is within my heart. My heartfelt appreciation goes out to: Mark and Paul, for being there through want and plenty—thank you for loving your sister; my newfound angels—Barbara, Khadijah, Michelle, Micah, Olivia, and Michael; my sister friends—Vonda, Charmaine, Angie, Dianne, Guilene, Stephanie, Charleen, Lessie, Robyn, Latisha, Linda, and Kathi, who encouraged and supported me through some tough times—I know that your prayers and advice guided my footsteps in this process; my brother friend, Marlon, who showed me that true friendship is not gender specific; Reverend Mother Ruth, who saw potential in me and refused to accept anything other than my best effort; Sister Penelope Mary, who hid all the new books in the library until I had a chance to read them; my high school writing teacher, Madeleine L'Engle, who kept saying "one day you'll write a novel"; my fourth grade teacher, Ellen Kronowitz, who always encouraged me to dream; my Louard family—Agnes, Rita, and Diane— thank you for taking me into the fold; my fabulous agent, Denise Stinson—I am blessed to have you as an agent, and I thank you for everything that you have done and continue to do; my wonderful editor, Glenda Howard—thank you for all your encouragement and for believing in my work; Shirley Hailstock, for her endless patience and good advice; Bebe Moore Campbell, for her advice and inspiration; and the original Mama Laurel, my grandmother Mary Louise Coore—I love you, Loudear, and even though I miss you, I know that you are one of God's angels, protecting me and guiding me with your love!

Prologue

February, 1975

Olivia Darling stood apart from the small group of mourners at the gravesite. Snow fell from a gray sky and blanketed the cemetery with thick, white powder. Olivia was as oblivious to the snow as she was to the cold air that stung her face. Instead, she stared at the two brown coffins in front of her. Her parents were going to be buried together. Didn't these people know that her mother was afraid of the dark? It had been a family joke. Her mother had always slept with at least one lamp light on, and the few times Daddy was away from home, her mother had kept every light in the house blazing bright. At least this time Daddy would be there to protect Mama from the dark, but knowing Mama, she would still be afraid.

"Don't put my mama in that dark hole," she'd told her grand-mothers. "She's afraid of the dark." *Hush, baby, hush.* "My mama's afraid of the dark," she told them, even as they ignored her words. Her grandmothers wanted to comfort her, but Olivia knew that their own grief was too strong for that. Like the rest of the family, her grandmothers were trying to cope with their own pain. They didn't have the strength, despite their inclination, to deal with anyone else's grief.

Just beyond the grave Olivia could see her sisters, Brynne and Camille. Flanked by their grandmothers, her sisters stood beside each other. Brynne was crying, but Camille stood erect, her eyes dry and clear, her right hand balled into a fist. There was not many years' difference in the ages of Olivia and her sisters. Brynne, the oldest sister, was thirteen, Camille was twelve, and Olivia was ten.

Somebody, a distant relative or perhaps someone from the congregation of her grandmother's church, came and stood next to Olivia. She felt the person take her hand, but Olivia pulled it away. She did not want to touch a stranger's hand. She wanted her mother's hand. She wanted her mother's arms to envelop her as they had done so many times before. She did not want a stranger's comfort.

Olivia watched as the minister made the sign of the cross over the two coffins. The ceremony was coming to an end. Her sisters placed roses on the brown coffins. Brynne began crying louder and she was led away. Camille remained standing by the coffins, her eyes now defiant, as if she were trying to challenge death for her parents. In Camille's light brown eyes, Olivia could see her refusal to accept that their parents were gone. Camille was not ready to say good-bye, not just yet.

The gathering at the gravesite began to sing now, their voices competing with the minister's prayer. *"Amazing grace, how sweet the sound that saved a wretch like me . . ."* Her parents' coffins were lowered into the ground. *"I once was lost, but now am found . . . was blind but now I see . . ."* Olivia wanted to tell them all to be silent. What need was there for songs now? Songs that her parents could no longer hear. She watched as the funeral director and his assistant took the flowers from the tops of the coffins. Olivia felt herself moving forward now, as if some unseen hand were pushing her toward the grave. They were going to throw dirt on her parents. They were going to throw dirt on her mama.

There was somebody else sobbing close by. *Stop it!* she wanted to scream. *Stop everything. Stop!* She opened her mouth to tell them that her mother was afraid of the dark, but there were no words. Instead, she began to scream. She watched as the mourners ran in her direction. Their eyes were worried, their faces were drawn in concern. She kept screaming even as she watched the coffins descend into the earth. She kept screaming even as the hands of her relatives surrounded her. She kept screaming even as they led her away from her parents' grave. And although her voice soon grew tired, the screams in her head continued for a very long time.

One

1995
Brynne

Fifteen dollars for a pair of black stockings came close to Brynne's definition of a sin. Still, these fifteen-dollar stockings made her brown legs look very good indeed, and Brynne was certain that Malcolm Blackfoot would be most appreciative. Who would have thought that a chance meeting in a coffee shop would lead to a date? Despite the good intentions of her family and friends who had tried unsuccessfully to fix her up with every eligible bachelor that Cleveland had to offer, Brynne had steadfastly refused to date anyone. She was not ready. But six months of solo Saturday nights, and Malcolm Blackfoot's dimpled smile had convinced Brynne that it was time to rejoin the land of the romantically involved.

She was nervous. A date. She was going on a date with a man that she met, well, truth be told, picked up at a coffee shop. Inappropriate. Just not something she would ever do, and it felt great. For the past few weeks she'd seen Malcolm Blackfoot at the coffee shop. He'd look at her. She'd look at him. Polite exchange of greetings. Sly glances, and then finally wide, open smiles. He was undeniably handsome, but he was not her type. Usually she went for the thin, bookish type. The kind that wore schoolboy glasses and oxford shoes. The kind that looked like they would feel at home in the library. Like her husband. Ex-husband, she corrected herself.

She didn't go for men who looked like football players, who

smelled of spice cologne and cigars early in the morning. She didn't go for men who wore two small diamond-stud earrings. She didn't go for men who stared at her lips when she talked. She most certainly didn't go for men who wore blue jeans and black cowboy boots. But Lord help her, yesterday morning, after working up the nerve, she had walked over to where he was sitting, the same seat where he usually sat in the back of the coffee house, and introduced herself.

She felt bold, and brazen. She felt free. This was never the sort of thing that she would have done. But seven years in a marriage that went routine after three, ten years in a job that she was not sure she ever cared for, and a lifetime of doing exactly what was expected and not really getting the anticipated joy in return, had emboldened her. *What the hell,* Brynne thought. *I'm not asking him to get married. I'm just introducing myself.*

She'd had to talk to herself as she walked over from the counter to where he sat. Tell herself that it wasn't a big deal. He'd been looking at her just as much as she looked at him. *What if he's married?* she asked herself. No sign of a ring, but that didn't mean anything. *What if he's involved with someone?* No harm, no foul. She'd lived her life by the what-ifs, and she was tired. *Just introduce yourself and, if he acts like he can't be bothered, tell him you're doing a survey on the habits of coffee drinkers and then fade away.* Nothing ventured, nothing gained. Her mother used to say those words to her. *"Don't be afraid, Brynne. Nothing ventured, nothing gained."*

"Hi, my name is Brynne."

Malcolm had looked up from his newspaper. He'd been reading the comic section.

His smile had been wide, and inviting. "Malcolm Blackfoot. Have a seat, Brynne."

One hour later, she'd learned that he owned a bookstore that specialized in African-American books, was an Aries like herself, had been married twice, and yes, thank you, Lord, he was not currently involved with anyone. Toni Morrison was his favorite author, Donny Hathaway was his favorite singer, and he loved the color midnight blue. He'd asked her out on a date.

"Would tomorrow be too soon?" he asked.

So here she was, on a Saturday night, putting on fifteen-dollar stockings and hoping to squeeze herself into a size-eight black dress.

The dress fit when she was in the store, but it was now a little too tight for comfort. She still hadn't put on any makeup. It was seven forty-five, and Malcolm was due at her doorstep in fifteen minutes. Her living room and her first-floor bathroom were clean, but every other room in her condo looked as if all hell had broken loose. She'd wanted to clean up today, but she'd spent too much time running around Cleveland trying to find the right dress for tonight. Something sexy but not too overt. It was bad enough that she'd picked him up, but she didn't have to dress like a hussy. None of the simple, conservative clothes in her closet would do, thought Brynne. Those clothes belonged to the old, cautious Brynne—the Brynne who played by the rules. The new Brynne was going to wear something that showed her curves. By the time she'd found the perfect dress, the perfect shoes, new lipstick, and her fifteen-dollar stockings, it was too late to do the cleaning she'd planned. She had just enough time to straighten up her living room and bathroom—that would have to do.

The phone was ringing. Her first thought was that Malcolm was calling to cancel their date. Maybe something had come up. She felt her mouth go dry with disappointment. She'd been looking forward to this, maybe a little too much. *Don't be silly,* Brynne chided herself, *maybe he's just running late. Well, if he cancels the date, so what? Remember,* Brynne reminded herself, *you don't know this man, not really. You're not even emotionally invested. Pick up the phone, Brynne,* she muttered to herself. Where was the phone?

On the fourth ring, just before the answering machine came on, she found the cordless telephone receiver next to her pillow.

"Hello," she said, trying not to sound anxious. "Hello?" Brynne repeated the greeting.

"Hi, Brynne," the voice on the other end of the line spoke up, just as Brynne was going to hang up the telephone. It was her sister Olivia.

Oh, I don't have time for this, thought Brynne. *Not now. I don't have time to deal with Olivia's latest drama.* Olivia was the youngest sister in the family. She was, as Brynne would try to explain to folk who couldn't quite figure Olivia out, fragile. There was more than enough pain in Olivia's life to account for the sadness that seemed to cling to her, but there were times that Brynne got tired of rescuing her sister. Although she would never admit this, there were times when Brynne wished that she could run away from Olivia's troubles, just like her sister Camille did.

"Hi, baby girl," Brynne said, using her sister's nickname.

"You sound busy," Olivia said.

"Actually"—Brynne eyed the clock on the far wall—"I am kind of in the middle of something, baby girl. Let me get back to you?"

"I lost my job, Brynne."

Brynne sighed, and sat down on the bed. The timing was bad. It always was with Olivia. "I'll get you another job. Don't worry."

"I hate that you always have to save me, Brynne."

"Things are going to be different, Olivia," said Brynne, knowing that the words sounded false.

This was just another in a long line of jobs that Olivia had lost. Things always started out promising enough, but Olivia and her demons were usually too much for her employers to deal with. The last job that Brynne had found for her, as a receptionist at an architect's office, had seemed to be a little different. The architect was a friend of the family's. She knew about Olivia's problems, and still she'd tried to give Olivia a chance. But Olivia's unexplained absences, the forgetfulness, and the depression had proven to be too much. "I'm sorry, Brynne, but I'm going to have to let your sister go." How many times had she heard those words, or a variation on that particular theme?

"When, Brynne?" The voice on the other end of the line rose slightly. "When are things going to be different?"

I don't have time for this right now, thought Brynne, as she fought that small nagging voice, the one she referred to as her conscience, the voice that was telling her that her sister was fragile, and her sister needed her. *I'm not turning my back on her,* Brynne reasoned, trying to silence that voice. *I'm just postponing the inevitable. I'll talk to Olivia tomorrow. After church. We'll talk about all of this tomorrow.*

"Olivia, I really have to go, girl. I'm expecting company."

"I'm sorry," said Olivia. "I know you're busy—"

"Don't worry about it," said Brynne. "Something will work out."

She stifled a sigh. All her life, she had been the rock her sisters leaned on—the one to fix things when they were broken. She was tired of that role. She was tired of being responsible for other people's happiness—from her husband, ex-husband, to her grandmother, Mama Laurel, right on down the line to Olivia and Camille. Everyone looked to Brynne, the sensible one, to be there when times were hard. *New day,* thought Brynne, *this is a new day for me. I'm di-*

vorced. I'm free. I'm ready to start living. I'm ready to go out on a date.
Olivia's problems would be there when Brynne returned. Besides,
there had to be someone left in Cleveland that would give her sister a
job, and Brynne knew that she would find this person.

The doorbell was ringing. Malcolm was here early, and Brynne was
not ready.

"Someone's at my door, I'll have to talk with you tomorrow."

"Hey, Brynne—you're my hero, girl."

"I'm hardly anybody's hero, baby girl," Brynne replied as she
stepped into her black, patent leather pumps. "I'll talk to you tomorrow."

The doorbell rang again, and Brynne put on her new-date smile.
She was planning to have a good time tonight. Yes, indeed. New
woman. New date. New beginning. Lord knows, thought Brynne as
she opened the door and saw a handsome black man smiling at her, it
was time for a change in her life.

Olivia

Olivia sat down on her bed and stared at the termination letter the
human resources director had handed her yesterday. The words were
all too familiar. She'd seen them before. *We regret to inform you . . . effective immediately your employment with the company is hereby terminated. . . .
we wish you well in your future endeavors . . .* She'd lost track of the number of the "good-bye and good luck" letters that she'd received, as her
sister Camille called them. All her jobs ended the same—termination, let go, laid off, "good-bye and good luck," "don't call us and we
certainly won't call you."

She couldn't blame her long list of employers. They were all, to a
fault, fair and generous with her. You can't run a business with a raving lunatic in your employ. Well, Olivia reasoned, she wasn't a raving
lunatic, but she was close. She was very close. In this last job, she'd
been absent more times than she'd been present, and when she was
present, she was late, uninterested, and sometimes, felt she was losing
her grip with reality. Her paranoia came and went without warning.
Where it went, Olivia did not know. But then, it would come back and
settle in like an old friend.

Looking back, Olivia believed that she had always been a little crazy. Even when her mama was alive, Olivia knew that she had always been a little different. When other children were playing with their playmates, she was talking to trees. Olivia remembered that, apart from her family, she'd had an aversion to talking with people. It was more than an aversion. She was scared. Afraid of getting hurt. Maybe in some small way, she had known the pain that was eventually going to come her way. She'd made friends with a great old oak tree in her backyard, where she'd sit, curled up for hours, at the roots of that tree, with nothing but the tree and her imagination to keep her company. She was, as folks in her old hometown of Goshen, North Carolina, would say, "peculiar."

Peculiar had started turning to mentally unstable when she lost her parents, although she hadn't really known her daddy too well. She always thought that he'd secretly preferred her sisters' company, but he was always kind to her, even though he was distant. Her mama was her heart. Her mama understood her, even though no one else did. Brynne came close to understanding her, but Brynne wasn't Mama. When her mama died, the voices started visiting her, but they didn't come to stay until her cousin Ray had started messing with her. He was the only son of a long dead relative, whose name Olivia couldn't remember. This deceased relative had meant a lot to Mama Laurel, and she'd had a soft spot for cousin Ray, even though everyone knew that cousin Ray gambled, smoked pot, had been in and out of prison for various petty crimes, and rumor had it that he'd stolen money from his mama. Mama Laurel wouldn't hear of it. Blood sticks together, she'd declared and she'd taken cousin Ray in, although all of the other relatives turned their backs in unison when he came knocking on their doors.

He was thirty-five and she was thirteen when it started. At first, it was just long hugs in the middle of the night, and Olivia had to admit, while it was strange, he was comforting. He would hold her and chase the nightmares away. "This is our special time," he would whisper. "This is just between us." She had kept silent. Although she did not understand cousin Ray's actions, she felt warm and secure. She didn't remember how long after his first nightly visits that comfort became terror. His hugs changed into something much more. Something terrible. Something unspeakable. "Don't tell anybody," he'd whisper. "They won't believe you." "You know you want it." "Don't tell anybody." His final threat had kept her silent. "No one will believe you and if you do tell anyone, I'll do the same thing to your sisters." The thought of him hurting her sisters as much as he hurt her was unbearable. She'd remained silent for months as he raped her, sometimes nightly, sometimes weekly. Olivia didn't know how long this would have gone on if Camille hadn't caught him coming out of her room in the middle of the night.

His glib words did not provide a reasonable explanation for his actions. Ray was banned from the house and from the family, but Mama Laurel had never pressed charges. Her opinion was that Olivia had been through enough, and dragging this situation into the court system would only hurt her youngest granddaughter more. That had been her reason, but Olivia knew better. Mama Laurel didn't want the nasty little family secret to come out. It was scandalous. It was shameful. It was dirty. Mama Laurel didn't want her family to be subjected to gossip. The facade of the perfect, upwardly mobile black family had to be preserved at all costs. It didn't matter that a child got hurt in the process. Olivia had never forgiven Mama Laurel for this.

Ray died two years later in a construction accident. "What goes around, comes around," Mama Laurel had declared. "What doesn't come good in the morning, won't be good in the evening." As far as her family seemed to be concerned, Ray's death wiped the slate clean. "He got what he deserved," was Camille's opinion. Even peace-loving Brynne was firm in her belief that cousin Ray was roasting in hell somewhere. Everyone was satisfied with the outcome. Death was just retribution for rape. Olivia alone was not satisfied. She had wished Ray dead enough times and she was convinced that God had heard her. She was certain that she had somehow summoned death to Ray, and while there was a large part of her that tasted relief when she heard the news of his death, there was another part of her that felt guilt. He deserved to be punished, yes. But did he deserve to die?

Olivia had been pushed from one psychiatrist to the next, but her demons were never acknowledged by Mama Laurel. The few times that Olivia would speak about her experiences to Mama Laurel, she would gently change the subject. *"Hush now, girl. That man can't hurt you anymore. You just have to move on now, girl. Don't let your mind dwell on that. Nothing you can do about it now except move on."*

How do you move on? Olivia wanted to ask. How do you move on when you are a thirteen-year-old girl whose body and whose innocence have been abused? How do you move on when every night, you can still smell the one who violated you? How do you move on when even your sisters' touch makes your flesh grow cold and your breath stop in fear? How do you move on when every day you wonder what you have done to attract this evil into your life? How do you move on when everyone pretends that your pain, as tangible as the lamp that you keep lit every night, does not exist? How do you move on?

"Olivia, we wish you well," the human resources director, Marie, had said to her after she gave her the termination letter. "This job just wasn't the right fit. When there's a position more suitable to you . . ."

Marie had looked at her with sympathetic eyes. She was a friend of Brynne's, and Olivia knew that letting her go was hard for Marie. She probably felt that she was being disloyal to Brynne. Still, you couldn't keep an unproductive employee around for too long. Friendship only went so far. "Good luck, Olivia."

Her coworkers weren't as kind. She'd heard the sly laughter behind her back. As she'd walked back to her station, she'd heard two secretaries talking about her in the lunchroom. "What took them so long to fire that crazy nut?" "Her sister's some big-time lawyer, they probably thought she'd sue them." "Sue them for what? She can't type and she can barely answer a phone." "All these hardworking folks out here that can't find a job and they go out and hire that fruitcake." "Just goes to show you, it ain't what you know, it's who you know." "Ain't that the truth."

The words were cruel, but they were true. She was mentally unstable and the only reason she'd gotten the job was that someone owed Brynne a favor. Brynne couldn't keep saving her, as sweet as she was. No one could save her from her demons. She could get another job but what good would it do? *You can't run away from the voices, the irrational feelings,* no matter what the psychiatrists said. *You can't run away from the past. You can't run away from memories of Ray. You can't run away.* The drugs that the psychiatrists prescribed might help manage the pain, quiet the noise, but the pain was still there. Would always be there. Damaged. Peculiar. Crazy. *Mama, if you had been here, would things have been different? Would you have protected me, Mama? Would you have stood by me?*

There were no answers to these questions. The pain that had been with her, constant and unyielding, would always keep company with her. Even Brynne, the one person who had stood by her, was growing tired of her. She could see it in Brynne's eyes—hear it in her voice.

She couldn't blame Brynne. She'd been rescuing her for years now. Even superheroes got tired sometimes. There was no one to help her now. Nobody.

Downstairs, she could hear her grandmother, Mama Laurel, moving around in the kitchen, putting dishes away, cleaning up after dinner. Olivia had offered to help, but Mama Laurel had waved her away. Olivia knew that Mama Laurel felt that she would just get in the way of things. Many times she'd heard her mutter under her breath, "It's easier to do things myself." To be grown and still living in your grandmother's house was a bitter thing for Olivia. That was failure. After all these years she was still dependent upon her grandmother's goodwill—not that Mama Laurel minded, Olivia was sure. Mama Laurel liked to have somebody to rule over, and it was much easier to run folks' lives when they were in close proximity.

Sometimes she wondered what it would be like just to float away from here—go somewhere new—leave behind the pain, leave everything behind. Starting over sounded so good. *Can't be accomplished,* she thought as she covered her face with her hands.

"Mama, why did you leave me?" Olivia whispered to the empty room. "Why didn't you take me with you?"

Brynne

The restaurant was dark and smoky, illuminated by candlelight and the dim lights of strategically placed lamps. The food was delicious, Indian. There was a jazz band playing soft music. The steady murmur of chatter and laughter enveloped Brynne, and the second glass of sweet wine caused any apprehension she had about the evening to ease away. Malcolm was holding one of her hands across the table and looking at her intently. It had been a while, a long while, since anyone had looked at her like that.

"You're a beautiful woman, Brynne."

Brynne laughed at this. The candlelight at the table must have been playing tricks on this man. She looked all right—with a little powder, lip gloss, and mascara, she would do. But she was hardly beautiful. She was ten to fifteen pounds heavier than she should be, and her weight showed in her round face. She had inherited her mother's smooth brown skin, and her mother's large almond-shaped eyes—they were her best feature. But her chin, which came from her father's side of the family, was too stubborn, too pronounced. Instead of Camille's full lips, hers were thin and in general nondescript. She'd cut her thick waist-length hair after the divorce and now wore a shoulder-length bob. Mama Laurel protested, but it was much easier to manage. Her body had gotten soft with age, and her long brown legs, once a source of pride for her, had now begun to look just a little bit chunky. She was far from beautiful.

"You should see my sister Camille," said Brynne.

Folks always wondered why Brynne was never jealous of her sister's beauty. Brynne was used to her sister's beauty. It was not a big deal for her. She loved her sister and she was secretly proud of the expressions of astonishment that usually accompanied a first look at Camille. *That's my sister,* she wanted to say, *and doesn't she look good!*

"She couldn't be more beautiful than you at this moment," Malcolm said, his voice low, his hands caressing Brynne's palm.

Brynne laughed again. Oh, this felt too good. To be sweet-talked by a good-looking man. "I think you've had a little too much to drink."

"I've had one glass of wine and I know a good-looking woman when I see one."

"Let's change the subject," said Brynne. She'd always been uncomfortable with compliments.

Malcolm raised his hands in mock surrender. "Okay. What do you want to talk about?"

"Anything else."

"Fair enough," said Malcolm. "I'm curious how any man let you slip through his fingers."

Another dangerous subject. She didn't want to talk about her ex-husband Jose with Malcolm. It seemed somehow disloyal, although she wasn't sure why she felt that way. Jose was now a part of her past. This was what she wanted, needed—something different. Jose was a good man, but he was a man who believed in control. The length of her hair, the kind of clothes she wore, her weight, her friends, Jose always had comments. He never told her directly what to do, but his carefully crafted comments with their mild tone of disapproval were enough to cast the deciding vote on all of her decisions, both great and small. They were a good team, everyone's favorite couple—two people who finished each other's sentences and threw good parties. They lost each other too easily. In their second year of marriage Brynne had miscarried. They'd tried for years to have another baby but she was unable to get pregnant. Brynne was certain that Jose blamed her, even though he insisted that their marriage would withstand this pain. Looking back Brynne wondered if she'd been desperate to have a child to save their marriage, to reestablish a connection between them that had been severed. She walked out of their home one day, surprising him almost as much as she surprised herself. Jose still wanted to try, but after seven years of trying, Brynne was ready for something new, something other than the perfect, sterile marriage that she found herself in. She still loved her ex-husband. He was her first and, she was sure, her last true love, but love in their case was far from enough.

"Any man that let you walk away had to be out of his mind," Malcolm continued.

"How do you know that he let me go?" she said lightly. "Maybe he walked away from me.."

Malcolm shook his head. "I don't think so," he said. "No man is going to walk away from you, Brynne. You're special, Ms. Darling. Very special."

The words came out before she had a chance to stop them. "What's so special about me?"

"You're a good woman, Brynne."

"There are lots of good women," said Brynne, embarrassed that she'd let him glimpse her insecurities.

"True. But there are not a lot of good women that have such wide, open hearts. The way you look at the world, Brynne—the way you still want to believe the best in people."

"Most people call that being naive," said Brynne. "That's not exactly an admirable trait."

"They're just jealous, Brynne. They want what you have, and they know that they can't have it."

"What I have?"

"Absolutely." Malcolm's voice grew husky, and Brynne didn't know if the second glass of wine was playing tricks on her, but she could swear that he wanted to kiss her. "They want a pure heart. That's what you have, Brynne."

"And you know this in the short time since you met me?"

Malcolm nodded his head slowly. "I'm a good judge of character."

Have mercy, thought Brynne, as she licked her lips. *Lord, have mercy on me.*

"Would you care to dance?" Malcolm asked.

"Here?" Brynne looked around. There was no dance floor.

"Yes, Ms. Darling. Right here. I love this song."

Brynne recognized the song. Donny Hathaway's "A Song for You." It was one of her favorites.

Malcolm stood up and held out her hand and Brynne found herself standing up. He took her into his arms and together they danced slowly by the table. The other customers applauded and someone sent over a bottle of wine. It was the start, thought Brynne, as she felt herself yielding into strong arms, of a very nice evening.

Camille

Camille hated Saturday nights. They reminded her of what she didn't have. A steady relationship with someone who mattered to her, and to whom she mattered. She thought of the many Saturday nights she'd spent with Harold. Nights when he'd make excuses to his wife and they would go somewhere, somewhere where his friends, or other folks who knew him, were not bound to be. At first, all the sneaking around had been exciting. She'd never been one who thought she could be with a married man. But there was something fun, something dangerous about tasting the forbidden fruit. *This will be a temporary thing,* she had thought. She was bored, and he was fun. At the beginning, he was a lot of fun. Too much fun. Now, he was nowhere around. They were growing tired of each other. She'd wasted too many Saturday nights with him, and in the process, she was certain that she'd passed up the chance to be with available men, men who could wine and dine her out in the open on any given night.

She sat on her bed and watched television. She was watching the movie channel that showed all the old movies. She had the nerve to be watching a love story. There was a woman and a man holding each other in a tight embrace. The way they looked at each other only happened in movies, Camille was sure. That true love nonsense didn't happen in real life. It was just passion, and then the dying of passion—that was how relationships went, in Camille's opinion. If folks wanted true love, unconditional love, they were better off with a good dog. *That's the truth.*

Camille wanted a cigarette. She wanted one badly. But she had given up that habit three months ago, and loneliness, or whatever this funk could be described as, was not worth the nicotine habit that had held her tightly in its grip for the past six years. She was finally butt free, and it looked like she was Harold free too. He'd called with some excuse about not taking her out, but she knew the truth. In his own way, he loved his wife. She didn't fool herself. Harold was out for thrills, for passion. Marriage becomes mundane, or so she'd heard. Look at Brynne and her ex-husband, Jose. If anyone had ever told her that these two lovebirds would end up in divorce court, she'd have laughed and called them every kind of fool. But here it was, Brynne divorced him and another so-called solid marriage bit the dust. Harold's marriage probably wouldn't end in divorce—he didn't want to let his wife go—but he was a man who had a wandering eye, and he'd ended up with Camille.

She was tired of this. Lately, everything was making her plain-old tired. She was tired of winters in Cleveland. She was tired of her family's meddling, of her grandmother asking her when she was going to get married, of grown men who had nothing better to do than use the same lines she heard back when she was in college. She was tired of feeling tired. *To hell with this,* she thought as she used her remote control to change the channel. This romance stuff was getting on her nerves. *I wonder what's happening on CNN.*

Two

Brynne

"Can I get an *amen?*"
Pastor Simmons had been preaching at Shiloh Baptist for over forty years, and he did not believe in making things easy for his congregation. The more confused his congregation looked, the happier he was. Confusion, for Pastor Simmons, was the first step to true understanding. The way he saw it, if folks looked confused, that showed that they were thinking about his words and not just sitting there in the church pews taking up space, or worse, trying to look cute in the house of the Lord.

Brynne struggled to keep her eyes open. She was sitting in the third row of the church, in the direct line of vision of the pastor and all the deacons behind him. They would certainly see if she nodded off. Her late night with Malcolm Blackfoot was starting to take its toll. A very enjoyable evening, which started with dinner at an Indian restaurant, had turned into a very late night. The thought of that very late night and what happened with Mr. Blackfoot made Brynne blush in the house of the Lord.

Pushing all thoughts of late-night passion quickly away, Brynne tried to concentrate on the pastor's words. He was getting to the main point of the sermon, and she leaned forward, ready to receive God's word. Shiloh Baptist was starting to rock. Some folks were standing up, moving around as if the Spirit just wouldn't let them be still.

Others were starting to testify right there in their seats. Testify about just how good the Lord was. How the Lord had made a way when there was none. How the Lord had brought them back when they had gone astray. How the Lord had looked down and He had been merciful. Brynne knew that she could testify to that. It wasn't too long ago when opening her eyes in the morning took more effort than she thought was possible. The fact that she was here, sitting upright in church this Sunday morning, was testimony enough that the Lord heard the prayers of her grandmother. She was sure of it.

"Work with me, church!" The pastor's voice brought Brynne's thoughts back to the present.

Pastor Simmons pulled out a handkerchief from somewhere in the deep folds of his ruby-colored robe, and wiped his forehead. "I need to preach this morning!" he roared.

"Take your time, Pastor!" someone called out. "Preach the Holy Word!" said another. "Bless His Holy Name!" "Come on with it!" "Amen!" The voices rose in unison, urging their pastor to deliver what they came to Shiloh Baptist for, something to hold on to, something to get them through whatever lay ahead in the coming days.

Shiloh Baptist was known to most of the black community in Cleveland as Buppie Baptist. The congregation was well heeled and unashamed of their prosperity. Doctors, lawyers, judges, politicians, hair dressers, civil leaders, and others who were intimately acquainted with making money came every Sunday to catch the Spirit. Brynne often wondered about the allure of Shiloh Baptist. There were several churches with dynamic preachers in Cleveland, yet this was the place where the majority of the wealthy and the wealthy wanna-bes came to worship. Brynne suspected that Shiloh's attraction was based on the comfort one felt immediately when one recognized other members of their tribe. Generally, folks at Shiloh were too busy climbing that ladder of success to be too envious about other people's successes. If anything, the high rate of achievement found at Shiloh served as a beacon to others who were aiming to get to that particular promised land. You could always find out who was doing what to whom and what was going on in the community when you worshiped at Shiloh. And there was no better preacher, after he got warmed up and on the right track, than Pastor Simmons.

"There is," said the pastor in his slow, southern drawl, "no time like the present! Beloved, tomorrow is not guaranteed!"

Brynne leaned forward to listen to the pastor's words. He was preaching to her this Sunday morning, as sure as night follows the day. If there was one thing these past two years had taught her, it was that there were no guarantees.

"We know not the day, nor the hour!" bellowed Pastor Simmons, fanning the flaps of his ruby robe, and walking back and forth from the pulpit to the very edge of the stage. "So you ought to get your house in order, beloved!"

"Amen!" Brynne called back, swaying in rhythm with the pastor's words. "Yes, Lord!"

"You need to get your house in order, beloved! Because soon, and very soon, there will come a day of reckoning, beloved! When the Lord is going to hold you accountable, beloved! And you know, beloved, the Lord is not going to take a postdated check! I say, here me now"—Pastor Simmons's voice rose into a roar—"the Lord is not going to take a postdated check! You need, you need, you need, you need, you need, you need—"

Here the congregation, as well as the entire choir, was on its feet. The organist started playing one of Brynne's favorite songs, "We've Come this Far by Faith."

"You need, you need, you need to get your house in order, beloved!"

Brynne lifted her long brown arms to the ceiling and closed her eyes. She was far from being in the place where she wanted to be, the place where she was certain of all of her decisions, and satisfied with the life God had given her, but she was moving forward. She was taking chances and that felt good. She'd gone out on a date with someone so completely different from anyone she'd ever met. Malcolm Blackfoot was the kind of man that her family would disapprove of. He had bad credit, had already been through two divorces, and was too handsome for his own good. He wasn't impressed by Ivy League schools, where people summered, or who had just made their first million. He drove the same car for the past ten years, and upward mobility was definitely not on his agenda. Brynne's lips tugged into a smile.

They'd spent last night kissing and talking about their dreams, their past, getting to know each other. When he'd finally walked her to her front door, she felt as if they'd been friends for a while. He'd hinted at coming in, but Brynne had kissed him firmly on the cheek. It wasn't that kind of party. Not yet.

Malcolm had left her with a promise to call later on that day. Brynne had fallen asleep with a smile on her face. She knew that she wasn't like her sister Camille, who thought that not having a man in her life qualified as a national disaster. Still, it was nice to have romance again. It had been missing for so long from her marriage. She gave a little sigh. She didn't know where this was going, but for now she was just going to hold on and enjoy the ride.

Olivia

Olivia poured the bottle of pills onto the white bedspread. The brightly colored red pills looked like candy. It would not be a surprise to her family that she had reached this particular destination. She had told them all too often that there was just too much pain and confusion in living. She had tried to do this once before when she was fifteen. A cry for help was the term the psychiatrist had used. Well, her cry had apparently not been enough, not enough to stop the voices in her head, not enough to wipe away cousin Ray's touch, not enough to wipe away her sadness.

She had tried substituting one pain for another. That was what the razors were about. She didn't remember how soon after Ray began hurting her that she began slashing her arms and her legs with razors. At first, she would just make little nicks on her arms. The momentary sting of pain brought a temporary release from her thoughts of Ray and his nightly visits. Then she began slashing herself, making deeper cuts, cuts that still left faint scars. It took a while for the rest of the family to discover what she was doing. Self-mutilation was the way her psychiatrist described it. Once again, drugs were prescribed, and they did help control the urges. But sometimes the appetite to hurt came back strong and Olivia gave in. This was no way to live. Running from pain, inflicting pain, and running from pain once more. *Time to get off this train,* Olivia thought. *It's been time.*

Her family would be hurt. Mama Laurel would be angry. Suicide is the coward's way out, Camille had said on more than one occasion. She was right. Olivia could not deny that what she was doing was wrong. She just couldn't see a way out of the pain. It's a sin, Brynne would say. Plain old ungrateful, would be Mama Laurel's commentary. Gram Naomi, her paternal grandmother, would undoubtedly blame her actions on Mama Laurel. and call her selfish. Everything that Olivia knew was going to be said was completely accurate, but there was just too much pain in living and, as much as she loved her family, she could no longer put up with the pain, even for them.

She swallowed another pill, and then another. Olivia lay down and let the feeling of peace wash over her. She had taken these pills many times. They calmed her down and did the job quickly. Maybe she should have provided a better explanation for her actions in the note she'd left on the refrigerator. All she'd written was *I'm sorry*. It was the truth. She was sorry. But this place, this exact place, was where she needed to be. On her way to a place that was pain-free. She placed another pill in her mouth and bit down hard into its center, tasting its bitterness. "Good-bye," she whispered to no one in particular.

Mama Laurel

Mama Laurel leaned over and whispered to her granddaughters, Brynne and Camille, "One of you is going to have to take me home. My heart is hurting something terrible!" When her granddaughters stared at her with blank expressions, she explained, "I mean, now!"

Mama Laurel heard Camille mutter something under her breath. Apparently, Camille was in no hurry to escort her home. Mama Laurel sighed. What did she expect from her? Undoubtedly the prettiest of her granddaughters, Camille was as spoiled as two-month-old milk. There was no good deed that child would not run away from; she was damn selfish. She was born that way and she would probably leave the earth the same way, as far as Mama Laurel was concerned. She had long since given up hope that Camille would one day change and become the woman her mother Antoinette had been, God rest her soul.

"Mama, can't you wait just a bit?" Camille's husky voice sounded like a blues singer's, but it was a voice that had brought down many a strong man. What the voice didn't accomplish, her face did. Camille was the family beauty, and she reveled in this fact. The once chubby, bispectacled child had turned into a stunning woman.

While Brynne was no raving beauty, her pleasant features and equally pleasant demeanor would, in Mama Laurel's mind, take her further than the heart-stopping, head-turning beauty of Camille. Sometimes Mama Laurel wanted to shake Brynne and tell her that self-confidence was not a sin. But Brynne was going to have to come to this realization on her own, she thought. If Mama Laurel lived to be a hundred, she would never understand how someone who excelled at everything she ever tried could be so insecure. *The divorce didn't help, but then that was her own damn fault—excuse me, Jesus, for using that word in your house, but Brynne should never have let a good man like Jose go. And, who divorces her husband knowing damn well, excuse me, Jesus, that she still loves him?*

She wondered if things would have turned out differently for her grandbabies if their parents had raised them. Olivia was a mess. She just lost her last job and was not taking her medication like she was supposed to. Camille was stomping through life not caring who got hurt in the process, and Brynne, her one granddaughter that had sense, had gone and divorced her husband for no reason that anyone could understand and was now talking crazy about leaving her good job to find herself.

She felt a tiredness come over her. Although she had been feeling all right during the pastor's sermon, afterward she started feeling weak and washed out. And her heart seemed to be beating to a rhythm all its own. She needed to go home and check on Olivia. Usually Olivia came to church every Sunday, but she had looked so tired and washed out that Mama Laurel had acquiesced when Olivia told her that she wasn't up for church this morning.

"I need to go home now," Mama Laurel hissed at Camille, annoyed that she was getting too old to drive herself to church. The hardest part about getting old for Mama Laurel was the way her body had started to turn on her, forcing her to do something she had successfully managed to avoid for most of her life—depend on others for their help. Sometimes, thought Mama Laurel as she looked at her two granddaughters, it was hard to accept old age with grace.

"Which one of you is taking me home?" she asked again.

Brynne said automatically, "I'll take you home, Mama. Come on."

"No," said Camille with such emphasis that both Mama Laurel and Brynne looked at her. "I'll take Mama home."

Now, this is peculiar, thought Mama Laurel. What had accounted for this sudden and decidedly uncharacteristic change of heart? Mama Laurel, who hadn't reached seventy-nine years of age by being foolish, looked around the congregation quickly. It did not take her long to see the reason for Camille's change of heart. Harold, Camille's

sometime beau, was sitting in the front row of the balcony next to his
wife. As the congregation stood to join the choir in song, Mama
Laurel had saw that Harold's wife was pregnant. Very pregnant. The
couple hadn't been to church in a month of Sundays, not since Mama
Laurel had told him off last fall. Camille certainly was not going to
volunteer the information that Harold's wife was pregnant.

As Mama Laurel looked at them, Harold's wife returned her stare
with a grim smile and angry eyes. Mama Laurel looked away. She
couldn't blame the child for disliking anyone that had a blood affilia-
tion with Camille. But it seemed to her that this woman's anger was
misplaced; she ought to turn those blazing, black eyes on her husband. She felt a surge of sympathy for Roxanne. She knew what is was
like to have someone you love betray you.

"Mama, I thought you wanted to go!" Camille snapped, interrupt-
ing Mama Laurel's thoughts.

"Don't use that tone of voice with me, miss lady," snapped Mama
Laurel as she gathered her fur, her cane, and her Bible. "I may be in
the house of the Lord this Sunday morning, but that will not prevent
me from putting your sassy behind in its place if the need arises."

"Mama, please!" whispered Brynne as she bent her head close to
her grandmother. "People are looking!"

Mama Laurel looked from one granddaughter to the other and
shook her head. Somewhere in raising them, she had failed. How else
could she explain the messes that they had made with their lives?

"Come on," said Mama Laurel, who was now tired and alarmed that
her heart seemed to be keeping time to a melody she could not hear.
"My heart is really starting to hurt now."

Three

Camille

The wind sliced across Lake Erie and blew the falling snow in several different directions. The cheerful radio announcer let it be known that although the temperature had risen to five degrees, with the windchill thrown in, it was more like twenty below.

Every year Camille swore to herself that she would leave Cleveland. But each year she found herself in the city that she had never made peace with. "I want to go home," she had cried when she and her sisters had first moved there.

"This is your home now, honey," Mama Laurel had said.

"This ain't my home," Camille had declared, earning a lecture about ungrateful children who should know better than to sass their elders, and the proper use of the English language. After that day she would always associate her birthday with the gray skies of Cleveland, the loss of home, Goshen, North Carolina, and the loss of her parents.

She maneuvered her Jeep Grand Cherokee up the narrow lanes of Carnegie Drive. The snow was making her progress difficult and the road was covered with a thin sheet of ice.

"I have got to get the hell out of Cleveland," said Camille.

"Looks to me like Cleveland has been pretty good to you," was Mama Laurel's quick reply.

"A good job isn't everything, Mama," said Camille, repeating the same tired refrain she always seemed to repeat whenever Mama Laurel was around. Camille's job as the director of human resources for a state agency sounded good. When people heard what she did, they were impressed, which suited Mama Laurel just fine. Mama Laurel had wanted at least one of her granddaughters to be a physician, but Brynne was squeamish, Camille wasn't interested, and Olivia had bigger issues than building a career in medicine. Still, Mama Laurel was satisfied that both Camille and Brynne had outstanding jobs. They would never have to depend on any man for an income, and that, in Mama Laurel's eyes, was a good thing.

Camille liked her job well enough, but she was getting more tired than usual of Cleveland's winters. Lately, the all too frequent clashes between Camille and her family over Harold was strengthening her resolve to put as much distance as she dared between herself and them. Besides, the thought of being in a city where neither Harold nor the bad luck that followed him was present was appealing.

She had recently gotten an offer for a position at a university in Atlanta as a vice president of human resources and recruiting. The offer came with a promotion and more money. Camille was definitely considering it. Atlanta had nice weather, an upwardly mobile African-American community, and a decent percentage of good-looking men.

As the snow blew about Carnegie Drive, Atlanta's appeal was looking downright irresistible.

"I know that a good job isn't everything," said Mama Laurel, a person who had never learned the fine art of dropping an uncomfortable subject. "But it's a start. Besides, if you let go of that situation that you're in, you'd be surprised to see how your life would turn around."

Camille sighed. *Here it comes.* It had been almost two weeks since Mama Laurel had spoken Harold's name. She had not expected this lull in the battle to last too much longer, and she was not disappointed.

"Mama, if you've got something to say, just go on and say it."

Mama Laurel turned and looked at Camille. Her voice sounded tired. "Camille, you know the Lord does not like ugly. You need to leave that man alone!"

Camille's bottom lip curled as she concentrated on the road. On more than one occasion her wheels had skated over the icy surface. Dangerous to be on the road at a time like this. *That's all I need,* thought Camille, *to get into an accident.*

"Mama, you've had your say. Let's drop the subject while I still have control of this car."

"You'll keep hearing this subject as long as you keep fooling around with him. Camille, honey, you could have your pick of any man in Cleveland."

Camille knew that Mama Laurel was trying to reason with her. That was never a good sign. For Mama Laurel, attempts to be reasonable were usually a prelude to all-out warfare.

"They say he beats his wife," said Mama Laurel, repeating a refrain she used often with Camille. But Camille was used to hearing that song and it didn't move her.

"People say a whole lot of stuff about other people. You can't believe everything folks tell you. Look at all the stuff folks say about me!"

"Most of that stuff is true," Mama Laurel muttered under her breath.

Camille heard that comment but decided it was best to let it go. After all, Mama Laurel did have a point. Camille knew that her scandalous behavior gave people some interesting conversation. But Mama Laurel didn't need to worry about Harold ever laying a hand on her. He would never do that. She wasn't the kind of woman who would stand for that. A man had to know his limits and Camille was damn sure that Harold knew his. Besides, Harold was on his way out and he knew it. The excitement she had felt at the beginning of their relationship was long gone. The sex was still good, but it wasn't enough for her. She wanted someone that was her very own. She was tired of sharing.

"His wife is pregnant, for God's sake!" Mama Laurel's voice rose with indignation, cutting through Camille's thoughts. "And all of Cleveland knows your business. A woman in your position! It isn't right, Camille, and you know it. It isn't decent. I raised you better than that."

Mama Laurel wanted her to be decent. Camille would have laughed aloud but she knew that this would have moved Mama Laurel's tirade into high gear. *Mama Laurel is dreaming impossible dreams if she thinks that she can appeal to my sense of decency,* thought Camille. *I haven't been decent since Michael Jackson had his original nose.*

Camille waited for the inevitable comparison to her mother Antoinette. She knew that it was coming. *Why can't you be like your mother?* It was a refrain that she had been hearing all her life, even before her mother was killed in the car accident. Everybody expected Camille to be like Saint Antoinette. *I only look like her,* Camille wanted to scream. *That's it. Just a family resemblance. Don't expect any more than that.*

Unlike her sister's memories of their mother, Camille's were not accompanied by any particular good feelings. They were bitter and vivid. Antoinette was a beautiful woman, and people expected her off-spring to reflect this beauty. Although Camille was now the family beauty, she had been an awkward, overweight child who disappointed, just by her very appearance.

All Camille had to do to disappoint was to show up. When they were children, Brynne was the cute, bookish one and Olivia was high yellow, which for most folks was enough. Camille was distinguished only by her weight. "It's a shame," folks would say, not even bothering to lower their voices, "her mama is so pretty. Just goes to show, just 'cause your relatives are cute don't mean nothing for you."

Every time she looked at her mother, Camille could see exactly what her own imperfections were, and she held her mother accountable for every slight she received because of her looks. If her mother had not been the beauty she was, no one would have had any such expectations of Camille. They were never close. Camille knew that her mother tried, but she would push her mother away. In time, her mother stopped trying. She did everything a mother was supposed to do. She provided for her. She took care of her. There was nothing Camille wanted or needed. But, the affection her mother provided Camille's sisters was denied to her. Her mother did not include Camille in her circle of warmth.

Thank God for her father. The finest man that God had ever made, Camille was convinced of this. It was her father who came at night to chase her nightmares away. Her father never made her feel fat, ugly, or unimportant. The least of her accomplishments were always a big deal to him. "Don't you worry, sweetheart," he'd say to chase away the tears that came when the kids at school teased her about her weight. "You're already a beauty, baby, and someday the world is going to know it."

Camille remembered the last day of her parents' life with a clarity that was undimmed even after all these years. They had been arguing. Camille's mother had wanted her father to accompany her to a lawn party given by one of her sorority sisters. Her father had not wanted to go. He laughed at her mother's pretentious friends. "None of them are more than two steps removed from the plantation, but they got a little education and a little money and suddenly they're putting on airs." That was her father's description of her mother's high-society friends. People who did their best to distance themselves from the rest of the black race in their single-minded quest for upward mobility.

Her mother had won that argument, just like she won all the other arguments. Her father could never say no to her mother. That was what killed him. His following her foolish mother to some party of people whose names Camille no longer knew had gotten both her parents killed. The car they were driving was hit by a man who had just come from visiting the neighborhood bar. Her father, who was driving, died instantly. Her mother died the next day.

Camille gripped the steering wheel and concentrated on the traffic around her. She needed to stay focused. There was a Honda Civic behind her that was entirely too close. One nasty patch of ice could send this fool skidding into the back of the Jeep. Camille pushed her foot gently down on the gas pedal and tried to put more distance between her car and the Civic. Thinking about the traffic, the snow, the road, anything, was better than getting into a fight with Mama Laurel. Camille knew that Mama Laurel was upset about her relationship with Harold, and she also knew that Mama Laurel had every reason not to like the fact that her grandchild was running around with a married man. But, Mama Laurel and the rest of the family had to learn to stay out of her business. They had to understand that she was a grown woman. From the stubborn look on Mama Laurel's face, Camille saw that, grown or not grown, Mama Laurel disapproved of her relationship with Harold and she was not averse to another fight with Camille to show her disapproval.

They drove the rest of the way home in silence.

Brynne

Brynne forced her thoughts back to the church service. The sermon was over, the choir had sung, the offering had been taken, and tithes had been given. It was now time for the testimonials. To say that church was an all-day affair at Shiloh was only a slight exaggeration. Once she got to Shiloh, she would settle in for the ride. From ten-thirty to eleven, there would be prayer and devotional hymns. Service began promptly at eleven, but usually it wasn't until about twelve-thirty when Pastor Simmons would ascend to the pulpit for his sermon. That usually took a good forty-five minutes, or sometimes an hour. After that, the choir had to sing and other church business had to be addressed. Then came the testimonials. Folks would stand up and testify about the Lord. That process could take a while. There were a few times when not too many people stood up, and at those times the pastor would shake his head and say in his booming voice, "Beloved, I *know* the Lord has been good to *somebody* today . . ." and either shame or gratitude, or a mixture of both of those emotions, would bring forth some more testimonials.

This particular Sunday there was no need for any exhortations from Pastor Simmons. Folks were trying to outdo each other with their testimonials. Brynne wanted to stand up and testify about her date last night with Malcolm, but somehow, in addition to being downright blasphemous, she was certain that her little date did not qualify as one of God's miracles.

The sun was shining through the stained-glass windows of Shiloh, giving the sanctuary an almost heavenly look with cascading gold and red hues blanketing the church. Shiloh was home. She had been baptized at the fountain behind the church altar. She had been married here. Even though she went to an Episcopal church with her husband, she was a Baptist by birth and by inclination.

Maybe one day she would bring Malcolm here, but no time soon. Everyone in the church knew her and her business. They were protective of her, and those who weren't were nosey. Camille had already given Shiloh enough gossip from her family. A new man in Brynne's life would only get loose tongues to wagging even more. She didn't need that. Still, Shiloh was an important part of her life, and if Malcolm was going to continue to be a part of her life, she wanted him to understand what Shiloh meant to her.

At the thought of last night, a slow blush crept up her cheeks. Lord, she was acting like a schoolgirl. All they'd done was kiss, but there was the promise of more. She'd felt like a perfect harlot. She'd kissed on first dates before, but not *those* kinds of kisses—kisses that left her hot and breathless and wanting more and more and more. In his car, parked right in front of her condo, they'd kissed like a couple of teenagers. Jose had never kissed her like that—with complete and unadulterated passion—as if he could not get enough of the taste of her. Jose's kisses had been pleasant and, as time went on, uninteresting. *Stop thinking about him. That's part of your past. Let the past be.*

"Sister Brynne, I see your smiling face." Pastor Simmons's booming voice startled Brynne out of her reverie. "I *know* that you have something to be thankful for, Sister Brynne."

Pastor Simmons was known to call folks out in church. No one was safe.

Oh Lord, though Brynne. *Why me?* Pastor Simmons knew that unless she was in a courtroom, she didn't like to speak in public.

She stood up and addressed the congregation. "Good afternoon, church."

The unified reply of Shiloh washed over her like warm, soapy water. "Good afternoon, Sister Brynne."

All right, here goes. Brynne took a deep breath. "I just want to thank the Lord for waking me up this morning," she said. "You all know that I've gone through a difficult time these past few months."

Sympathetic murmurings and a few calls of "yes, Lord" were their response.

"But I want to say that I know the Lord is leading me to a new direction, and I want to thank the Lord for that."

"Let the church say amen." Pastor Simmons's voice rose up from the pulpit.

"Amen."

Four

Camille

Camille let out her breath slowly when her grandmother's pale yellow colonial home came into view. Relief. She didn't know whether it was Mama Laurel's age or her general disposition, but Camille was finding it harder than usual to be in her company. More than once, Camille wished that Brynne's ability to get along with difficult people were a family trait.

Camille pulled the Jeep into the driveway. She kept the motor running.

"Aren't you coming in?" asked Mama Laurel.

"I'd love to," Camille lied easily and without remorse, "but I've got a lot of work to do this afternoon."

Freedom was so close, Camille could almost reach out and grab it.

Mama Laurel was not impressed. "Come on in. Olivia looked down this morning. Why don't you come in for just a minute?"

"And I'm the one to cheer Olivia up?" asked Camille. "Brynne is much better at finding silver linings than I am."

Mama Laurel's voice was low and controlled, but her eyes clearly showed that she was on the thin side of evil. "Your sister," she said, drawing out each word for emphasis, "needs some cheering up." There was no mistaking it, Mama Laurel was not going to take no for an answer. Camille turned the motor off. So much for freedom.

Camille got out of the car and walked around to the passenger side, opening the door for Mama Laurel. She helped her out of the car, closing the door behind her. She walked with her to the front door and waited while she took her time finding her key. After what seemed like an excessively long time, Mama Laurel took out her key from her purse and opened the front door.

The stereo was cranked up and Aretha Franklin's voice filled the house. *"You make me feel like a na-tu-ral woman . . ."* Aretha's voice wailed. Mama Laurel walked over to her stereo to turn the music down, but halfway there she stopped.

"I think the music is coming from Olivia's room," she said.

"Sounds like she's having a party up there," Camille said.

"I don't like this," said Mama Laurel. "Something's wrong. Why on earth is she blasting the stereo like that?"

They were silent for a moment, each woman looking into the other's eyes.

Later, looking back, Camille could not say what made her heart fly to her throat and her mouth go dry with fear. But in that moment, when the only thing she could hear was Aretha's voice and the sound of her own racing heartbeat, she knew that her sister was in trouble, and all thoughts of being annoyed with Olivia flew out of her head.

Camille took the steps two at a time, with Mama Laurel following close behind, despite her age and medical troubles.

Both women called out Olivia's name, but there was no response.

"Olivia!" Camille was screaming now. She did not know what to expect. They reached the top of the staircase and ran down the hallway to Olivia's room, all the way at the end.

Olivia's bedroom door was open and Camille entered the room first. She saw that Olivia was sleeping. Camille's relief was immediate.

"Olivia, wake up, girl!" she called. But Olivia did not move. Camille walked quickly over to her sister. Olivia lay on her bed curled up like a baby in her mama's stomach. Her hands were clasped as if in prayer.

Camille saw the open bottle of pills lying next to Olivia's knees; then she saw Olivia's lips. They had turned blue.

"Sweet Jesus!" Camille whispered.

Mama Laurel moved into action as she half lifted, half dragged Olivia to a sitting position. Olivia's head flopped to the side like a rag doll's.

Mama Laurel snapped at Camille, "Call emergency, girl!"

Camille stood still, tears streamed down her face. "Is she breathing?" she asked, unable to move her legs and tasting the salt from her tears.

"Yes!" cried Mama Laurel. "Call emergency, now!"

Olivia was breathing. Camille ran to the phone on Olivia's desk and dialed 911 with unsteady hands. She felt something wet and warm running down her legs. She had urinated on herself. *Olivia's still breathing.* Camille held on to that thought as she waited for the operator to answer the phone.

"Nine-one-one, what is the nature of your emergency?" The operator's voice sounded like God to Camille when she finally answered.

The tears were choking Camille's throat as she struggled to get the words out. "My sister!" she cried, when she finally found her voice. "My sister needs . . . help."

Brynne

Brynne felt the tap on her shoulder and turned to see Sister Leneda, one of the church's ushers and an old friend of her grandmother. Sister Leneda bit her lip and her eyes had that bright glassy look of someone who has recently shed tears. "Come on, honey," she said. "You've got to come with me."

Brynne didn't ask questions. She got her coat and her Bible and followed Sister Leneda. *Something has happened to Mama Laurel,* she thought as she hurried behind Sister Leneda. Mama Laurel had said her heart was hurting her and now something bad had happened. She braced herself for the worst. From the look at the thin, grim line that used to be Sister Leneda's mouth, that something was very bad.

As they walked down the church's center aisle, the congregation turned their well-coifed heads to watch them go. Their eyes were openly curious. Sister Leneda was known to the congregation as the bearer of bad news. Any emergency at Shiloh Baptist went first to Sister Leneda before it went anywhere else. Although Sister Leneda had just celebrated her seventy-second birthday, Brynne had to walk quickly just to keep up with her. By the time they got outside the main sanctuary, Brynne was out of breath.

"What happened to Mama Laurel?" she asked as she put her coat on.

"Your grandmother is as well as can be expected," said Sister Leneda. "It's your sister who's in trouble."

"Camille?" asked Brynne. "What happened to Camille?"

"It's Olivia," said Sister Leneda, her dark eyes large and sympathetic. "She tried to hurt herself. It sounds serious."

Hurt herself? What on earth is Sister Leneda talking about? wondered Brynne. "What are you saying?" she asked.

"I'm sorry, honey," said Sister Leneda, placing her hand on Brynne's arm. "She tried to kill herself this morning."

Brynne felt the blood rushing to her head. Her mouth went dry even as her knees buckled beneath her. Sister Leneda's arms were quickly around her, giving her support. Olivia had tried to talk to her last night, but she'd been too busy getting ready for her date with Malcolm.

Brynne's mouth formed the words several times before they came out. "Is she dead?"

"No, honey," replied Sister Leneda, "but she's in bad shape. They need you over at the hospital. She's at Cleveland Medical. I'm going to get one of the deacons to take you over there."

Brynne shook her head. She didn't want to be with anybody except her family right now. "It's okay," she told Sister Leneda. "I can drive myself over there."

"Are you sure?"

Brynne forced her voice to remain calm. "I'm quite sure, Sister Leneda. Thanks just the same."

A few moments before, she'd been thanking God as if all her troubles were over, and now it looked as if she'd be calling Him soon to help her through this. *Oh please, Lord,* she prayed silently. *Don't take my sister. Please, Lord.*

Brynne walked out of the church quickly and headed for her car.

Five

Naomi

Naomi Darling was a person who didn't have any time for tears. She'd buried her husband, her parents, and her child, and she had refused to let the tears come. For her, tears were a sign of weakness, and she did not tolerate the weak. In the seventy years she'd lived on this earth, she could count on one hand, with some fingers left over, the times she'd cried. Even as a child, her parents had remarked on their child's unnatural ability to withstand pain and disappointment dry-eyed. Today, however, as she placed the telephone back in its cradle, she felt the unfamiliar sting of tears in her eyes.

She sat back on her sofa and tried to grasp what she'd just heard. Her granddaughter Olivia had tried to kill herself. God knows that the child had been through hell, but still, she'd hoped that Olivia would exhibit the Darling backbone and face her troubles the Darling way—head-on without much fuss, and with determination.

Olivia was in the hospital. Her granddaughter Camille had called her to give her the details, which were sketchy. Camille had been crying throughout the conversation. That wasn't like Camille. Of all of her granddaughters, Camille was most like her. Tough. Determined. A person who kept her emotions in check. But, Camille had cried like a baby, talking about how Olivia was going to die.

"She is not going to die," Naomi had said, more to calm herself than her granddaughter. "She is going to make it through this. Your sister is a survivor. Look at all she's already been through, bless her heart. She is going to make it."

Camille had kept on crying.

"I'm coming to Cleveland," Naomi had said before she hung up. She looked outside her window at the garden. It was a warm February, even for Goshen, North Carolina. She had even seen some buds starting to bloom. Her bridge club was supposed to meet at her house this afternoon. She would have to call and cancel. *Think, Naomi, think. How fast can you get to Cleveland?*

She was surprised that her hands were shaking when she dialed the only airline that serviced Goshen. She'd have to change planes in Charlotte or Raleigh. "Lord, I hate to fly," she muttered to herself.

"Reservations, may I help you?" a cool, impersonal voice greeted her from the other end of the receiver.

Naomi cleared her throat. "Yes, I need to get to Cleveland."

When she had left Cleveland the last time, after an argument with Laurel, she'd told her granddaughters that it would take death or some other significant occasion to bring her back to that city. As far as Naomi was concerned, any city that Laurel was in was definitely a place to avoid. Their mutual dislike had deepened over the years and it was only their love for their granddaughters that kept them from severing their relationship completely. Well, her granddaughter had just tried to kill herself. That was enough for Naomi to come back to Cleveland. Even if it meant seeing Laurel again.

Brynne

Cleveland Medical Center, previously Cleveland General, was located east of the downtown area. Four imposing gray buildings all connected by covered walkways, Cleveland Med resembled a large college dormitory or a correctional facility, depending on your particular point of view. Although Brynne had been to Cleveland Med on many occasions, she always forgot which of the many doors on East Sixty-first Street was the main entrance to the facility.

Brynne parked in the parking lot across the street. As she got out of her car, she said another quick prayer for Olivia. She'd been praying for her sister during the short drive from the church to the hospital, but her prayers, like her thoughts, were scattered—frantic pleas to

God to save her sister. Thoughts of last night's telephone conversation with Olivia made her prayers even more fervent. Prayers fueled by guilt. *I should have listened to her last night. I should have talked with her.*

Pushing her uncovered hands into her coat pockets, Brynne tucked her head down against the wind and crossed the street. She walked quickly down the block in a direction she hoped would lead her to the main entrance, all the while praying to God to spare her sister's life, to forgive her for turning her back on her sister last night.

As she walked she heard a familiar male voice call her name.

She turned and saw her ex-husband, Jose, quickly walking toward her with determined strides. She wasn't surprised to see him. Dependable, steady Jose would naturally be here in a time of crisis. It was when he was at his best. Providing a shoulder to lean on, producing a tissue when needed, making difficult phone calls, difficult decisions. Calm, steady, the type of person who always rose to the particular occasion in which he found himself.

There was a time, long ago, when she had yielded to his strength. It was so easy having someone take care of you, especially when life was handing you some tough situations. But those days were long gone. They were divorced. She no longer needed anyone to lean on. As Mama Laurel told her often enough, "You're the firstborn child, Brynne. Firstborn children can handle their own stuff." It took her some time to come to this conclusion, but she was here now, and she wasn't going to let her well-meaning ex-husband hand out any more life preservers. She was going to swim this particular sea on her own.

"What are you doing here?" Brynne asked her ex-husband as he stood in front of her.

"Mama Laurel called me."

She noticed the new strands of gray around his temple. They had not been there before. His eyes looked tired, and there were now faint lines around those eyes that she had not noticed before. Tall, thin, and the color of dark coffee, with brown eyes that seemed to be able to see past any defenses Brynne put up, wide full lips the color of blueberry stain, sharp, high cheekbones, Jose was solidly but not spectacularly good-looking. Brynne could see the pain in his eyes, pain that she knew she had caused.

"Jose, I don't think you should be here," she said. "This isn't the time or the place to discuss this but this is a family matter. We're divorced, Jose. You don't have to rescue me anymore."

She watched the pain cross his eyes and she was instantly ashamed. She was not a cruel person. Why was she acting this way?

"Is that why you think I'm here?" Jose asked. "To rescue you?"

"Yes," Brynne replied.

"Brynne, you've never needed anyone to rescue you. Not when we were married, and not now. I'm here because I care about you. I care about Olivia. I care about all of your family."

This would not be so damned difficult if she didn't still love him. She didn't want to hurt him. She just wanted to get on with her life. Why couldn't he understand this? He was part of her past, part of something she wanted to leave behind.

"Jose, I appreciate you coming, I do," said Brynne. "I just don't think it's appropriate."

"Appropriate?"

"I know I sound crazy."

"Not crazy, Brynne. It's a tough time. I understand."

Why did he do this? Why was he being so reasonable? She'd just told him that he wasn't welcome in her family drama. She'd been downright rude, but here he was, being reasonable. Hell, he was being nice. He was being Jose.

"Look, we can stand here and argue about this, or we can walk into that hospital and see what's going on with your sister."

She felt small. She felt petty. Her sister had tried to commit suicide and she was arguing on the sidewalk about whether someone who cared about her sister should come and be with her family. She had been put in her place, effortlessly and effectively.

"I'm sorry," she said.

"Come on," he said, gently taking her arm, "let's go find Olivia."

Mama Laurel

Mama Laurel sat in the corner of the intensive care waiting room, which was thankfully empty of people except for herself and Camille, who sat on the far side. The room was painted bright blue with a bright red and green sofa in the corner and some orange and yellow chairs scattered around. Mama Laurel thought that whoever had designed this was obviously under the mistaken belief that if you give people enough color, enough paintings of different flowers on the walls, a television, and a candy machine, they can forget that they are in an intensive care waiting room wondering if the person they came to see is going to live or die. All these bright colors did was hurt Mama Laurel's eyes and give her a headache.

She stood up and walked over to one of the two large windows in the room. Outside, Lake Erie's gray waters glistened in the afternoon sunlight. It had stopped snowing, finally. She hated the snow. It reminded her of her daughter Antoinette's funeral. She had buried Antoinette in a ground covered with snow. After all this time, the pain was still there.

A knock on the door interrupted Mama Laurel's thoughts. Olivia's doctor had finally come to talk to them. He had kept them waiting awhile, and the longer Mama Laurel waited, the more nervous she'd become. A short, stocky man dressed in a white coat entered the room.

"I'm Doctor Trahan. I will be taking care of Olivia."

There was nothing particularly striking about his appearance. He had a medium brown complexion, as if he were a mix of half a cup each of dark chocolate and milk. His features were pleasant but nondescript. His face was just beginning to show signs of a beard in progress. A funny-looking man, Mama Laurel decided as she sized him up. His chin was a little large for his face, and his nose looked as if it had once been broken, broad and slightly off center. A boxer's nose. It was his eyes, however, that caught Mama Laurel's attention. They were large and dark, with long, almost feminine lashes. And they were kind and compassionate. These were the kind of eyes you wanted to look into if you were ever in trouble.

"I'm Mrs. Redwood," said Mama Laurel. "I'm Olivia's grandmother and this is her sister, Camille."

"You're the ones that found her?" asked the doctor.

Mama Laurel nodded her head.

"Tell me, Mrs. Redwood, has she ever done anything like this before?"

"Not that I know of. She talked about this kind of thing, but I never thought she would do this to herself. She has—has emotional problems. She's been getting help. I thought things were getting better." Mama Laurel's voice cracked. *Lord, let me keep it together,* Mama Laurel pleaded. *My grandchildren need me whole and strong. I can't fall apart now.*

"Mama, the razors," Camille said, her voice soft and urgent. "Tell him about the razors."

Mama Laurel shook her head. Camille ought to know better than that. Making family business public. No need for the man to know about that stuff anyway. All he needed to do was get her grandbaby better. That was all he needed to do. He surely didn't need to hear any family business, especially Olivia's kind of family business.

"What about the razors?" Dr. Trahan asked, keeping his eyes steady on Mama Laurel.

As if he sensed her hesitancy, Dr. Trahan prodded, "What about the razors, Mrs. Redwood?"

"Those razors don't have anything to do with this," said Mama Laurel. She was feeling her anger rise. This man should be here telling them about Olivia's condition, not prying into Olivia's personal business.

Camille spoke up. "My sister occasionally tries to hurt herself with razors."

Mama Laurel flashed her an angry look. That girl just had no sense of boundaries. This was not the doctor's business. This information wasn't going to help him get her granddaughter better. All the information did was confuse matters. This man wasn't a head doctor. If he was, then Mama Laurel could see talking about this, but what good did discussing all of this do?

"How is my granddaughter?" Mama Laurel asked.

"We'll get to that," Dr. Trahan said. His manner was easy, but he was not going to let the subject drop. "Let's talk about the razors."

"For heaven's sake, Mama," said Camille, "why keep it a secret?"

"We don't need to discuss this here," said Mama Laurel, once again feeling her temper rise.

"Doctor Trahan," Camille said, "since her teenage years, my sister has slashed herself with razors. No big cuts, really—just nicks, all on her legs and her arms. Once she slashed her cheek, but she never did that again."

"Is she getting psychiatric treatment?" asked Dr. Trahan.

"Off and on," replied Camille. "She's supposed to be on medication, but she doesn't take that too regularly."

"She's been getting better!" said Mama Laurel. Camille was making Olivia sound crazy. Now, she would be the first to agree that Olivia had a few emotional problems, but her grandbaby wasn't crazy.

"Obviously not, Mama," Camille shot back. "She is not getting any better. That's why we're here this afternoon."

"Mrs. Redwood, I understand that this is a difficult subject to discuss," said Dr. Trahan. "And, I also understand that you want to discuss your granddaughter's condition, which we will get to shortly. I just wanted to know a little bit about her history. In treating my patients, I like to know as much as I can about them."

"How is Olivia?" Mama Laurel asked.

"She's holding on," Dr. Trahan replied.

"What does that mean?" asked Camille. "Holding on to what?"

The doctor's voice sounded weary to Mama Laurel's ears. "Life," he said. "Your granddaughter is holding on to life. Olivia is young and she seems to be—otherwise in good health. Those are both things in her favor. But, she is still in a coma and we're uncertain whether or not there's been any damage to the brain—"

Mama Laurel let out a small cry. She was trying her best to deal with the news as calmly as possible, but the thought of Olivia lying helpless in this hospital was wearing away any resolve she had of holding on to her emotions. She felt something squeeze her heart tight and she closed her eyes until the pain quickly disappeared. *Not now, not now,* thought Mama Laurel. *I can't deal with this heart right now. My grandbaby needs me. Not now, Lord.*

She held on to the back of one of the leather chairs. Why was it so hot in the room? It had to be at least ninety degrees. It was making her dizzy, all this heat. She closed her eyes again.

"Mama, are you okay?"

Mama Laurel opened her eyes to find a worried-looking Camille and Dr. Trahan standing in front of her. "I'm fine," she said quickly. "I'm just concerned about Olivia, that's all."

Although Dr. Trahan addressed Camille, he never took his eyes off Mama Laurel as he spoke. "There is a water fountain with some cups out in the hallway. I wonder if you could get your grandmother some water? I'll stay with her for a minute."

Camille left the room quickly without further comment.

"Ma'am, why don't you sit down?" said Dr. Trahan.

Mama Laurel obeyed the doctor and sat down quietly.

"Are you feeling ill?" he asked.

"No, but I'm a little hot."

"You're telling me the truth, aren't you, ma'am?" The doctor was persistent. "If you weren't feeling well, would you tell me?"

"Right now, I have to focus on Olivia," replied Mama Laurel, embarrassed that her fear was obvious, even to this stranger with the kind, dark eyes. "Just take care of her . . ."

Mama Laurel's words trailed off. She was afraid to speak any more. She didn't want to cry and if she continued talking she would start bawling like a newborn baby.

Camille came back with the water. "Drink up, Mama. You don't look so well."

Mama Laurel took the paper cup filled with water and drank quickly. She did feel a little better. The cold water felt good.

"Thank you, Camille," she said. "I do appreciate your kindness."

Camille's eyes narrowed speculatively as if she wondered whether her grandmother's words were genuine. The hesitation before her answer was not lost on Mama Laurel. "You're welcome, Mama."

"I have to be on my way, but as soon as we get any new results, I'll come back," said Dr. Trahan, who still looked concerned. "Mrs. Redwood, perhaps it would be better if you waited at home. You'd probably be more comfortable in your own surroundings."

"I'm not going anywhere." Not until she knew her grandbaby was going to be all right.

"Very well then," said Dr. Trahan.

As he turned to go, Mama Laurel caught his hand. "Take good care of my baby," she said.

"That I will, ma'am. I promise you."

Mama Laurel still did not release his hand. "Make sure," she said, her voice now getting stronger. "Make sure you tell her we love her when you see her."

"Yes, ma'am."

Camille gently pried the doctor's hand from Mama Laurel.

"Mama," she said quietly, "let the man go and do his job."

Mama Laurel let go and they watched as the short man in the white coat departed.

Six

Camille

Camille looked up to see an unhappy-looking Brynne walking through the door of the waiting room with an equally unhappy-looking Jose walking behind her. She shook her head. Trust Jose to be here by Brynne's side. Divorce was not an impediment to him. No matter what the divorce decree said, Jose was not going to let go of Brynne.

"It took you two long enough to get here." Mama Laurel's greeting was querulous and to the point. "But thank God y'all are here."

"Mama Laurel." Jose walked over and kissed his ex-grandmother-in-law on the cheek. "I see you're holding up well."

Mama Laurel sucked her teeth at Jose's comment, but her eyes were soft and loving. Jose was as much a part of her family as if he shared their blood, as far as Mama Laurel was concerned. Camille watched as Mama Laurel patted the cushion on the sofa where she sat and said to Jose, "You sit down here beside me. Truth be told, I'm glad you're here. Even if you are late." Mama Laurel was not one to let go of a point.

As if noticing Brynne for the first time, her grandmother said, "Brynne, you come on over here with me and your husband."

Brynne ignored Mama Laurel's comment, but Camille saw a flicker of exasperation cross Brynne's features, which just as quickly was replaced by her usual placid exterior.

"How's Olivia?" asked Brynne, who remained standing by the door.

"We don't know. Doctor says she's hanging on—whatever that means," Camille replied. She forced her voice to remain calm even as her heart hammered in her chest. *Please, Lord,* she prayed silently, *I know I'm in no position to bargain with you, but please let my sister be all right.*

"What happened?" Brynne asked, her voice small and frightened.

"She swallowed some pills," Mama Laurel said. She sounded almost calm, as if she were explaining that the winter months were cold in Cleveland, or why she preferred Pepsi to Coke. But Camille knew that Mama Laurel was scared. She had a good reason to be scared. Olivia might have finally gotten her simple self in some deep trouble.

"She's in a coma," Mama Laurel continued.

The silence that followed Mama Laurel's statement was unnatural. It was as if each person in the room struggled to deal with this information.

Brynne broke the silence. "She's going to pull through this, Mama. She's been through hell and she came back from that."

Camille tasted white-hot anger as she remembered what Olivia had already been through. Ray had destroyed her sister, and even though he was long dead, Camille was certain that he was the cause of her sister's actions. The psychiatrists, the screams at night, the cuts on her body, Olivia's whole sorry life had been destroyed by one evil bastard.

"I shouldn't have left Olivia alone this morning," said Mama Laurel.

Maybe now the family would take Olivia's problems seriously. Camille had tried many times to get Mama Laurel and Brynne to deal with Olivia. Mama Laurel believed that being crazy was the same as being weak. Camille tried to get her to see that if Olivia was crazy, she had just cause. First, losing her parents, then the rape, and worse, the family's steadfast determination to bury the incident as if it never happened, had more than helped to push Olivia way past crazy. As for Brynne, she would firmly believe that the family could handle Olivia's problems for her. She was always trying to rescue Olivia herself—either getting her a job, driving her to the doctor's, picking her up from strange street corners from which Olivia would call with no explanation as to how she got there or why she was there. Brynne had been rescuing wounded animals and wounded people from as far back as Camille could remember.

Whenever Camille talked about getting Olivia committed to an institution with people who were trained to handle these kind of situations, both Mama Laurel and Brynne would look at her as if she had just suggested dropping off her sister with a pack of wild dogs. "We don't do that in this family," Mama Laurel would say. "We take care of our own. We don't pay folk to take care of business that we can take care of ourselves."

"Mama." Camille turned to Mama Laurel. "Olivia needs help and, if she does make it, we've got to see to it that she gets it. If this doesn't convince you that she needs help, then I don't know what the hell else will."

"Camille!" Brynne was clearly distressed. "We just got back from church!"

"Oh, Brynne, grow the hell up. Don't you think God has heard cuss words before?" *I swear,* thought Camille, *sometimes Saint Brynne gets on my nerves.*

"Olivia's no crazier than you are, Camille," said Mama Laurel. "She just needs a little help, that's all."

Camille threw her hands in the air. "I give up, Mama. I don't know what it's going to take for you to realize that this is past the point of having a bad day and feeling stress. She tried to kill herself, Mama!"

Brynne intervened. "Camille, this is not the time, nor is it the place. We can discuss this when we're home."

"When is the time, Brynne?" asked Camille, raising her voice and not caring who heard her. "When is the time? When Olivia finally succeeds in killing herself? Can we talk about it then, Brynne? Or do we have to wait until after the funeral?"

Camille didn't even see it coming. Mama Laurel walked over to where she was standing, raised her right hand, and slapped Camille across her beautiful mouth. "You're hysterical," Mama Laurel said quietly before she turned and walked back to the sofa.

Camille raised her hand to her lip and tasted blood. Damn, Mama Laurel had busted her lip!

"This family," said Mama Laurel, pointing her walking cane toward Camille, as Moses had lifted his staff to part the Red Sea, "is falling apart."

Mama Laurel

Mama Laurel watched as night fell over Lake Erie. She was hungry, but she didn't want to leave the room. She wanted to be close by when

Olivia awoke. Mama Laurel thought about asking one of her grand-daughters to go to the cafeteria to get her something, but she didn't want them out of her sight. She needed them here with her when the doctor came, even though Brynne and Camille had spent most of the afternoon in silence and doing their best to ignore each other.

After the last conversation with Camille, Mama Laurel was grateful for the silence. Anything was better than hearing Camille's bitter mouth. Mama Laurel had given up trying to figure out just what made Camille so hateful. The Lord had blessed her with good looks, a good job, and a damn good family. If anything, she should be count-ing her blessings, but instead the girl just spent her time helping folks feel bad.

A knock on the waiting-room door announced the arrival of Dr. Trahan. He looked tired. And he did not look hopeful.

Mama Laurel opened her mouth to speak, but fear had taken her voice away. Folks only looked the way he did when they were ready to give bad news.

"How is she?" Brynne asked.

"Stable," said Dr. Trahan. "The next forty-eight hours are crucial. That will determine if she's going to rally or not. But her vital signs are improving—"

"Is she still unconscious?" asked Camille, cutting off the doctor in midsentence.

"Yes."

"When can we see her?" asked Brynne.

"You can go into her room now," said Dr. Trahan, "but don't stay too long. I think it would be best if you all go home afterward. If any-thing happens during the night I'll call you."

Mama Laurel spoke up. She had been thinking about this for a while, but until this moment, she had not expressed her thoughts to anyone. "I'd like to stay with my granddaughter tonight. I don't want her to be alone."

The doctor clearly was not pleased with this scenario, but he agreed, in a tone that sounded too begrudging to Mama Laurel's ears for her liking. "All right, since she's stable. But we may have to revisit the issue later."

"Fine," said Mama Laurel, satisfied that the doctor had not given her a hard time, but she had been prepared to deal with him if he had tried. She understood the importance of rules, but there were times that rules needed to be bent, broken, or twisted into something that accommodated what was right. And what was right for Mama Laurel was that she stay with Olivia tonight. Her granddaughter, like her beloved Antoinette, was scared of the dark, and Olivia's demons would come out in the night. Mama Laurel was not going to let Olivia be alone with those demons. Not tonight.

"Mama, you're tired," said Brynne. "I'll stay with Olivia."

"You go home, Brynne." Mama Laurel was determined. "I'm staying with Olivia tonight."

Brynne

Brynne stood behind her family as they crowded around Olivia's bed. She hung back a little, letting Mama Laurel, who led the way, Camille, and Jose surround the bed. The sound of a machine with its intermittent beeps, the hospital smell of antiseptic, and the sight of Olivia's pale drawn face overwhelmed and frightened Brynne. Memories of the last time she saw her mother alive came back with an unexpected force.

A time long ago she had stood in another hospital room, this time with Gram Naomi. She had looked down at her unconscious mother, whose pretty face had been swollen and battered so that it was almost unrecognizable. Brynne had not wanted to come to the hospital, but Gram Naomi had insisted. It was time to say good-bye to her mother. Gram Naomi didn't believe in sugarcoating hard facts. "Your mother's going to die," she had told Brynne. "Camille and Olivia are too young to understand, but you're old enough to handle this." Since that time, hospitals had terrified her.

"Come on in, Brynne," said Mama Laurel.

Brynne obeyed her grandmother's order and walked into the room. The door closed behind her with a soft click. She went over to her sister's bed and stood between her grandmother and Camille. Brynne looked down at Olivia's still body, feeling her legs go weak and her body start to shake as if she were standing on a ground that was undergoing a mild and continuous earthquake. Brynne leaned on Camille, who silently wrapped her arms around her. Not once did Camille ask her if she was all right. Not once did Camille look in her direction. Still, Camille kept on holding her until Brynne's trembling ceased.

Brynne could not look at Olivia's face. She remembered when she had looked at her mother after the accident. She had seen death in her mother's face. She did not want to see the same in Olivia's face. Instead she stared at her sister's hands until her eyes became blurry from her tears.

"Come on, Brynne," Camille finally said. "Let's go."

"Good," Mama Laurel joined in. "You all need to go home to get some rest."

"What about you, Mama Laurel?" asked Jose.

"I'll be just fine," replied Mama Laurel, and the way she sounded, Brynne could almost believe her. But Brynne knew that it was going to be a difficult night ahead for Mama Laurel. Staying here with nothing to keep her mind off her troubles.

She knew what Mama Laurel was doing. Trying to keep death away. That was the way Mama Laurel was. She was going to do everything in her power to watch over Olivia, fighting the angel of death if she had to. And, if death won this battle, then Mama Laurel wanted to be here with her granddaughter. She wasn't going to let her die alone.

Brynne heard the door open and turned to see a nurse hurrying into the room. From the look on the nurse's face, she meant business. She looked at her watch pointedly and said, "It's time to go. Doctor Trahan's orders."

"I'm staying," said Mama Laurel.

"I understand that," said the nurse. "The rest of you have to go, however."

Mama Laurel started calling out orders. "Jose, make sure you take Brynne home. She can get her car in the morning. Camille, I want you to stop by my house and make sure everything is in order. And, Brynne, don't forget to call Pastor Simmons in the morning. Let him know what's going on."

"Yes, Mama."

Brynne watched as Camille leaned over and kissed Olivia's cheek. Then she walked outside into the hallway and waited for Jose and Camille.

Seven

Brynne

Brynne stood in the parking lot and said calmly to Jose, "I don't need a ride home."

Camille had driven off and left them arguing in the cold. The frigid air stung Brynne's face but she was grateful. It gave her something to think about other than Olivia.

"I told your grandmother that I was taking you home and I intend to do that."

Jose stood in front of her, his arms across his chest. He was exasperated with her, as she was with him. He was acting like a husband—concerned, protective, loving, all the things he no longer should be.

The wind swept through the parking lot, bringing a fresh bout of frigid air. Brynne pulled her coat closer. Except for the parking lot attendant in his booth who was staring at them with open curiosity, they were alone in the parking lot.

"I appreciate your offer," said Brynne, "but I am not a child and the sooner that both you and Mama Laurel accept that, the better for all concerned. I can drive myself home."

"Brynne, I'm not arguing with you anymore. Get in the car."

"No."

He was doing it again. Telling her what to do. Acting as if she were a child, as if she couldn't take care of herself.

"Please." Jose spoke the word quietly. "Please."

That was not a word Jose used often.

"Why?" asked Brynne.

"I gave my word to Mama Laurel. I don't want her to worry about you. Please get in the car, Brynne," he said. "It's cold and I'm tired."

"I told you before that I don't need you to take care of me. Mama Laurel has to understand that and you do too."

"Do you hate me that much, Brynne?" He stared at Brynne's face as if he were searching for something. "Do you hate me so much that you can't stand being around me?"

"I don't hate you," Brynne said quietly. "I just want to get on with my life. These are terrible times, Jose, but I can't use this—what's happening to Olivia to run back to you."

Jose cleared his throat. His voice was gruff when he spoke. "If you ever need me, Brynne—give me a call."

Brynne watched as he walked away.

Camille

Camille drove through the streets of Cleveland listening to her favorite jazz station. She loved jazz. It calmed her down. On the radio Billie Holiday was singing "God Bless the Child." How appropriate, she thought as she pulled into Mama Laurel's driveway. The downstairs lights were on. In their rush to get to the hospital, they had forgotten to turn off the lights.

Camille was surprised that either of them had the presence of mind to lock the door behind them. Although her grandmother liked to brag about her Shaker Heights neighborhood, crime was still a fact of life, whether you lived in the 'hood or the Heights. She turned the engine off and for a moment stood staring at her grandmother's house. She was tired. She wanted to go to her own home and throw herself on her bed, but Mama Laurel had asked her to make sure her own house was in order, and as tired as she was, she still didn't want to hear Mama Laurel's mouth in the morning if she disobeyed her orders.

Camille fumbled in her purse for the keys.

Her big black purse was like everything else in her life, a complete mess. Still, Camille refused to indulge in any self-pity. She had contributed to whatever state her life was in, and if she wanted things to be different, she was going have to be different. *When Olivia gets better,* Camille promised herself, *I'm heading to Atlanta.* Atlanta, land of warm weather, new opportunity, and distance from her family.

Camille pulled out every set of keys she had in her purse before she found the right ones. She had keys for her apartment, for her grandmother's house, for her office, and for Brynne's condo. *What the hell do I need with so many sets of keys?* she thought as she opened her grandmother's door.

Closing the door firmly behind her, she looked warily around her grandmother's house. When she was a little girl she used to think that there were ghosts in this house. Ghosts of people who had once lived there or who had just passed through. She felt their presence tonight. They were sitting around watching her and her family as the various dramas unfolded. She wondered if they were amused, disappointed, or just plain-old fed up with her family, just as she was.

Her grandmother's house had always brought out conflicting feelings in Camille. This was a place filled with as many good memories as bad. She had grown up here. She had lost count of how many times she had sworn that once she left home for college she would leave this house and her family's various problems behind. She loved her family, but it was no lie that there were times when they drove her crazy. Still, this was a house where she had shared a lot of laughter with her sisters. Looking back, it was hard to believe that she and her sisters had ever shared a closeness, but there was a time, long ago, when you couldn't tell where one sister began and the next one ended. They were each other's best friends. What had happened to pull them all in different directions? Growing up was only part of the explanation, but Camille did not know what the other reasons were that accounted for the estrangement between her and the rest of her family. True, they had long disapproved of her choices, from the men she dated, to the friends she had. Even the clothes she wore elicited disapproving comments—too tight, too short, too red, too black. "Girl, how do you walk in those high heels?" Wasn't family about acceptance? thought Camille. Where was her family when that lesson was taught?

Camille heard the doorbell ring. Who the hell could that be, at this hour? It was past ten o'clock. She walked over to the front door and looked through the peephole. It was Harold. Camille's mouth dropped open in surprise. What on earth was he doing here? They'd had a fight last week and they hadn't spoken since. Seeing him in church this morning had brought all his angry words back to her. Harold had been upset because Camille had accepted a dinner invitation from an art teacher that she had recently been introduced to at a party she hadn't wanted to go to in the first place. His name was Omar and he was not the type of man that she was interested in, tall, attractive, with smooth brown skin and a clean-shaven head. Camille admitted to herself that the outward package looked good. But he had two basic problems. He did not have a big bank account and he did not act in any way impressed by her. His invitation to dinner was one of the most casual she had ever received and she would have told him no quickly if Harold had not been getting on her nerves quite as regularly as he had been.

Harold had been furious. He had called her every name in the book. When that didn't work, he tried whining, which yielded even worse results than his name calling. He finally resorted to threats. He started with the "if I can't have you, no man can" nonsense and Camille had put a quick stop to that by walking out on him, but not before telling him about himself. She had not heard from him since. The whole thing was ridiculous anyway because she ended up calling Omar and left him a message on his answering machine canceling the date. She never heard from him after that. *Just as well*, she thought. *What can a high-school music teacher do for me?*

Camille hesitated before opening the door but she knew the nature of this particular beast. He was not going to go away. He'd seen her car in the driveway, and he'd ring the bell until someone answered the door. "What do you want, Harold?"

"I'm worried about you, girl."

She hated when he called her that. She was thirty-five, for God's sake. "Harold, you haven't answered my question. What do you want? I'm tired. It's late and I really don't want to talk to you."

"Where's Mama Laurel?" Harold asked, warily.

"At the hospital with Olivia," Camille replied. "What are you doing here?"

"I heard about Olivia," he replied. "I went by your house and then I came here. I wanted to see if there's anything I can do for you, Camille."

"There's nothing at all you can do for me, Harold, except to leave."

"Are you sure about that?"

Harold leaned in closer to Camille as if he wanted to kiss her. Camille stepped back and surveyed her married lover. He looked good. His looks were definitely never the problem. Harold had the thick, firm build of someone who played football, as he had in college. He was medium height, with tight, jet-black, curly hair, which provided an interesting contrast to his pale skin. Camille knew that she wasn't the first woman and probably wouldn't be the last to make a fool out of herself over Harold Bledsoe. The collar of his dark coat was turned up and gave him a rakish air. He reminded her of Ron O'Neal in *Superfly*, all smooth, slicked back, and trouble.

He said, "Let me hold you."

Camille shook her head. "No, Harold. This isn't the time and it damn sure isn't the place."

He ignored her words and took her in his arms. He stroked her back and whispered words that she had heard before. He told her what he wanted to do to her tonight. He told her how he was going to love her, and how she was going to feel. This was wrong. Their whole relationship was wrong—a relationship built on secrets, on other people's pain. They had hurt so many people—Harold's wife, Mama Laurel and the rest of Camille's family, Harold's unborn child. Had it been worth it? No. The passion was great, but even that wasn't real— there was no responsibility, no bills to pay, no diapers to change, no everyday dinners to cook, no laundry to wash, nothing but fun— which grew old quickly. Camille wanted more. She knew that she deserved more. She'd known some foolish women who'd fallen in love with their married lovers, but Camille had not allowed herself to get caught in that particular trap. Instead, she'd taken the temporary passion the same way other folks took drugs to dull an unspecified ache. The ache had been there for a while—not painful enough to do anything drastic about it, but still persistent enough that the sex and the lies that came with a relationship with Harold Bledsoe provided a welcome relief.

"You need me, baby girl," he whispered, "just like I need you."

"No." Camille choked out the words, even as she felt her body responding to him as it had so many times before. She could forget a lot of things in Harold's arms, just as she had done before. She pressed her hands against his chest to push him away; instead he pulled her tighter, and she felt whatever resolve she still had to tell him to go home drain away from her. She wanted to be with him tonight. It was wrong. It was temporary. But she wanted someone to take her away from this place, from this time, from this pain, even if just for a few moments.

"We've had some bad times, Camille." Harold's voice was husky, and Camille knew that he was feeling the same passion that she felt. "Let me be there for you. Don't shut me out, Camille."

He kissed her then. He kissed the corners of her mouth, the tip of her nose, her earlobes, her eyebrows, her chin, the base of her neck. Camille wrapped her arms around his neck, drawing him closer. *Just for tonight. I need to forget, just for tonight.*

Harold lifted her then, and carried Camille inside her grandmother's house.

Brynne

Brynne heard the telephone ringing as soon as she opened the front door to her apartment. *Olivia,* she thought, *someone's calling about Olivia.* She felt her heart start to pound as she reached to answer the phone. Bad news, she thought. Folks only called this late if they had bad news.

"Hello," she said.

"Hello, Brynne." She heard Malcolm's voice on the line. If she hadn't been in such a hurry to go out with Malcolm Saturday night, then maybe she could have helped Olivia chase away whatever demons had caused her to hurt herself, she thought, as a fresh wave of guilt washed over her.

"I know it's late," Malcolm continued, "but I just wanted to hear your voice. I tried calling you a couple of times before, but you weren't home."

"I was at the hospital," Brynne said stiffly. *Now why did I mention that to him?* Brynne thought with a flash of annoyance. *There I go again, spreading my family business. Mama Laurel is right about me. Everyone doesn't have to know all my business.*

"What happened?"

Brynne shook her head. How could she explain what happened? She wished in heaven's name she knew what happened, why her sister had done this to herself. Why her sister never seemed to be able to put her past where it belonged, firmly behind her. She wished she knew what made Olivia's brown eyes just stay sad. She wished she knew where her sister had gotten lost and left behind. Was it the rape? Brynne seemed to remember that sadness had clung to her baby sister like strong perfume, even before that terrible time. She felt the tears roll down her face. *Again, Lord, I don't have any more tears to cry,* she thought, even as the sobs rose in her throat.

"Brynne, what's wrong?" Malcolm's blues-bass voice was concerned. "Can you talk about it?"

"No." Brynne choked back a sob. "No. No. No. No."

She put the telephone back in its cradle and walked over to her sofa. She cried like a newborn baby. Her tears provided some comfort. They provided a release. She didn't hold back. There was no one around to tell her to be strong. There was no one around to stop her, to hand her tissues, to soothe her. No one.

She lay down on the sofa and cried until her eyes closed from exhaustion and from sadness. She cried until she finally fell asleep.

Then there was someone knocking on her door. The sound roused her from a dreamless sleep. Disoriented, she looked at the clock on the wall. It was almost midnight.

She sat up and stared at the door, debating whether to go and see who had come by this late or to go to her room, to get into her bed, and pull the covers over her head.

Oh, hell, she thought as she got up and walked to her front door. Whoever this person was, pounding on her door like some maniac, it had better be important.

She looked through the peephole and saw Malcolm.

"Brynne," he called out. "I know you're in there. The doorman let me in. He said he saw you come in earlier. Let me in."

Brynne opened the door. At another time she might have been concerned about the mess she must resemble. Her hair was all over her face, her clothes were wrinkled, and she knew from previous crying jags that her eyes were red and swollen. Now, however, her baby sister had taken a bunch of pills and was in a coma at Cleveland Medical. She had other concerns to get her attention, and looking pretty for Malcolm Blackfoot was not one of them.

"Malcolm, this really is not a good time," said Brynne. "I'm kind of falling apart right now."

He didn't say anything in response to her declaration. Instead, he drew her into his arms and held her.

Brynne didn't know how long they stood there in her doorway, holding on to each other. She lost all sense of time while she clung to a man whom, when all was said and done, she hardly knew. This didn't make sense. She had refused Jose's comfort earlier and now she was clinging to a stranger as if he were a long-lost friend.

He held her tight, while she talked to him. She told him about Olivia, about her sorrow for not being there for her sister when she'd called, about her fear that she would lose her sister just as she had lost her mother and her father. Told him she should never have hung that telephone up when Olivia needed to talk with her.

"I could have helped her," said Brynne. "I could have stopped her."

He didn't say anything. He just kept on listening, and when she was finished, he led Brynne to her bedroom, where he laid her down on the bed. Then he lay down beside her, and held her, once again, in his arms.

She felt, inexplicably, safe. *I hardly know this man,* Brynne thought as her eyes grew heavy with the promise of imminent sleep. Still, the warm scent of him, the way that he held her, strong, and steady, even his silence, all of it gave her comfort. The last thing she remembered before sleep came and carried her peacefully away was the feel of a soft kiss against her forehead.

Naomi

Naomi did not like flying. The way this plane was bouncing all over the sky confirmed her deeply held belief that if God had wanted folks to fly, He would have given them some wings just like He gave those birds that flew way below the plane. The plane hit a rough patch of turbulence and Naomi gripped the hand rest and tried to calm herself. When the turbulence stopped, Naomi said a quick prayer of thanks. Her thoughts turned to her granddaughter Olivia. She wondered when the turbulence in Olivia's life would end.

A sense of sadness gripped Naomi as she thought about Olivia and her latest troubles. She had tried to tell Laurel to keep a close eye on Olivia. The last time Naomi saw her, last Thanksgiving, Olivia had seemed more fragile than ever. But Laurel always felt as if she knew everything. Nobody could ever give her advice, and now her granddaughter was in a fight for her life. Naomi wondered, not for the first time since she'd heard this news, where Laurel was when this was going on.

Don't you worry, baby, Naomi made a silent promise to her grand-daughter. *I'm coming to Cleveland. Help is most definitely on the way, and if I have to get on a plane that looks like the last time it saw some action was in World War Two, then so be it.* Everything was going to be all right. She just knew it. Somewhere, deep inside her, she had faith that Olivia was going to pull through this.

"First time in Cleveland?" asked the friendly stranger to her right.

Naomi shook her head but did not speak. This man had been try-ing to get her into a conversation since before the plane even left the ground. The only thing worse than being on an old plane during tur-bulence was being on an old plane, during turbulence, and stuck be-side a friendly, overly talkative stranger.

"Great city!" chimed in the friendly stranger to her left. "Gets a bad rap about the weather, but hell, if you want sunshine, I say move to Florida!"

I stand corrected, thought Naomi. Being stuck between two friendly, overly talkative strangers was worse.

"Ever been to Florida?" asked her other neighbor, as if they were a tag team.

Once again, Naomi shook her head and remained silent.

"My daughter's down in Florida. I go there every chance I get."

Wish you were there now, thought Naomi wearily. All she wanted was some silence, some peace. She needed to focus her energies on deal-ing with the drama that was sure to await her in Cleveland. She did not need to talk about Cleveland, Florida, or any other subject with these folk.

"So what brings you to Cleveland?" asked the friendly stranger on the left.

"My granddaughter tried to kill herself."

Nothing like the truth to shut folks up, thought Naomi as she ob-served the immediate embarrassed silence that met her reply. The friendly stranger on the left raised his eyebrows in surprise and mur-mured something about being sorry. The friendly stranger on the right hid behind a *Golf Digest* magazine. Any attempt at polite conver-sation had ended, Naomi thought with a sense of satisfaction. She knew that she needn't have been quite so direct, but sometimes folks with the best of intentions would try her, and anyone who knew her knew that Naomi Darling and the concept of patience were strangers.

She closed her eyes as the turbulence had finally stopped, and she felt the plane sway back and forth as if gently rocking its inhabitants. For the rest of the flight, Naomi's neighbors were silent and she thanked the Lord for His mercies. She did not think she could have endured even one more minute of the nonsense that was coming out of the mouths of these two strangers. Not when her baby was lying in some hospital in Cleveland fighting for her life.

Eight

Camille

Camille woke up with a sour taste in her mouth and the sunlight shining in her eyes. She was lying on her grandmother's floor, with a blanket thrown over her body. She looked over to see if Harold was still around, but Harold and all traces of him were long gone. As Camille knew, he was like a vampire. He was always gone by the morning.

It was clear that he had gone back to his wife in the middle of the night. That was his pattern. A long time ago this used to bother her. Now she didn't care. She just wanted him out of her life. Yet, as strong as her desire to be away from Harold was, the desire to be with him had been stronger. He was like a drug for her. Something forbidden and destructive, but something that had been irresistible. Lately, irresistible had given way to fed up. She wanted more than what Harold could give her. It was time to move on.

Camille groaned as she turned over. Her bones ached from a night on the floor. She was glad he was gone. Last night after they'd made love, he'd argued with her. He'd wanted to see her today, and she'd explained to him that her sister was in the hospital. He'd accused her of cheating on him. Once again, he'd brought up Omar, the teacher she'd met at the party. She'd tuned him out and fallen asleep, but she'd awoken more determined to get him out of her life. She was tired of the drama that came with Harold. The passion was good, but it didn't outweigh all the other nastiness that came with sleeping with someone who was promised to another. She couldn't go on like this.

Camille sat up and surveyed her surroundings. Everything seemed to be in order. Her clothes were folded and placed on her grandmother's couch. Camille remembered in the early days of their relationship that after they had made wild love, she would watch in amazement as Harold went from one end of the room to another, picking up clothes and placing everything in order. Back then she thought it was cute. Now she recognized the excessive neatness for what it was, Harold's need to have control over whatever environment he found himself in.

Camille got up and walked naked through her grandmother's house. She was thirsty and she needed to drink something cold. Her stomach started to growl as if it knew that it was about to be fed. Few things in life were certain, but Camille knew that she could bet her last nickel that her grandmother's refrigerator would be well stocked.

There was a note taped on the refrigerator door in Olivia's handwriting. She picked it up and read the words *I'm sorry.* Camille folded up the note and placed it on the countertop. She forgot about her hunger, about Harold, about everything else but her sister Olivia. She needed to go to the hospital. She needed to see her sister.

Mama Laurel's words came back to her as they usually did in times of great stress. *"Always remember, blood is thicker than water, you remember that, Camille. You might get mad at me and your sisters, and none of us is perfect, but when the chips are down, there is no one who will stand by you like this family. Your family."*

Camille started moving around the kitchen quickly and with specific purpose. She was going to make herself some coffee and after that she would head over to the hospital to relieve Mama Laurel. She hadn't heard from Mama Laurel last night, and that was a good sign.

If anything had happened to Olivia, Mama Laurel would have immediately gotten in touch with her. Camille's mind raced as she thought of the several things she had to face this day, including a desk at work full of telephone messages to be returned.

Well, thought Camille, as she turned on Mama Laurel's coffee-maker, everything would get done once she got herself ready and went over to the hospital. Her job would have to wait.

Brynne

The smell of strong coffee welcomed Brynne to a new morning. She eased open her eyes and saw Malcolm standing in her bedroom with a breakfast tray, filled with food. For a moment, she was disoriented. This picture was unfamiliar. Then she remembered. Olivia. Had she made it through the night?

"Good morning, sunshine." Malcolm smiled at her. "I hope you're hungry. I've got Blue Mountain coffee, turkey bacon, eggs, and grits for the lady's pleasure. There's also some whole-wheat toast here— enough to feed two very hungry people."

"I know you didn't get all that from my kitchen," said Brynne.

It had been a while since anyone used her kitchen for anything except heating up food in the microwave. Brynne couldn't remember the last time she'd even plugged in her coffeemaker. Since her divorce, Brynne's inclination to explore her culinary skills had all but disappeared.

"No, I've been busy this morning. I went to the supermarket and believe me, I've come back with enough provisions to last you the week."

"Malcolm, this is really kind of you . . ." This was awkward. Every bit of it. Last night . . .

Sleeping in the same bed with him, even though nothing had happened, was awkward. Waking up to him. Seeing him here in her room, in her space, as comfortable and natural as if he belonged here even in the midst of all the drama, was confusing. One week ago he was a handsome stranger she flirted with in the coffee shop. This morning he was something else, although she wasn't exactly sure how to define this new change in his status.

"I'm worried about Olivia," said Brynne. "I really need to get back to the hospital. I appreciate—uh, everything—especially last night. I needed a friend, and, well, thanks."

Malcolm sat down on the bed beside her. He placed the tray in front of her and said calmly, "You need your strength to get through this. You have to eat something. Once you've eaten, then I promise you, you'll feel better able to deal with what the world is offering you today."

He had a dimple in his left cheek, Brynne thought absently, watching his lazy smile.

"You sound like my grandmother." Brynne returned his smile. "She believes that good food cures most ills."

"She's a wise woman," said Malcolm, as he handed her a cup of strong-smelling coffee.

"Besides, my food is special, Brynne," he said, drawing his words out slowly. "It has a secret ingredient that not only gives sustenance, but also strength—strength enough to deal with troubling times."

"But I have to get to the hospital," said Brynne, taking the cup from his hands.

"Has anything happened?" asked Malcolm. "Have you heard anything?"

"No." Brynne shook her head. "I haven't heard a word."

"All right, then," said Malcolm, "drink your coffee, eat your breakfast, and then you can go to the hospital."

"Malcolm—"

"Remember what I said about the powers of my food, Brynne. You don't want to miss out on this, trust me."

The grits did smell good.

"I am hungry," she said, taking a sip of the coffee.

"Well, eat up then," he said, "and remember there's plenty more where that came from."

He had a small diamond earring in his left earlobe. Usually, Brynne found men who wore earrings a little too flashy for her taste, but it looked good on Malcolm. Everything looked good on Malcolm, but that was a whole other topic to concern herself with at a later date. Right now, she had to go on and eat this food; then she needed to get over to the hospital.

She tasted the grits and immediately her senses went heavenward. "This *is* delicious!"

"You sound as if you're surprised."

"I just never knew a man who could cook," she answered before thinking how stupid that comment sounded. Jose did not cook, but that didn't make him the general representative for the male species.

"Actually, cooking is just one of my many talents," Malcolm replied, his tone mild.

"Did your wife teach you how to cook?"

Malcolm smiled. "I've had two wives, remember? Neither of them could cook—I think that was part of the reason why they married me. No, my daddy taught me how to cook. He was a cook on the railroad."

"Well, maybe wife number three will be such a good cook she'll keep you out of the kitchen."

Malcolm picked up a piece of the turkey bacon and took a bite. Then he said, "There won't be a wife number three. I'm not the marrying kind, Brynne."

"I'm sorry," Brynne said quickly. "It sounds like I'm trying to get into your business."

Malcolm shrugged. "No problem, I like to be straight with everyone."

"Sometimes I think that I should probably give up on marriage—after my experience with my ex-husband."

Malcolm smiled at her. "Oh, you'll get married again. There are too many men out here looking for a good woman."

"What about the good women looking for a good man? You're a good man. Somebody's bound to scoop you up."

Malcolm laughed. "I like my freedom a little too much to be good company for any wife. Both of my wives found that out."

"Were you unfaithful to them?" The question left Brynne's lips before she had a chance to stop herself.

"No," said Malcolm. "I left them before it got to that point. I like the company of women, Brynne. I have a lot of women friends, and truth be known, I like hanging with women a lot more than I like hanging with men. I'll probably end up a lonely old man—you know, the kind that always talks about the one that got away."

"Well, at least you know who you are," said Brynne. "I'm still trying to find myself."

Malcolm raised a glass of orange juice in salute. "Here's to the search, Brynne—and here's to the beginning of a very nice friendship."

Brynne raised her orange-juice glass in response, and then took a sip of the juice. She glanced at the clock on the wall and saw that it was almost nine o'clock.

"I've got to get to the hospital," she said.

"Do you need a ride?" Malcolm asked.

"Thanks," Brynne said as she got out of bed, "but I think I'll take my car. After I go to the hospital, I need to go to work to straighten out a few things."

"Work?" Malcolm was surprised.

"Yeah," said Brynne, "but not for long. I have a meeting and then I'll go back to the hospital."

"I think I've just met the African-American superwoman."

Now it was Brynne's turn to smile. "I'll be glad when I get to take that big old *S* off my chest."

Mama Laurel

The telephone in Olivia's room rang once and Mama Laurel moved quickly to answer it. "Hello," Mama Laurel said into the telephone receiver. It was Camille.

"What's going on with Olivia and why haven't you called me?"

Yesterday Camille was complaining about her sister and this morning she was acting all concerned. Mama Laurel couldn't help smiling. No one ever accused Camille of being predictable. "Nothing's going on with Olivia at this point," Mama Laurel replied. "She's the same."

"You sound like hell."

The Lord giveth and the Lord taketh away. "Well, pardon me, Miss Camille, if I'm not here doing jumping jacks so early in the morning. I guess spending the night in the hospital doesn't bring out the best in me."

"Okay, okay, okay," Camille said quickly as if she wanted to avoid any warfare. I just thought you sounded worried."

"I am worried, Camille."

"Well, I don't want you to worry, Mama."

"Wish for something else, Camille," Mama Laurel responded. Not worrying at this point was like not breathing. Olivia should be awake by now, Mama Laurel reasoned. She knew that this feeling was based on nothing more than hope and prayers, but that should be enough.

"I'm coming to get you, Mama," said Camille.

"No," said Mama Laurel quickly. *That's the last thing I need. My blood pressure is already high enough.* She was too tired and too down to face Camille this morning. She wanted to go home and she wanted to be alone. If her granddaughters saw her now, they would be worried and they had enough to deal with already.

"I can take a cab."

"Mama, let me take you home."

Mama Laurel would not be moved. "I'm taking a cab."

"Mama, don't be a martyr," said Camille. "I can be there in half an hour."

"I'm not being a martyr. I'll see you later."

"But, Mama—"

Mama Laurel hung up the phone. The conversation was over.

She looked over to where Olivia lay, and said, "Olivia, your sister means well, but she sure can try you sometimes. Anyway, I'm going home now, but I'll be back later on. Your sisters are coming to see you today. We all love you, Olivia—just please, come on back to us. Please."

Camille

A dozen white roses in a clear crystal vase were waiting for Camille in her office. There was a note with the bouquet, but she didn't bother reading it. She knew who the roses were from and she had a pretty good idea what the note would say. The theme of undying love was getting as old as it was false. Harold knew that he'd annoyed her when they argued about Omar, and this was his way of making up. No one could accuse Harold of being original.

Camille's head hurt as she surveyed her small office. She'd put off going to the hospital. She needed to get some things done first. Olivia's condition hadn't changed, according to Mama Laurel, so she'd come to the office with the intention of staying a short while and getting some work done before going to spend the rest of the day in the hospital. Her secretary, Jim, had placed all her files in order and she was grateful. When she'd left work on Friday, her office had looked as if a hurricane had descended on the little room and took nothing for granted. All the papers she'd left strewn over the desk were now placed in neat piles with yellow stickers on them, identifying both priority and identity. Jim was worth his weight in gold, and then some, Camille thought as she sat down in the worn, brown leather chair behind her desk.

There was a lot to do today and she needed to get organized. She'd gotten a late start. She had called Jim to reschedule all of her meetings. "Family emergency," she'd told him, "I'll fill you in later." Family emergency. That phrase could be used to describe the general state of her life. There always seemed to be some drama with the Darling sisters, from Olivia's demons to Brynne's recent divorce, to Camille's own turbulent love life.

Camille heard a knock on the door and looked up to see Jim striding into her office. Most people, particularly those who knew Camille as well as Jim did, would wait to get some sort of response before being summoned into her domain. But with Jim, Camille counted herself lucky if he bothered to knock before coming into her office. According to the rumor mill, Jim had played football in college, although this was just one of the many rumors that Jim would neither verify nor deny. He was at least six feet six and a good two hundred and fifteen pounds of solid man. Jim was, Camille was quick to admit, a departure from any stereotype she had about assistants. After she had gone through a series of them, Jim was the best she'd ever worked with, and he did not hesitate to remind her of this fact whenever he felt this necessity arose.

Jim observed the bouquet with one raised eyebrow and said, "I guess homeboy hasn't left his wife yet."

Jim knows entirely too much of my business, thought Camille, *and if he wasn't so damn invaluable I'd tell him about himself.*

"Thanks for straightening out this mess for me. What would I do without you?" said Camille, refusing to let Jim bait her this Monday morning.

"Let's hope you never have to find out," said Jim. "By the way, what is the nature of the family emergency? Is everything okay?"

"It's Olivia," said Camille in a clipped, tight voice that clearly expressed her desire not to go into any more detail than she had to. "She's in the hospital."

Jim knew when to back off. "I'm sorry. I'll pray for her."

"Thanks," said Camille, anxious to change the subject. She knew that eventually she would tell Jim the exact nature of her family emergency, but she wasn't ready to talk about Olivia now.

"I need to look at the Mitchell House file," Camille continued. "I'm supposed to be interviewing the director tomorrow."

"Right here, boss." Jim was in his element. He might be the nosiest, tell-it-like-it-is secretary around, but he was organized and he knew his stuff. They had been together for three years, and although he'd threatened to quit frequently, he seemed as happy to be with her as she was with him. Camille knew that she was difficult to deal with. As Mama Laurel stated often and loudly, Camille was born difficult. But Jim gave as good as he took, and then some. It didn't hurt that he was the smartest person she had ever met, with not just book smarts but people smarts. He could read people within minutes of meeting them. Camille wondered how she was going to do without him if she took the job in Atlanta. She knew that Jim was not leaving Cleveland.

He had lived all over the country before he found acceptance and happiness in Cleveland. Jim's wife had died of brain cancer five years ago, and it had taken him a long time to rejoin the living. He'd found support and sustenance here in Cleveland, and he'd found a fresh start. Camille was not about to ask him to give that up.

Jim handed Camille a thick manila folder. "Happy reading."

As he turned to walk out of Camille's office, Camille said to him, "If Harold calls, tell him I'm not in, okay?" *What a difference a day makes,* thought Camille. In the light of day, her sanity had returned as well as her headache.

Jim shook his head. "Why do you play these games, Camille? If you don't want to talk to him, tell him. This cat-and-mouse stuff is wearing on my nerves. Especially since I'm the one that has to deal with the adulterer—oops, sorry."

"Yeah, well, life is tough and then you die."

"Oh my, aren't we Miss Sunshine today! You know if he starts getting all funky with me, I'm going to have to tell him about himself."

"Again?" A smile played about Camille's lips as she remembered the last time Jim told Harold off, after a particularly nasty conversation where Harold made the mistake of trying to pull rank.

"Oh well, what can I say? You can take the man out of the ghetto . . ." said Jim before he made his exit, with a dramatic slam of the door.

Brynne

Brynne sat in Olivia's hospital room and held her hand. After Malcolm left her apartment, she'd come over to the hospital. By the time she'd arrived, Mama Laurel had already left. The nurses, in particular, seemed relieved by Mama Laurel's departure. It didn't take a Rhodes Scholar to guess that Mama Laurel was as hard on them as she was on everyone else who crossed her path. Sometimes she was just plain-old impossible. There was just no reasoning with her. She lived her life as if she'd earned the right to be disagreeable. Brynne's other grandmother, Gram Naomi, was just as difficult as Mama Laurel. But Gram Naomi still had a little tact left. There were some things that even Gram Naomi wouldn't say, in the name of good manners. Mama Laurel, on the other hand, had never met a thought that she didn't care to share with whoever was in her presence at the time.

Brynne wondered when Gram Naomi was going to get into town. Camille had told her that Gram Naomi was on her way to Cleveland, but that was yesterday, and no one had heard from her yet. Brynne knew that Gram Naomi was no fan of Mama Laurel. The last time Gram Naomi had been in Cleveland, open warfare had been declared and Gram Naomi had sworn she'd never set foot in that city again. Still, even Gram Naomi would have to let go of that Darling pride that ran so deep in her, and in Camille, to come back to be with Olivia. Where was her grandmother?

She turned her attention back to her sister who lay so unnaturally still in her hospital bed. It was as if death had already come to Olivia. "Fight, Olivia, Fight," Brynne whispered to her sister. "Don't give up. Don't leave us. We need you, just as much as you need us. We need you." *If only I had taken that telephone call,* Brynne thought again. *If only.* The two most terrible words in the English language, thought Brynne. *My life seems to be made up of if-onlys. If only I had married someone else. If only I had chosen another career. If only I had gone to art school instead of law school.*

Brynne had always loved to sculpt. Her teachers had all told her that she had a special talent. When she was sculpting, she felt completely free. It was the only time in life when she felt in control of herself and her surroundings. Mama Laurel and Gram Naomi had both told her that sculpting was a fine hobby, but "you need something stable—a job that will put food on your table."

She'd easily given up her dream of a career in sculpting. She hadn't put up a fight. Camille was the only one who had objected to Brynne's giving up her dream so easily. "Follow your heart, Brynne. With all due respect, Mama Laurel and Gram Naomi have already lived their lives. It's time for you to decide how to live your own life." As tempting as Camille's words were, her grandmothers were right. She'd done well as a lawyer, and the fact that sometimes she was a little dissatisfied, well, that was just life.

Olivia stirred and Brynne caught her breath. "Olivia," Brynne called out. "Olivia!"

There was no response, and after a few minutes, Brynne became convinced that she'd imagined Olivia's stirrings. She leaned over and whispered in her sister's ear, "Come back to us, Olivia. We need you. I need you."

Nine

Mama Laurel

Mama Laurel opened the front door to her home and found Naomi sitting on her couch watching television as if she had a right to be there. A cigarette was dangling from Naomi's mouth and she remained focused on the television show until Mama Laurel cleared her throat. Mama Laurel knew that Naomi had heard her open the door, but this was just Naomi's way. She wasn't going to acknowledge you before she got good and ready.

Naomi turned her head in Mama Laurel's direction. "Laurel," she said, "how's my grandbaby?"

No hello. No how are you? No explanation for the reason she was sitting in Mama Laurel's house. No warning that she was going to arrive. *Some things just don't change,* Mama Laurel thought, shaking her head.

She didn't answer the question; instead Mama Laurel had a question of her own. "How did you get in here, Naomi?"

It had been three years since she'd last seen Naomi. At that time she'd told Naomi to get the hell out of her house. In all the years she'd been on this earth, she'd never thrown anybody else out of her house. Naomi had insulted Mama Laurel's daughter, Antoinette.

She'd had the audacity, there was no other word for it, to say that Antoinette had been spoiled by Mama Laurel. Then Naomi had crossed the line from being wrong and opinionated to being plain-old spiteful when she'd said that Mama Laurel was spoiling her grand-daughters, and was preventing them from being the women they ought to be. "They haven't grown up yet, Laurel," she'd declared, "and that's your fault."

Mama Laurel had felt the heat rush straight to her head. For one terrible moment she thought she'd pass out, the dots in front of her eyes having signaled that fainting was a possibility, but Mama Laurel was too stubborn to let that happen. She'd be damned if she let Naomi get the better of her.

"Get the hell out of my house, Naomi," she had said, her voice calm, but her insides shaking with her rage. Since that time, they hadn't even spoken on the telephone, despite their granddaughters' attempts to heal the feud.

Once long ago, when their children had married, they were friends. They would call each other up and chat for hours about the latest spat the newlyweds were having. When Antoinette became pregnant with their first grandchild, they were overjoyed, each one good-naturedly trying to outdo the other with decorations for the nursery and presents for the baby. But something changed their relationship shortly after Brynne was born. Antoinette had a brief fling with an ex-boyfriend who showed up when she was feeling neglected. Antoinette's husband, Sherrod, forgave his wife and their marriage grew stronger despite, or perhaps because of, their trials.

Mama Laurel was disappointed in her daughter, but she stood by her Antoinette. However, Naomi never forgave Antoinette for betraying her son, and from that time the battle lines between Laurel and Naomi were firmly drawn.

"I remembered that you always kept a spare key in the flowerpot," said Naomi.

Mama Laurel shook her head. Was there any of her business that Naomi didn't know?

"How is Olivia?" Naomi asked again.

"She's holding on," said Mama Laurel, closing the door behind her. "She's still in the coma and the doctors don't know when she's coming out of it."

Naomi took a long drag on her cigarette and exhaled slowly, blowing smoke through her nose. "What are you doing home?" she asked.

"This is my house," said Mama Laurel, the hairs on the back of her neck starting to rise. "Last time I checked, I live here."

"I know where you live," replied Naomi, looking up at Mama Laurel through a cloud of smoke. "But I would have thought that you'd be in the hospital with Olivia."

"I've been in the hospital all night," said Mama Laurel. "I just came home to get some rest. I'm going back this afternoon."

"Oh," replied Naomi in a tone that said it all. Disapproval that Mama Laurel had come home and left Olivia in the hospital. "What about Brynne and Camille? Did they choose to stay with their sister?"

"I left Brynne with Olivia. She's spending the morning with her. Camille's supposed to go to the hospital later on this morning."

"For all you know, Laurel, Olivia might be there in that hospital all by herself."

"She's being well taken care of," replied Mama Laurel, trying unsuccessfully to keep from sounding defensive.

"Well, it looks like I got here just in time," said Naomi, taking another drag on her cigarette. "You know I vowed never to set foot in this place after you threw me out. But because of Olivia's situation, I put aside my natural inclination to avoid both you and this place. It's times like these when family should be rallying around Olivia. Can't just rely on the doctors. They can't give her the kind of support family can. The kind of support she obviously has been missing."

Mama Laurel had to count to ten twice before she answered. She didn't want to end up shouting at Naomi. There was already too much drama in the family and she didn't want to engage in any arguments with Naomi. She was not going to let this hateful woman get on her nerves.

"If you want to go to the hospital, Naomi, then that's what you should do."

"That's what I'm going to do. It's high time somebody took this situation in hand. Things have been out of control, not only with Olivia, but with the other girls, Laurel, as I've been saying for a while. If you couldn't handle it, you should have called me and asked for some help. Too much pride is not a good thing, Laurel."

The words were said softly, but the venom came through loud and clear.

What little self-control Mama Laurel possessed snapped. "Naomi, I just spent a night with my granddaughter who tried to kill herself. I don't have any time for your mess. I won't have you coming into my house, where I pay the mortgage and everything else up in here, and insult me. I won't have it! I threw you out once before and before God, if you continue down this road, I'll be throwing you out again. You sit there down in your high-society home, jetting to different social events, throwing your lawn parties, sending the girls money on their birthday and on Christmas, visiting them once a year when it's convenient for your busy schedule, and you have the nerve to talk to me about what I haven't done for them?"

"You know those girls come first in my life! How dare you suggest that my social engagements are more important to me than them?"

"I call it like I see it, Naomi! Straight, right down the middle!" Mama Laurel realized that she had lost the battle not to scream at this hateful woman. "Being a special-events grandmother is not enough. The girls needed more and I gave them more!"

"Well, obviously," said Naomi, getting up from the couch, "it wasn't enough."

Mama Laurel walked to the antique desk in the corner of the living room and opened the top drawer. Finding what she was looking for, she pulled out a pink ceramic ashtray with the words *Martha's Vineyard* emblazoned in gold on the sides of the ashtray. She closed the drawer and walked over to where Naomi was standing.

"I know that it's been a while since you've been in my house," said Mama Laurel, "but I don't allow people to smoke in here. It's a nasty habit and the smell stays a lot longer than the smoker ever does."

She was being rude and she didn't care. She wanted Naomi out of her house and she didn't care what she had to do to accomplish this goal. If she had to get down on Naomi's level, which, as far as Mama Laurel was concerned, was beneath her, then that was exactly what she would do.

Naomi took the ashtray from Mama Laurel and put out the cigarette without any comment.

"I hope that you've made a reservation for a hotel," said Mama Laurel, not caring that now she was way past rude. "There's no room for you here."

Naomi raised her left eyebrow. "Six bedrooms and no room? I guess that's what they call northern hospitality, Laurel. Never you mind, I'll stay with one of the girls. They might have been raised here up North, but they haven't forgotten their southern manners. It's in their blood."

"Naomi," said Mama Laurel, her voice shaking as she tried to control her anger, "I'm going to ask you again, what are you doing here in my house?"

"I'm waiting to get some information about my granddaughter. I couldn't find Brynne or Camille, so I figured I'd wait here. All roads seem to lead to your house anyway, at least where the girls are concerned. Keeping them so close to you, Laurel, is just not healthy, but I guess by now you realize that."

Mama Laurel knew that Naomi resented the time her granddaughters spent with her. Growing up, they had spent three weeks each summer with Naomi, and every other Thanksgiving, but now as adults whose lives had all taken different directions, her granddaughters had grown out of the habit of visiting Naomi, although Laurel knew that they talked to her frequently by telephone.

"I just don't know how you could just leave my Olivia at the hospital!" Naomi blurted out.

That's it, thought Mama Laurel. *She's got to go now before I kill her.* "I'll call you a cab. You can go to the hospital now."

"Now, that is a good idea," said Naomi thoughtfully. "I do want to see for myself how Olivia's doing. I guess that after you provide me with food, you can call a cab."

"Food?" Mama Laurel raised her eyebrows. First this hateful woman insulted her and now she wanted food?

"That's right," Naomi replied. "I'm hungry."

Mama Laurel sighed. It didn't make any sense to fight that battle. If feeding this woman was going to be the only way to get her out of the house, then Mama Laurel was prepared to cook a three-course meal. Already, her heart was starting to pound in a most unnatural way.

"How does a ham sandwich sound?" asked Mama Laurel.

Brynne

Jose entered Olivia's hospital room without knocking. Brynne fought an immediate feeling of annoyance. She didn't want to see Jose, but she knew that he was here to support her and her family. He was also here because he loved her sister. He looked tired, as if he hadn't slept much last night. There were dark shadows under his eyes. Her feelings of annoyance gave way to worry. It seemed almost natural to worry about him, even now. After all, she had worried about him—his health, his happiness, his job, anything that touched his world—for years now.

"How's the patient?" Jose asked, walking over and then sitting in the chair next to her.

"About the same," Brynne replied, repeating the latest information that Olivia's doctor had given her.

"Well, that's good news," said Jose.

Brynne turned to look at him. He was too close to her. He made her uncomfortable. The way he stared directly into her eyes, as if he were trying to see if the sadness in his own eyes were reflected in hers.

"How is that good news?" she asked.

"She hasn't gotten worse, Brynne," he replied, calmly. "She's holding on, and that's damn good news."

He was right. That had always been the difference between them. She had always looked at things in their worst light. Jose had a way of running his life using a healthy dose of optimism. He had looked at their marriage in the same way. "We're just having a little trouble, that's all," he'd said when she asked for a divorce. "We can work this thing out, Brynne. We still love each other." *Yes,* thought Brynne, *we do love each other. That hasn't changed.*

Brynne cleared her throat. "This waiting—it's hard," she said. "I just keep wanting her to wake up."

Jose nodded his head. "She'll wake up when she's good and ready, Brynne. Trust me, Olivia is going to come out of this. She's going to be all right."

Brynne felt the tears spring to her eyes. She wished she could share Jose's certainty that this particular story was going to have a happy ending. Before she could stop herself, she said to him, "Olivia called me the night before she did this."

He didn't reply. Instead, he sat quietly, waiting for her to continue.

"I was going out—I didn't talk to her," Brynne said.

Jose interrupted her. His voice was gentle and firm. "Stop right there, Brynne. Stop blaming yourself. Brynne, you can't save the whole world, although God knows that you try."

Brynne looked into Jose's dark brown eyes and saw compassion. She saw love and hurt, but no bitterness. How could he not be bitter after what she'd done to him? She'd walked out on their marriage, not caring that he still loved her and was still willing to do anything to save the marriage. If she were in his shoes, she could not be so forgiving.

"I wish I could be so certain that life is going to work out, no matter what the odds. How do you do it, Jose? After everything, how can you still be optimistic?"

"Is that what you think about me?" he asked, clearly surprised.

Brynne nodded.

"Then you really don't know me at all," Jose said. "I stopped feeling that way the day the woman I loved walked out of my life. Now, Brynne, I just hang on."

"I'm sorry," Brynne said, and she meant it. "I never wanted to hurt you."

Jose put his hands up. "Enough with the true confessions, Brynne. Listen, I know you probably have a lot to do at work. Warrington and Smyth needs its star lawyer. I've cleared the decks at work for the next few hours. I'm going to hang out with Olivia for a while. Why don't you go take care of business and then come back? If anything changes on this front, I'll call you."

Brynne hesitated. She didn't want to leave her sister.

As if reading her thoughts, Jose said, "There's nothing you can do for Olivia now except pray, and you can do that from work. I'm here, don't worry about her being alone. Go on and do what you need to do. Then, come on back and spend time with your sister."

"Thank you," Brynne whispered. "I know that I don't deserve your kindness—but thank you."

"Don't thank me, Brynne," Jose replied. "We're family, no matter what that divorce decree states."

Brynne leaned over and kissed his cheek. As she had so many times since the divorce, she felt regret. Leaving this good man was a hard thing to do, but she was convinced that she needed to do this to find herself. Still, it hurt her, even now that they were no longer a team. She hadn't realized until this moment that through the divorce she'd lost more than a husband, she'd lost her best friend.

Brynne

Warrington & Smyth ruled the Cleveland legal community from the top five floors of the tallest building in Cleveland. Filled with the best, the brightest, and the most connected, Warrington & Smyth had an impressive client list, not only of midwestern regional companies, but of several Fortune 500 companies. Although W&S, as the firm was known about Cleveland, was not hurting for clients, it was helpful for an associate, particularly when one had aspirations of becoming a partner, to develop a client base. Although Brynne had been at W&S for six years, she had only brought in one client, Patton Communications. Brynne was in danger of being late for her appointment with Reggie Patton, the CEO of Patton Communications. Unlike other clients, however, Reggie was a friend, and it was more than likely that Reggie would be late for the meeting himself.

Brynne had known Reggie for most of the time she had lived in Cleveland. His mother, Philomena, was in the same sorority as Mama Laurel. Mama Laurel and Philomena had hatched a misguided scheme to throw Reggie and Brynne together in hopes that they would one day discover that they were right for each other. It never happened. Reggie was always more interested in Camille. Brynne was more interested in her books, and then Jose. Yet, the two of them had become friends, and through their friendship Reggie had become Brynne's client.

Reggie owned a successful African-American radio station in Cleveland. Brynne entered the wood-paneled elevator and pressed the button for the sixty-fifth floor. She wondered what Reggie wanted to talk to her about today. His message last week, when he'd set up the meeting, had been vague. He probably had come up with some get-rich-quick scheme that he needed some legal advice about, thought Brynne. Reggie was a fool with everything else, including his personal life. When it came to business, however, Reggie was nothing short of a genius. Anything he touched turned to gold. Unlike Brynne, who had been an honor student with straight As, graduating at the top of her class at Wellesley College and the University of Pennsylvania's Law School, Reggie had been a C student on a good day, and had dropped out after three semesters. Reggie was one of the most successful and confident people that Brynne had ever met. He always believed he was going places, and if school didn't get him there, he was going to find another way. He hustled and, using nothing but a small inheritance and his shrewd business sense, he had bought a struggling AM radio station and turned that initial investment into Patton Communications.

The elevator door opened and Brynne stepped into the lobby of W&S. She was surprised to see Reggie standing by the receptionist's desk. He appeared to be flirting with the receptionist, from the look of the wide smile on her pretty face. With the exception of the Darling women, Reggie had no trouble whatsoever attracting members of the opposite sex. Women flocked to him like bees to honey and he reveled in this indisputable fact. Brynne would have called him a dog, except he was just so charming about his flirtation, and he was unfailingly candid with all of the many women who moved in and out of his life with apparent ease. His motto in his relationships was "for a good time, call." Brynne watched as Reggie whispered in the receptionist's ear. Her light laughter and quick blush confirmed Brynne's initial suspicion that Reggie was in a serious rap mode.

Brynne cleared her throat and both Reggie and the receptionist looked in her direction. Reggie's face lit into an easy smile when he saw Brynne. "Don't look so surprised that I'm on time."

Brynne noticed that the receptionist was eyeing her warily. The receptionist was new and Brynne did not know her name. Young, mid-twenties, with skin that looked as if it were freshly scrubbed and glowing, and a slim aerobicized body, Miss Receptionist was definitely Reggie's type. She was even the right complexion. Reggie liked his women high yellow. Brown sisters need not apply. The only brown woman that Brynne had ever noticed him interested in was Camille.

"I'm sorry I'm late," said Brynne. "Family emergency."

"Is Camille okay?" Reggie's concern was immediate.

So, thought Brynne, *he's still carrying a torch for Camille.*

Brynne was not the only one who noticed Reggie's concern about Camille. Miss Receptionist did too. Judging from those tight, clamped-together lips, thought Brynne, Miss Receptionist was not happy.

"Camille's fine. It's Olivia," said Brynne.

"Oh." Reggie's eyes were sympathetic. He knew about Olivia's problems. "Is she going to be okay?"

Noting Miss Receptionist's eyes on her, Brynne quickly replied, "Why don't you come on into my office, and let me take a look at that agreement that's giving you all this trouble?"

Reggie turned and gave his card to the receptionist. "Send me that demo tape and I'll take a listen. I have a lot of producer friends in the business. Maybe there's something I can do to get the tape to the right people."

The receptionist's voice was downright reverential. "Thank you, Mr. Patton, I appreciate anything you can do to help."

"Please," said Reggie, "it's my pleasure. And, Cynthia?"

"Yes, Mr. Patton?"

"Call me Reggie."

"Yes, Mr. Patton—oh, I mean Reggie."

Brynne shook her head. The boy was smooth. She had to give it to him. She hoped that Cynthia knew what she was in for. Reggie might be more good looking and rich than he had a right to be, but he was a whole lot of trouble. And Brynne knew that many women could attest that no matter how nice the ride was with Reggie, it always ended badly. Still, she had many things to worry about, and the current state of Reggie's love life did not interest her. She needed to take care of business in order to get back to the hospital.

Camille

Camille sat in her office with one clear thought in her mind—her family was going to drive her crazy. She sat at her desk, holding the telephone receiver, listening to Mama Laurel's voice. Her head was pounding, as she tried her best to concentrate on what she was saying, but as usual, Mama Laurel wasn't making any kind of sense. She was whispering into the telephone and Camille could hardly make out a word she was saying.

Camille tightened her grip on the phone, took a deep breath, tried to count to ten, but stopped at three before she interrupted Mama Laurel in midsentence.

"Mama Laurel, why are you whispering?"

"Because," whispered Mama Laurel, "I don't want that woman to hear what I'm saying!"

"Don't call her that," said Camille. "She's not that woman. She has a name."

"Stop lecturing me, Camille. I am in my own house and I can call that woman any name I damn please. She's lucky I'm saved, or I'd call her a few other names, so help me, Jesus," whispered Mama Laurel.

I am going to lose my mind, thought Camille. She had already canceled two meetings this morning, and she was dodging Harold's calls. The argument they'd had last night after making love had been the final breaking point. If she'd forgotten who Harold truly was, his angry words had brought his true nature into focus—nasty, petty, deceitful, and cruel. They'd used each other last night, and nothing had changed. Olivia was still in the hospital. Harold was still married. His wife was still pregnant. And the relationship was still dead wrong. The morning had not gone well. Now, Mama Laurel was calling on the phone complaining to her about her grandmother Naomi.

"Mama, I'm really, really, really busy."

"Not too busy to call Naomi, I see. What possessed you to call her? As if we don't have enough drama around here without her adding to the mix! What can she do but just stir up trouble? Now she's in my house, sitting here talking about everything I haven't done for you all."

"I called her because she is Olivia's grandmother also. She has as much right to be here as you do," replied Camille. She was tired of the feud between her two grandmothers. Two past-grown women acting like children squabbling over toys.

"You always took up for her," said Mama Laurel. She was no longer whispering. "I remember how you wanted to go and live with her after your mama died."

Camille sighed. She'd known that it was just a matter of time until Mama Laurel mentioned Camille's first unforgivable sin—her decision at age ten to go back to North Carolina to live with Gram Naomi. Mama Laurel had blocked that move, and although Gram Naomi had first agreed to this arrangement, she'd let Mama Laurel talk her out of it. Mama Laurel had reasoned that the sisters should all be raised together, and once Gram Naomi had neither the patience nor the inclination to raise three motherless girls, Camille had remained with Mama Laurel. Still, Mama Laurel had forgiven Camille for this.

Camille had always felt a sense of closeness to Gram Naomi that she hadn't felt with anyone else, even her sisters. Perhaps it was Gram Naomi's strong resemblance to Camille's beloved father that explained the strong affinity between the two women. Whatever the reason, it had always been easy to talk to Gram Naomi, and Camille had lost count of the many times Gram Naomi had given advice, sympathy, cash, or whatever she needed. Camille knew that Gram Naomi was always there for her.

"What do you want me to do, Mama?" Camille knew that Mama

Laurel was on a roll, and once she got going, this tirade could last for a good long time.

"I want you to get over here and get this woman out of my house!"

"Get her a cab, Mama. If she wants to go to the hospital, I'll meet her there."

"I tried that. At first she agreed but now, just to be disagreeable, she says she wants one of you all to come and bring her to the hospital."

"Mama, I can't. I have something to clear up here before I go back to see Olivia."

"Brynne's tied up in a meeting or something. The receptionist won't put me through. I tell you, Camille, you've got to get over here quick! She's downstairs snooping. I can't take it. I keep telling you all that my heart is weak! You'd better come on over here quick before you have to start visiting me in the hospital!"

"Mama, I'm really busy here," said Camille even though she knew that it would not make much difference. Mama Laurel's mind was set on Camille coming to get Gram Naomi.

"Just get her out of my house," said Mama Laurel, whispering furiously, "or I will not be responsible for anything that transpires after this phone call."

"Lord, Mama, don't we have enough drama in this family already?" asked Camille.

"I've put up with that woman's meddling and her sour tongue for you all's sake, but I'm here to tell you that I'm tired and all bets are off. She told me she would take a taxi to the hospital after I got her some food. As tired as I was I made her some food, which she ate without one word of thanks to me. Then she tells me that since Olivia's condition is stable, she'll just wait here until one of you all comes to drive her to the hospital. This is after she argued at me for not being at the hospital with Olivia. I tell you my heart can't take another five minutes with the woman! You've got to come home and get her, Camille. If you don't you just might find the heifer outside on my front lawn where I have a good mind to toss her—"

Camille put her pen down on the desk. Work was going to have to wait. What happened in normal families? Camille wondered. One thing was certain, she'd never know. Her family had left normal a long time ago.

"I'll take her to the hospital, Mama."

"Thank you," said Mama Laurel, "and, Camille, please hurry."

Camille heard a click and the dial tone. Mama Laurel's way of saying good-bye on the telephone was simply to hang up whenever she decided that the conversation was over.

Camille picked up her phone and buzzed Jim. When he answered, she said, "I've got to go to Mama Laurel's house. Cancel the rest of my appointments."

T en

Brynne

Brynne looked out of her office window and stared out at downtown Cleveland. Cleveland in February was not a pretty sight. There were times during the year when Cleveland was glorious with warm, hazy summer days, when the ever-present Lake Erie shined a brilliant blue in the sunlight, or when bright colorful autumn with its trees of flaming orange and red leaves made life's occasional blues seem far away. But, Brynne thought as she stared out at the gray skies, with tufts of cotton-white clouds hanging low over the skyline, winter in Cleveland was depressing. Sunshine was a fond yet distant memory, and served to confirm Brynne's black mood. Optimism died an easy death in those gray skies.

Brynne tried to concentrate on what Reggie was saying but her mind was visiting too many different places. She thought of Olivia lying in her hospital bed, oblivious to the chaos her actions had caused. She thought of Malcolm and how easily he had entered her life. She thought of Jose and how difficult it was to get him out of her life. She thought of Pastor Simmons's words about faith, and she thought of what the partner's reaction would be when he found out that she would not be able to make the deposition scheduled for this afternoon. She thought about everything and anything except what her client was saying to her.

Reggie cleared his throat.

"Brynne, you could pretend you're listening to what I have to say."

Brynne turned and faced Reggie. "I'm sorry, Reggie. I've got a lot on my mind. I'm worried about Olivia."

"Is there anything I can do?"

Brynne smiled at him. Even though he was a womanizer, Reggie's friendship was one of the few things she could count on. "No, there's nothing you can do, but I appreciate your asking."

"What hospital is she in? I'll send over some flowers, or better yet, I'll stop by."

"She's at Cleveland Medical," said Brynne, "but she's in ICU. No visitors except immediate family."

"And I'm not immediate family?"

"You're family." Brynne laughed, easing some of the tension. "You're just not immediate."

"Okay," said Reggie, "you're not listening to me, so why don't you tell me what's on your mind and I'll listen to you?"

"I wasn't there for Olivia when she needed me," said Brynne, repeating the words that kept running through her head. It didn't matter what other people said, how other people tried to make her see reason. In her heart, she knew she could have stopped Olivia from doing this if only she had taken the time to listen.

Reggie shook his head. "Brynne, when are you going to stop this? When are you going to stop going through life blaming yourself for everything that happens? Sometimes bad things happen. Period. End of sentence."

Brynne felt a familiar sadness creeping over her. "I've just been unhappy for so long."

"And being in a job that you hate is not helping matters, is it?"

"I don't hate my job," Brynne replied. "I'm just going through a period of dissatisfaction."

"Let's deal with Olivia first. Brynne, it can't be a surprise to you that she needs help. Real help, like from a psychiatrist. There's nothing you can do for her but keep being supportive. Olivia's demons aren't your fault, so you can stop blaming yourself. Blame isn't doing you or Olivia any good. Now about your job situation, I do have a suggestion . . ."

Reggie hesitated, as if he was trying to find the right words. Then he said, "Why don't you come and work for me?"

"You!" Brynne was so shocked that her mouth snapped open in surprise. "Work for you?"

"What's wrong with working for me?" asked Reggie. "You do it anyway."

"Yes, but—work for you?" Brynne repeated the question.

"Look, I need someone in the organization that I can trust. You're bright. You know the law, and even better, you know me. You understand me. I think we'd make a good team."

"Work for you?" Brynne repeated the question one more time, as if she didn't quite understand his words. "As what?"

"I don't know. My right hand. We'd create a position for you. Legal consultant. Vice president of operations. Whatever."

When Brynne finally regained her voice, she said, "I'm flattered, Reggie, but what would I do working at your radio station? I know the legal side of your business, but the corporate side is totally foreign to me."

"Look, you breezed through law school. You passed the bar, for God's sake. You can learn the business side."

As tempting as his offer was, she could never work for him. He was disorganized, trifling, and a few other unflattering adjectives. She was on the partnership track here at W&S, and as remote as that possibility now seemed, she still had a chance. She wasn't about to give that up to work for Reggie and his organization, although the thought of starting over, starting something new was compelling. She did not want to hurt him. So she did the next best thing to rejecting him, she lied. "I'll think about it, Reggie."

"Good!" Reggie clapped his hands together. "Take your time. I know it's a big step and all, but you're not going anywhere here—let's face it, you and I both know that."

Brynne's pride was hurt. Reggie was too close to the truth. "Reggie, I'm on track to be a partner."

Reggie laughed. "Get real. It took W and S twenty years to make a Jewish partner. It's probably going to take them another twenty to make a black woman partner."

"You don't know that," Brynne said quickly.

"No, I don't," said Reggie, "but if I were a betting man, I just wouldn't bet on that, Brynne. Look, the only reason I'm here is because of you. You can do better, Brynne. This is not the right place for you. Has anyone talked about partnership with you recently?"

"No."

"Do you enjoy what you do?"

"Give it a rest, Reggie," said Brynne. "Let's talk about something else."

"I'll let the subject drop," said Reggie. "You have enough things to deal with right now, but once things get less hectic, think about your future here. Realistically."

"I just don't share your pessimism," Brynne lied again.

"Well, at least give my offer some thought. It comes with a raise. A substantial raise. You'll have a lot more responsibility. Brynne, you're the sharpest person I know. You're wasting your talents here."

"I'll think about it," Brynne lied one more time for good measure. "Now, let's go over this contract that's giving you so many problems."

Camille

Camille got to Mama Laurel's house just in time. As she got out of her car she could hear the shouting through an open window. Only Mama Laurel kept her windows open in the dead of winter. "Closed windows make my house smell musty," Mama Laurel would reply whenever someone complained about the cold air. "Between you being cold and my house smelling musty, there is no contest."

Camille took a deep breath and silently asked the Almighty for strength. Her plan was to go in and get her Grandmother Naomi out of the house as quickly as possible. She fumbled in her purse, once again looking for the keys to her grandmother's house. The shouting was getting louder. She briefly considered ringing the doorbell, but quickly discarded the idea. She knew that neither party was going to leave the battle to answer the door. At last she found the keys and opened the front door.

The scene in front of Camille was all too familiar. No matter how things started out with Grandmother Naomi and Mama Laurel, it always ended up this way. They were standing a foot apart from each other, each one yelling at the other.

"It's your fault that my grandbaby is lying there in a hospital! You couldn't raise your daughter properly so what made you think you could raise my grandbabies?" Naomi's voice rose with each word until by the time she had finished her questions, the last word came out in a hoarse squeak.

"Don't you tell me about raising children! Look at how your son turned out! He could barely keep a damn job!" Mama Laurel was rolling up her shirtsleeves as she shouted. That was a bad sign, thought Camille.

The insulting of people who were long dead continued.

"He had a good job, until he met your daughter!"

"That's a lie! Naomi, I won't have you talking trash about my daughter! You can talk about me all you want, but I'll be damned a hundred times before I let you talk that way about her!"

Camille walked over and placed herself in the middle of the two women.

"Stop it," she said, without raising her voice. Both grandmothers looked at Camille as if her presence surprised them. It was obvious that their battle had prevented them from taking notice of her entrance.

Mama Laurel spoke first. "Camille, you get this woman out my house before I call the garbage man and ask him to take out the trash!"

Camille repeated, "Stop it."

Naomi touched Camille's arm. "Camille, come take me out of here before I do something I'm not responsible for."

Camille gave Gram Naomi a quick hug. Although they spoke frequently, it had been at least a year since she'd last seen her. She noticed that Gram Naomi was losing weight. Unlike Mama Laurel, who was tall and solidly built, Gram Naomi had always had a slight frame. At seventy years old, she was still beautiful. She was the color of wheat that had been in the sun for a while. Her gold eyes were still bright, and apart from a few laugh lines around those eyes, Gram Naomi looked years younger than her actual age.

"I'm glad you're here," Camille said to her paternal grandmother, even as she heard her maternal grandmother's murmured grumbling.

Gram Naomi sighed. "Take me to the hospital, Camille."

"Where are your bags?" asked Camille, still keeping an eye on Mama Laurel.

"Over in the corner by the kitchen."

"I'm just going to walk over there and get the bags," said Camille slowly. "If the two of you can't be civil while I do that, at least be silent."

"Camille, there is no need to use that tone of voice to me," said Mama Laurel. "I'm still your grandmother."

"Mama, please," said Camille, not bothering to hide her exasperation.

"Just get the bags, Camille," said Naomi. "I'm anxious to be away from here."

"Camille, you tell her," said Mama Laurel emphatically, "that I don't want her to be around when I go to visit with Olivia. I don't even want her on the same floor. You tell her that!"

"You tell her that I will visit my grandbaby any time I please! Go on, Camille, tell her!" Naomi was starting to raise her voice again.

"You tell her that I don't want her in the same building when I go to visit Olivia."

"*If* you visit Olivia! The way I see it, if I didn't come here, that poor child would be lying in the hospital without any family around!"

"Camille, get her out of here. Get her out of here, I tell you!" Mama Laurel spat out the words.

"Stop it!" This time Camille yelled. "Both of you, stop it! If you don't stop this, I swear I'll turn around and go back to work, which is where I should be anyway!"

Both Gram Naomi and Mama Laurel became instantly silent.

"Gram Naomi, when you told me that you wanted to come here to see Olivia, I hoped that you could come here without bringing any drama."

"I didn't start any drama," said Gram Naomi, drawing herself up, "but if someone's going to start something with me, they better be prepared to finish it!"

"No matter how high some folks climb up on society's ladder," observed Mama Laurel, "they still got one foot down in the gutter."

"Mama Laurel, please!" Camille felt her head pounding. She knew that no aspirin would cure this headache. Months away from her feuding family might do the trick, but she wasn't sure about this.

"If anyone is knowledgeable about life in the gutter," said Gram Naomi, "it's you, Laurel."

"Okay, I'm leaving," said Camille. "You two have to settle this on your own. Gram Naomi, if you want to get to the hospital, you're going to have to take a cab!"

"Now, Camille—"

"Olivia is in the hospital, do I have to remind you two? I don't care how you feel about each other. Right now it's not important. I don't have time for a lecture, and I don't have the heart for it. I'm going back to work and then I'm going to the hospital. You all are just going to have to deal with each other or not deal with each other, but I'm out of it."

"But what about my ride?" asked Gram Naomi.

"Sorry, Gram, but you're on your own with this one."

Mama Laurel and Gram Naomi both looked at her as if she'd just stripped naked and run the Cleveland Marathon. "Have you lost your mind?" Mama Laurel squeaked. "Don't leave me here with this woman."

Camille did not respond. Instead she buttoned her coat and walked to the front door.

She hesitated before she opened it. Turning to her grandmothers, she said, "Stop talking about my parents. Whatever they did or did not do for each other is none of your business. Maybe it's time to focus on your own lives instead of constantly putting yourself into theirs. They are dead and gone and the last time I checked, they've been leaving you alone. Why don't you return the favor?"

Camille then opened the door and walked outside, letting the frigid February wind sweep through Mama Laurel's living room.

Brynne

The phone rang three times before Brynne picked it up. Reggie had left shortly after their discussion about her joining his company. Brynne had sat in her seat for the last half hour staring out of her window at Lake Erie. She had a large office as befitted her status as a senior associate, but her window view left a lot to be desired. Although there was the lake, there were also industrial buildings, smokestacks, and brown hills in the distance.

"Brynne Darling," she said into the telephone receiver.

"Hi, Brynne." It was Jose.

Brynne took a deep steady breath. She felt her heart hammering in her chest, and her mouth go instantly dry.

"Olivia?" She managed to choke out the word.

"Nothing's changed," Jose said quickly. "I knew you'd be worried. So I just wanted to let you know what's going on."

"Thank you," said Brynne, touched by his concern.

She heard him take a deep breath; then he said, his voice quiet and distinct, "I still love you, Brynne."

"Jose ..." Brynne's voice trailed off. What could she say in response to his words? That she still loved him? She did. But she had made the decision to move forward in her life. Moving forward did not include her ex-husband.

"Listen," Jose continued, "let's just change this subject. You know how I feel about you and I know how you feel about me. I wish things were different for us, Brynne, but that's life. I don't know why I'm talking to you about this—I know that it's too late, I know you don't care. Forget what I said, Brynne. I'll talk with you later."

There was a moment of awkward silence between them. Then Jose hung up the telephone.

Eleven

Brynne

Brynne had been summoned to the offices of Winston Gray III, the head partner in the litigation department. His secretary had called her, saying, "Mr. Gray needs to see you right away, and he's not happy." It was never a good thing to be summoned to that particular office. Winston Gray had come from a long line of lawyers. He used to joke that if there were lawyers on the Mayflower, he was sure that they were related to the Grays. As he often told associates with great pride, the Grays were barristers in England long before their emigration to America. Because of his illustrious lineage and the wealth he had accumulated as a result of the law, Winston had a healthy respect for the law and an even healthier respect for W&S. Brynne took a deep breath as she worked up her nerve for what was undoubtedly going to be an unpleasant meeting with Winston.

She was going to miss a deposition in a case worth millions to the firm. Associates, people who had more connections and who were liked by those who had power in the firm, had been fired for less. It would not matter to Winston that her sister had just tried to commit suicide. It would not matter to Winston that she had gotten another associate to cover for her. Nothing mattered to Winston except W&S. She'd left Winston a message earlier to let him know about the deposition. She'd asked another senior associate who was familiar with the case to cover the deposition for her. The client didn't have a problem with the substitution, but Brynne was certain that Winston would not be as understanding.

She walked quickly down the hallway toward Winston Gray's office, trying to ignore the sympathetic looks that the secretaries were giving her. She was never quite sure how the grapevine worked, but it was alive and well in W&S. Secretaries knew all the gossip, usually before many of the attorneys. Keeping her head held high even as her stomach nervously tightened, Brynne forced her outward expression to remain calm. No one needed to know how nervous she was.

When Brynne reached Winston Gray's office, she stopped at the secretary's desk and asked, "Is it safe for me go in?"

Mary O'Reilly, Winston Gray's secretary, was the only person in the firm who was not afraid of him. They had worked together from the time of Gray's first job. When he yelled at her, she would yell back. Legend had it that at one time, before Brynne had started with the firm, Winston Gray had lost his mind and fired Mary. According to the story, which was widely circulated throughout the firm, it took three weeks of begging by Winston Gray, a substantial raise in salary, and a job for her sister Penny before Mary came back.

She was small, thin, devoutly religious woman who wore her black hair parted in the middle and pulled back into a tight bun—what you saw with Mary was exactly what you got. After spending much of her life among lawyers, people who are trained to always keep you guessing, Brynne had found Mary and the few folks like her refreshing.

"Is it ever safe?" Mary replied. "Go on in and take your medicine. He's been waiting for you."

Brynne took another deep breath and walked through the open doors of Winston's office. He was sitting at his desk with a phone at his ear. Winston had the face of a man who was once good looking but who had aged badly, the ruddy, florid face of someone who drank too much, and although firm legend held that he had been quite an athlete during his Yale College days, he had crossed the line from being chubby to obese. Small green eyes filled with contempt peered directly at Brynne. She sat down on one of the chintz chairs placed in front of his desk and waited.

His office, decorated in pastel colors, with antiques and portraits of various landscapes, had been decorated by his daughter, one of the more popular interior designers in Cleveland. It did not reflect either his temperament or his personality. From the heavy drapes with their floral motif to the matching floral cushions on the antique chairs, Brynne expected to see Laura Ashley herself walk through the door.

Winston Gray placed the telephone receiver back into its cradle. *Get ready,* thought Brynne, *it's show time.*

"Close the door, Brynne." Winston's command was said in a soft, neutral voice, but after years of experience working with him, Brynne knew better.

Brynne got up and walked over to the door and shut it. She liked it better this way; at least the whole office wouldn't be witness to the bloodletting that would surely occur soon. After she shut the door she walked over to the chair, sat, and waited.

She did not have to wait long.

"What in the hell do you mean that you're not available for the Byers deposition?" Winston's voice was tight and low.

"I'm sorry, Mr. Gray." Winston insisted on everyone in the firm, including his fellow partners, calling him by his surname. "I have a family emergency."

He raised one dark eyebrow and his voice rasped into a hoarse croak. "A family emergency?"

"Yes," said Brynne, feeling the hair on the back of her neck starting to rise. She knew that this man was incapable of compassion but she'd thought that he would at least fake some concern or in some other way pretend to be human. "A family emergency."

Winston leaned back in his chair, took a deep breath, and said, "The Byers case is one of the biggest cases this firm has now. I don't have to remind you of my initial reluctance in having you work on this case. I felt that this case needed a more seasoned litigator. However, up until now, I have been pleasantly surprised by your work on the case, so that is why I directed that you handle the deposition. So you can imagine my surprise when I found out that you will not do the deposition, and instead you are having Phillip Canzilotta, an associate distinguished only by his less than stellar job performance at the firm, do the deposition. What in the hell were you thinking?"

Brynne didn't know what made her do it. What made her jump up like a crazy woman and rush over to Winston's desk and yell back at him, spit flying in different directions. She had been abused by Winston on a regular basis for the past five years, and each time she did what all the other associates, partners, secretaries (except for Mary), mail sorters, messengers, three ex-wives, and five children did—she took it silently. But something about the way he was looking over the rim of his glasses, the way he looked at her as if she were a piece of garbage that was in his way, something about his insults, about the way he dismissed poor Phil who was the hardest-working associate at W&S and who had three mouths to feed with a fourth on the way, something just didn't sit right with her.

Brynne yelled at him, "I was thinking that my sister tried to kill herself and I didn't know whether she was going to live or die! That's what I was thinking! I wasn't thinking about a deposition of a minor witness that you didn't feel like doing!"

Winston's eyes were round and wide. Disbelief shadowed his face as he looked at Brynne as if seeing her for the first time. Brynne read his thoughts as if they were placed in an open book. *Crazy* was the one word she saw in his eyes. He thought that she had flipped out. Well, if he wanted crazy, she could give him crazy. She could give him so much crazy that he would be talking about it to his friends at the country club for years to come.

"Want to know what else I was thinking about, Mr. Gray? I was thinking about that lousy evaluation you gave me and the paralegal you fired because she mispronounced a client's name and all the countless other people you so nonchalantly step on to get to wherever it is you want to get to! That's what I was thinking of!"

Winston cleared his throat. He opened his mouth as if to say something; then he thought the better of it, and snapped his mouth shut. His eyes shifted around uneasily as if searching for something in the office to protect himself from this African-American female gone hog-wild.

"I am going to the hospital to see my sister. She's at Cleveland Med. If you want to fire me, that's where you'll find me." Brynne turned around and walked to his shut office door. Her heart was pounding, her hands were sweating, and her legs were shaking. But, all things considered, she felt more at ease than she had felt in a long time. *This honesty thing can create a lot of problems,* thought Brynne, *but I see why Mama Laurel does it. It feels damn good.*

When she got to the door, she turned around and said to Winston Gray III, her voice as steady as her nerves, "I would tell you to go to hell, but I don't wish to be redundant."

Mama Laurel

It had taken the taxi half an hour to get to Shaker Heights. Mama Laurel was just about to call the taxi dispatcher for the third time when she heard the sound of a horn in front of the house.

"It's about time," said Naomi as she got her coat.

Mama Laurel never thought that she would live to see the day when she agreed with Naomi, but for once, Naomi was right. The taxi had taken entirely too long. It would have been all right if the dispatcher had said that the taxi would arrive in half an hour, but instead the dispatcher had said it would be there "right away." When did half an hour become right away? thought Mama Laurel as she got her fur and followed Naomi out of the door.

After Camille left the house, Mama Laurel had called a cab for Naomi. She'd been anxious to get Naomi out of her house. Naomi had asked her whether she was going back to the hospital. The question, like everything else about Naomi, had annoyed Mama Laurel. "Of course I'm going to the hospital," Mama Laurel had replied. To Mama Laurel's surprise, Naomi had suggested that they share the cab. To Mama Laurel's greater surprise, she found herself agreeing to accompany Naomi to the hospital. She hated to give Camille any credit, but she made sense. Olivia was in trouble, and fighting with Naomi didn't serve any purpose. The family needed to pull together, even if it was only until Olivia got through her latest struggle.

The taxi cab driver was a young black man with dreadlocks and a wide, easy smile. "So which one of y'all been giving the dispatcher a hard time?" he asked, still smiling.

Mama Laurel decided right then and there that he was entirely too familiar.

"I called and told the dispatcher that you all were taking too long to get here," she said as she slid into the backseat.

"Suppose this had been an emergency?" Naomi chimed in as she got into the seat beside Mama Laurel and slammed the door behind her.

"Then y'all would have called nine-one-one; that's what it's there for. Where to, ladies?"

"We're going to Cleveland Med," said Mama Laurel, "and we're in a hurry."

The taxi cab driver chuckled and said, "Aren't we all?"

Mama Laurel had to hand it to him. He refused to let Naomi's sour disposition or hers dampen his enthusiasm. She was used to folks who went out of their way not to bring her any displeasure and here was this fool, half an hour late, just as cheerful as a day in June.

"You all comfortable back there, ladies?" asked the driver as he started the engine.

"I wouldn't call this comfortable," commented Naomi, "but we're ready."

"Yes, we're ready," agreed Mama Laurel, "and we're in a hurry, although not too much in a hurry for you to drive crazy. I heard how you tore up my driveway like a bat out of hell. I had to wonder what you were hurrying for, seeing as you were already half an hour late."

The driver shook his head and pulled the car carefully out of the driveway and maneuvered it into traffic. "Something terrible must be going on in the hospital. You two are just about the most disagreeable people I've met in a long time." He said this without rancor or emphasis. He was just stating a fact.

"H'mph!" said Naomi, glaring at the back of the driver's head. "Didn't your mama teach you manners?"

"Did yours?" was the smooth reply.

Mama Laurel hid her smile behind her hands. This man was too much! She looked up at the rearview mirror and found his eyes looking into hers. Underneath all those dreadlocks he was actually good looking. She liked his easy manner, the way he deflected every insult with ease and smiles. Her late husband, Turner, could have benefited from having an easy manner like that. Turner had taken life and its lessons personally, which was why by the time he died at thirty-nine, one of the mourners at the funeral said, without any disrespect, "I don't know what took Turner so long. I'd have thought he'd be dead a good ten years ago."

Naomi leaned forward in the seat and spoke to the driver. "Now, I want you to know, I already got cheated on a fare by one taxi driver this morning, so I'm watching your meter to make sure that history doesn't repeat itself."

"You know," replied the taxi driver, shaking his dreadlocks in amazement, "I don't usually recommend unnatural substances, but have you tried taking a Valium?"

Camille

Camille decided to stop at the Seventh Street Grill to get a Caesar salad for a late lunch. She'd just called her office on her cell phone and Jim had informed her that there were no messages about Olivia. She had to believe that in this case no news was good news. A sigh escaped Camille's lips. After work, she'd go over to the hospital. There was nothing she could do for Olivia anyway, and she needed to get away from the drama that her family inevitably brought with them. She'd deal with them later.

She found a parking space right in front of the restaurant, which was unusual. Daytime parking in downtown Cleveland was downright impossible. It was hard to find parking spaces even in the parking garages.

She got out of her Jeep and after slamming the door shut behind her, she walked quickly to the restaurant. Inside, she saw that there was not a long waiting line for take-out. Another good sign. Usually Seventh Street Grill was packed with people, and the take-out lines were legendary. Camille had once waited forty-five minutes in the take-out line, which showed, as far as Camille was concerned, her love of the restaurant. Camille was by nature an impatient person, but only a Seventh Street Grill Caesar salad could cause her to wait so long and be so patient. She knew that the meal was worth the wait.

She walked to the line, which snaked away from the counter. She could smell the hamburgers on the grill in the kitchen and she thought for a moment about having a hamburger instead of her usual salad, but she pushed the thought out of her mind. She had spent most her childhood being overweight and she was not about to eat anything that would bring her back to that time again.

Even though she'd lost the weight long ago, Camille had never made peace with her body. No matter how thin she was—and at a size two, she knew that she was thin—she still saw an overweight person in the mirror. She knew that she had a problem. She wouldn't call herself anorexic, but she was obsessed with her weight. Obsessed with how she looked. She could not forget what it felt like to be the ugly duckling in a family of swans. The end result was her refusing to eat high-calorie foods, exercising four to five times a week, and taking diet pills daily even though she knew she did not need them.

"Well, well, well." Camille heard a soft chuckle, and a vaguely familiar masculine voice behind her. "My day has just taken a significant turn for the better."

She turned and found herself facing Omar. A few weeks ago, she'd broken a date with him. She'd only agreed to go out with him to annoy Harold. She'd never had any intention of going anywhere with him. Earnest high-school teachers with small bank accounts did not interest her. He was dressed in blue jeans, a white oxford shirt, and a silk tie with an African-inspired print. His cleanly shaved head looked to Camille as if it had just been buffed and shined. The thought brought a small smile to Camille's lips.

"Hello, Omar."

"Hello, Miss Darling," he returned her greeting and her smile. If he was upset that she had called him half an hour before she was supposed to meet him for dinner and told him that something had come up and she couldn't make it, he didn't show it. Camille was grateful. She was used to Harold's pouting. A man with a calm demeanor was a refreshing change.

"How are you?" asked Omar.

Camille had met him at a party a few weeks ago. The hostess of the party, a friend of Camille's who wholeheartedly disapproved of Camille's relationship with Harold, had tried her best to throw Camille and Omar together.

They were the only single people at the party and so they had spoken together for some time, all the while under the possessive gaze of Harold, who was at the same party, with his wife.

Camille had not known that Harold was going to be at the party, but Camille's friend, Lessie, had invited Harold with the hope that if Camille saw Harold out with his wife, it would somehow dampen Camille's ardor.

It had been an uncomfortable situation, with Harold glaring at Camille and Roxanne glaring at Harold. Omar had been a welcome diversion. He had regaled her with stories, and he had acted interested, really interested in whatever Camille had to say. Not once during the evening did he make any comments about her looks, nor did he try to come on to her in any other way. His casual invitation to dinner just as Camille was getting ready to leave had come as a surprise. She probably would not have said yes, but Harold had chosen that time to walk up to her and put his hand very possessively on her arm. It had been embarrassing for Camille and she had no doubt that it was humiliating for Roxanne, but Roxanne had kept her distance. Omar had pointedly ignored Harold and escorted her to her car. He shook her hand and told her to get home safely. He stood on the sidewalk and waited until she drove off.

Camille dragged her thoughts back to the present. He really was a handsome man, in an Isaac Hayes/Michael Jordan kind of way. Bald, black, and beautiful.

"I'm fine," Camille said. "What brings you downtown today?"

"I took my students to the Rock-and-Roll Hall of Fame this morning," he said. "Now they're visiting the Science Museum with the biology teacher. I decided to skip the exhibit and grab some lunch. I'll catch up with them later."

"How did you like the exhibits at the Hall of Fame?" asked Camille, trying to make conversation while the line moved forward.

"They were great. They have a new exhibit coming about the blues singers from the fifties. Maybe you'd like to go with me sometime," he said coolly. "That is, if nothing comes up."

Okay, you got me, thought Camille. She liked the way he handled himself. Got his point across without throwing a fit. Harold could learn a lot from him.

Camille smiled at him and said, "I'm sorry about that."

She had seen grown men melt from the wattage of her smile.

He appeared to be unimpressed. "Are you?"

"Am I what?" Camille asked, confused.

"Sorry."

"Of course I am," Camille lied.

Camille was relieved that she had now reached the front of the line. She ordered her Caesar salad and hoped that they would be quick about getting her order taken care of.

"Maybe after you decide to leave Harold alone, you'll give me a chance." The words surprised Camille. Omar had not mentioned Harold to her that night, even when Harold had tried to intervene during their conversations.

Camille turned and looked at him. "Maybe."

Omar stared at her. His expression was as serious as his words. "I'm not saying this just because I find you the most interesting person I've met in quite a while."

Interesting? What happened to beautiful, attractive, fine, and all those other adjectives men routinely threw her way? *Interesting?*

Omar continued, "I think you can do better than that brother. Hell, I think his wife can do better than him. I hate to put another black man down, but he's the kind of brother that makes it hard for the rest of us good black men."

"Good black men?" Camille repeated his words.

"Yes, Camille. Good black men. Black men who respect their women. Black men who are faithful to their wives. Black men who recognize that women have more to give than a luscious body. Good black men, Camille. They do exist."

She did not want to hear this. She knew what Harold was. She had gone into the relationship with her eyes open. He was a married man who wanted to sleep with her. She wasn't some woman who thought she could make her man change. Hell, he wasn't her man. She was in it because it felt good. It was exciting. Life had been one long, tough journey. That true-love stuff that Brynne believed in did not exist. She wasn't looking for true love, although she didn't mind companionship, such as it was. She knew that her relationship with Harold was destined to end badly. But she was tired of everybody judging her and Harold. It was bad enough when her family got that party started, but when Omar, a stranger—no matter how good looking, no matter how pretty his full lips were, no matter how high his cheekbones were, and how deep brown his eyes were—talked to her about her life, that was too much for her to take.

Camille took her salad away from the counter and walked past Omar. As she walked away, she heard his voice, low and soft, "You keep running away, Camille, but no matter how far you run, you can't run away from yourself."

The lyrics were from one of her favorite Bob Marley songs, "Running Away." At least the teacher had good taste in music, Camille thought, as she walked out of the restaurant.

Twelve

Brynne

Brynne walked quickly down the hospital hallway. She felt ener-gized. The discussion she had with Winston Gray was probably the last she would have with him this side of the grave, and it probably cost her job, but she was feeling almost lighthearted. She'd never spo-ken to anyone else so bluntly. Unlike Camille or Mama Laurel, Brynne weighed every word before it came out of her mouth, and frankly, that was exhausting.

When she arrived at Olivia's room, she opened the door and was surprised to see that Jose was still sitting in a chair beside Olivia where she'd left him in the morning. He was holding Olivia's hand.

"You're still here," she said.

"Hello, Brynne," said Jose, his eyes inscrutable. "Yes, I'm still here."

"I thought you'd be at work by now." Brynne walked over to the empty chair next to him and sat down. This was awkward.

"Does it bother you that I'm here?" Jose asked.

Brynne nodded. "Yes."

"You can erase me out of your life, Brynne—but you can't erase me out of this family. Your family has been my family for too many years now for me to just walk away."

She watched as he raked his fingers distractedly through his thick curly black hair. He was angry. She preferred his anger to his pain. She could deal with his anger. He had every right to be upset and there was a part of her that knew that she deserved his wrath. She couldn't deal with his pain, however. She didn't want him to hurt. Ever. She still felt protective of her ex-husband. She suspected that those feelings would never end.

"How's Olivia doing?" asked Brynne, changing the subject and turning her attention to her sister.

"The doctor says that she's showing signs of improvement. She's responding to some tests that they're giving her, but I don't really know anything more specific."

"That's the best news I've heard today," said Brynne, instinctively reaching out to touch her ex-husband. She wanted to show him that she still cared, even though they were no longer a couple. She still cared.

Jose moved away from her touch. "Don't do that, Brynne." His black eyes flashed in anger.

"Do what?" she asked.

"Pity me," Jose replied, his voice tight.

"I don't pity you, Jose," Brynne said, surprised that he thought this.

"Like hell you don't." Jose stood up.

What was wrong with Jose? Brynne wondered as she stared at her ex-husband. This was not the mild-tempered man she'd known, this was not the man who even in the worst of circumstances never lost his composure. Was Olivia's condition getting to him, or was it something more? In all the years she'd known him, he'd never snapped at her, even when he was angry with her. His calm demeanor in the face of any crisis had irritated Brynne when they were married. She was always the one that panicked and he was always the voice of reason, but now she missed the reasonable Jose.

"Jose, please . . ."

"Please what, Brynne—go away? Should I go away, Brynne? Should I walk away from Olivia, from this family, just like you walked away from me?"

"Jose, if it's that difficult for you to be around me, maybe you shouldn't be here."

She watched as he turned and walked toward the door. She had hurt him again.

"Jose, wait—I didn't mean it."

He left the room without saying another word.

* * *

Brynne

Brynne heard the door to Olivia's hospital room open and she turned to see Mama Laurel and Gram Naomi walk in.

"Gram Naomi." Brynne walked over to her grandmother, and wrapped both arms around her. "I'm glad you're here."

It was good to see Gram Naomi, even under these circumstances. There had always been a calmness in Gram Naomi that was missing in Mama Laurel. Brynne would have used the word "unflappable" to describe her paternal grandmother, but that would not adequately have described the quiet strength that Brynne saw in her. Even when she was telling you off, she did it without breaking a sweat.

"I've missed you, Brynne," said Gram Naomi, kissing her cheek. "How is Olivia doing?"

"She's doing a little better," said Brynne, glancing over at her sister, who lay peacefully, as if in a deep sleep, in the hospital bed. "The doctor told Jose that she was responding to certain tests."

"Jose was here?" asked Gram Naomi, a sly smile playing on her lips.

"Don't get any ideas," Brynne responded. "He was just here to give support to the family."

"He's a good man, Brynne," said Gram Naomi. "There aren't a whole lot of men who would come to the hospital to be with their ex-wives."

Behind Gram Naomi, Mama Laurel cleared her throat.

"Mama Laurel," said Brynne, disengaging from Gram Naomi. She walked over to Mama Laurel and kissed her on the cheek. Everyone in the family knew that the two grandmothers were in constant competition for the affection of their granddaughters. Brynne loved both of her feuding grandmothers equally, but she'd always felt drawn to Gram Naomi. She secretly wished she'd inherited Gram Naomi's confidence, her absolute certainty that whatever she was doing at a particular moment was the right thing.

"Come here, Brynne," said Gram Naomi. "Come hold my hand. You too, Laurel. It's time for us to pray for Olivia."

Naomi

Naomi pulled her chair up to the side of Olivia's bed. She had tried to prepare herself for this during the cab ride to the hospital, but the sight of her grandchild lying in a bed, looking more dead than alive, took her breath away. Laurel and Brynne had gone to the cafeteria to get some coffee.

Naomi was certain that they were trying to give her some time alone with her youngest granddaughter.

She stared down at Olivia's pale face.

This was her son's daughter. One of the few remaining links she had with a son she had loved even when he turned his back on her way of life and even when he married a woman whom she would never have chosen, a woman who had hurt him terribly. Still, no matter what her son did, she loved him. She could never understand mothers who cut their children out of their lives because of an argument. Didn't make any sense to Naomi. She'd carried Sherrod in her womb for nine months. She'd taken care of him, worried about him, did everything in her life either because of him or in spite of him. Ever since her husband's death, when Sherrod was only five, Naomi had groomed her son to take her husband's place in Goshen's black society.

But Sherrod had fought her every step of the way, starting with his choice of a career and his choice of a wife.

Naomi was the product of four generations of doctors, lawyers, educators, and preachers. She had planned her only son's life with the same single-mindedness and determination that she attacked everything with in life. She had wanted him to be a doctor, like his father and his father's father. But Sherrod had instead chosen to be a coach of a high-school football team. Football was his passion, and against his mother's strenuous objections, he had played football professionally until he injured his back and ended his undistinguished football career. He came back to Goshen, and was hired to be the coach at the same high school where he'd played football. Naomi had taken to her bed for a week after he told her what his choice of work was going to be. But Naomi was a practical woman. She knew when she had been beaten. Still, she decided that she would spend the rest of her life working on getting him a real career. Something with potential, even if it wasn't something that had an M.D. after his initials.

After recovering from her shock about her son's career, Naomi had to deal with a second and more devastating shock. Her son's wife. Sherrod met Antoinette on his one and only trip overseas, a vacation in Bermuda. He had met and married her in the space of ten days. She was a woman who knew nothing of the South or southern ways, a woman whose bohemian style went against everything Naomi believed in. Sherrod's choice of a wife had both shocked and angered her. Naomi would have chosen any one of her friends' daughters for her son. Good southern women who understood their culture, who understood what it meant to marry into the Darling family, one of the oldest, most established, and certainly one of the wealthiest black families in their little section of heaven, North Carolina. The marriage would never last, she had warned her son, but it was clear that her son loved this inappropriate woman until the day they died. Antoinette's infidelity had only confirmed what Naomi had long suspected—the woman had no class. Naomi knew that Antoinette had tried to fit into what she thought Sherrod's world was. She tried to join the different charitable organizations. She attended the various lawn parties. She did all the things a society wife should do, but she was always an outsider.

Old ghosts, thought Gram Naomi, as a solitary tear rolled down her cheek. Sherrod and Antoinette were old ghosts, who after all this time still haunted her. Why was she holding on to this sadness? Sherrod had left her a long time ago, and as for Antoinette, the woman had been dead now longer than the years she'd known her. Old ghosts.

Camille

The rest of the workday passed uneventfully for Camille. She put her run-in with Omar out of her mind and turned her attention back to her work. She had gotten most of her work done for the day, further strengthening her belief in miracles, and she'd dodged four phone calls from Harold. Although it was almost six o'clock, she hadn't made it to the hospital as planned, but she had checked with Brynne a few hours earlier and was told that nothing had changed.

Camille closed her eyes and put her head down on her desk. She was bone tired, and the thought of driving over to Cleveland Med and spending a few hours with her family was not at all appealing, but she wanted to see Olivia so she was going to have to put up with the rest of her family, at least while she was in the hospital. At least Gram Naomi was there. It would be good to see her. She usually acted as an effective buffer between Mama Laurel and herself. Hopefully, her grandmothers had followed her suggestion and had formed a truce.

Her telephone rang and she picked it up automatically.

It was Jim. "Camille, you have a visitor."

"Could you be a little more specific?" Camille asked, wondering who this visitor was.

"Mrs. Harold Bledsoe," said Jim, his voice low. "I tried to run interference for you and told her that you were not in, but she said she knew I was lying and she wasn't leaving until she saw you. Should I call security?"

What else could happen? thought Camille.

"Send her in," said Camille. It was better to deal with Mrs. Bledsoe head-on, and hopefully avoid a scene. Camille sat up and pulled back her hair. *This should be interesting.*

A few minutes later, there was a knock on her office door.

"Come in," said Camille.

Jim entered the office first and for a moment looked completely lost. It was obvious that although he had dealt with a lot of drama in his short life, he had no point of reference in dealing with confrontations between wives and mistresses.

"Is everything okay?" he finally asked.

"Yes," said Camille, her voice steady. "Please bring Mrs. Bledsoe in."

Jim stepped aside and Roxanne Bledsoe stepped in. She was a small woman, as completely different in looks from Camille as night from day. She was barely five feet, and even though she was pregnant, she didn't look as if she were over 105 pounds. A good breeze would blow her over easily, Camille thought. Roxanne was the color of vanilla, and her hair, which she wore in a short curly Afro, was flaming red. There was a dusting of freckles over her small, slightly upturned nose. Her eyes, which were filled with anger, were coal-black. These eyes seemed to stare right through Camille.

"Do you need anything?" asked Jim, looking from one woman to the other.

"No, thank you, Jim. I'm fine," said Camille.

"Well, I'll be right outside if you need anything," said Jim, still hovering.

"Thank you, Jim," said Camille.

"There won't be any bloodshed," said Roxanne coolly. Her eyes never left Camille's face. "Don't worry, I won't be staying long."

Jim left the office without comment and quietly closed the door.

"Please sit down," said Camille, her eyes focusing on Roxanne's rounded stomach.

"I'd rather stand," said Roxanne in a voice that let Camille know that she would rather do anything, even eat dirt, than sit in Camille's chair.

"Why are you here?" asked Camille.

"I wanted to tell you to your face that my marriage to my husband is over. You can have him. You've got what you wanted. I also wanted to look into the eyes of the woman who has destroyed my family— with my husband's help, of course."

Camille did not respond. That it had taken this long for Roxanne to confront her surprised Camille. It was inevitable that they would have this conversation. Camille had expected it, and at one time she had wanted the conversation. Camille thought that this conversation would be just the kind of humiliation that she needed to prompt her into doing what she knew she should have done a hell of a long time ago: get rid of Harold. But Roxanne had kept silent. She had not acknowledged Camille's presence. Even at the party where Harold made a fool of himself in front of Omar, Roxanne had turned her anger toward Harold and ignored Camille, as if she were above the dirt that Camille and Harold were rolling in. It was obvious now, however, that Roxanne had stripped away any veneer of civility.

"There have been other women," Roxanne continued, her eyes never once leaving Camille's face, "and I thought that you would go the way they went, but apparently I underestimated your staying power. Last week Harold told me that he would not see you anymore. He said he was prepared to be a good husband and a good father. I assumed that meant that you had broken off the relationship. I was glad. I love my husband. I suspected, however, that he was lying. Last night I followed Harold to your grandmother's house and I waited outside until he left. I wanted him to see me waiting there for him. Isn't that pathetic? But I wanted to see his face when he realized he was busted, and do you know what, Camille? It was priceless. Anyway, he's all yours. I packed up his clothes and had someone deliver the suitcases to your house. I think they left all of it on your front lawn. At least those were my directions. I wish you exactly the same type of life with Harold that I had. You two deserve each other."

"I don't want him," said Camille honestly. Not anymore and probably not ever.

"Yeah, well, I guess you should have thought about that before you slept with my husband." Roxanne spat the words out at Camille. She was shaking as she spoke, and Camille felt ashamed. Ashamed that this pregnant woman was in her office trembling because Camille didn't have the strength to end a relationship that had never brought her anything but confusion. Ashamed that she had caused the pain she saw in this woman's eyes. Ashamed that she had played with fire and burned a whole lot of people the process, not only Roxanne, but her own family as well.

Mama Laurel's words came to her loud and clear as if she were standing in the room with them. *"What doesn't come good in the morning, won't come good in the evening."* Camille's relationship with Harold was built on another person's pain. It was inevitable that one day that pain would come around and slap Camille on her face as it had today.

"You're right," said Camille. "You're absolutely right."

Roxanne looked down at where Camille sat and said, "I will not allow myself to feel another minute of pain because of you, or because of Harold. You deserve each other."

She did not shut the door behind her when she walked out of Camille's office.

Thirteen

Camille

It took Camille longer than she intended to get to the hospital. After Roxanne left her office, she had sat for a long time staring at nothing. Roxanne's visit had left her shaken. She knew that she should be at the hospital with the rest of her family, but she had to work up the nerve, as Mama Laurel would say, to deal with everything that awaited her there. First, there was Olivia. Although her condition had not worsened, she was still in a coma. The longer she stayed in this condition, the worse her chances were for recovery, Camille thought. Her sister might die. It was a fact that had to be dealt with. No one else in the family wanted to think about that possibility. But Camille was dealing with it, although she was dealing from afar. But the thought of going to the hospital and waiting to see if her sister would live or die had kept Camille's feet firmly planted in her office. She knew that her family would think that she was being cold, but she couldn't handle saying good-bye right now. She also couldn't handle her anger toward her family for not seeing just how desperate Olivia was. No one wanted to deal with that unpleasant truth either. Whenever she talked about having Olivia committed, everyone would say, "There goes that old evil Camille." There was nothing evil about telling the truth, as far as Camille was concerned, even if the truth hurt like hell.

Then, there was the ongoing feud between her grandmothers. Camille didn't feel like being a referee. It was obvious that they had not put aside personal dislikes for the sake of Olivia. If anything, from what Camille saw this morning, their mutual loathing had flourished, even as Olivia lay in a hospital bed. It was disgusting, but Camille knew that she was no better. *Fruit don't fall too far from the tree.* She had not let Olivia's situation stop her from arguing with her family. Camille had always thought that her family would come together in a crisis but she was wrong. It seemed as if the crisis just gave everybody an opportunity to point a finger at someone else to blame them for feeling bad.

Finally, she had received a telephone call from Harold after his wife left. A call that left her with a lot to think about, as if her plate were not already full. The phone had rung after-hours and she would not have answered but she thought that it might be Brynne or Mama Laurel with some news about Olivia. The conversation with Harold had been brief and unpleasant. His wife had kicked him out and he was moaning about it. "Not that I want to be with her," he had assured Camille, "but imagine kicking the father of your child out the house." For Harold, this was apparently an unpardonable sin. He wanted to stay with her for a few days and when Camille refused he had gotten angry. Angry words had passed between them and Harold had issued the same threat that he always issued when Camille wanted to walk away. *"Don't think I'll let you walk away to another man. I'll kill you first."* Camille had never paid much attention to his threats before, but there was a desperation in his voice that Camille knew she shouldn't ignore. She slammed the telephone down in his ear.

This was the end, it had to be the end. Each time she had broken up with him she had let him back into her life. Loneliness. Boredom. Frustration. Pick any of the above. They had all at one point propelled her back to Harold. But there was one thing that Camille knew. The threats were becoming more frequent. It was a pattern. Threaten, then apologize. Profusely, and preferably with flowers. It was time to get away from Harold. Been time. When all this was done with Olivia, whatever way it turned out, she was leaving for Atlanta. New life. New start.

She had driven to the hospital with Harold's threats and Roxanne's words ringing in her ears. As hard as she tried she couldn't forget either. The words continued echoing around her as she walked through the corridors of the hospital and found the intensive-care unit waiting room. The room was filled with people tonight unlike the previous evening, and the presence of so many sad strangers had apparently helped to bring about a cease-fire between Mama Laurel and Gram Naomi, who sat on opposite sides of the room, doing their best to ignore each other. Brynne was pacing the room like a caged animal when Camille entered the waiting room, and the relief in Brynne's eyes when she saw her sister lifted Camille's spirits.

"I'm glad you're here, sis," said Brynne.

"Is everything all right with you?" asked Mama Laurel, looking at Camille intently.

Camille wondered how her grandmother was always able to sense when there was something going on with her. Even when Camille tried to put on her public face, Mama Laurel was always able to see right through her serene expression. She hoped a short and neutral answer would throw Mama Laurel off the scent of her latest troubles.

"I had a lot of work to do," she replied.

Neutral. The words sounded okay. Nothing argumentative there. Maybe she'd back off.

Mama Laurel was not buying it, but she kept that to herself. Camille knew that in time Mama Laurel would come back to her, like a dog digging up a yard to find a long-buried bone, but for now, with everything else facing the family, Mama Laurel dropped her inquisition.

Naomi put her arms around Camille's shoulders and said, "We're glad you're here."

Camille pulled away from her grandmother. She was afraid that any sign of sympathy would be her undoing. She fought to get some control. She was close to losing her grip and she had to pull herself together. She struggled to get Roxanne's face out of her mind. Even when Mama Laurel and the rest of the family were lecturing her about her loose morals, their words had not affected her like Roxanne's presence in Camille's office. She felt small and nasty.

Focus, girl, she told herself. *Focus on Olivia. Put all your energies on your sister.* Olivia was the one who needed help right now, Camille reasoned with herself. Any of her own problems could wait.

Camille walked over to one of the few empty chairs in the room. It was going to be a long night.

Brynne

It was decided after much discussion that Gram Naomi would stay with Camille that night. Mama Laurel would go home, and Brynne would remain at the hospital.

The doctors had come by the hospital room several times during the evening, but so far there had been no change in Olivia's condition.

At nine o'clock, her family left the hospital, with Mama Laurel and Gram Naomi arguing about the exact time they would return. Whatever fragile peace they had arrived at seemed to be at an end. Brynne was glad for the silence that followed their departure. This was difficult enough without her warring grandmothers trying to complicate things.

Brynne walked out to the hallway to the pay phone. She'd been thinking about Jose's angry words. He'd left the hospital room in anger and in pain. Anger and pain that she'd caused. She wanted to talk to him but she didn't know what to say. She wanted to comfort him, to make things right for him. Just because she'd walked away didn't mean that she didn't care about him.

Tonight for the first time since the divorce she'd dealt with her true feelings for her ex-husband. She loved him, still—she knew that. But she was also afraid of losing her independence. Afraid that she'd go running back to him. It would be so easy to do that—to abandon her desire to be free, abandon her wish to be, for once, her own person.

She dialed his telephone number quickly before she changed her mind. The telephone rang once and then Brynne heard her ex-husband's voice.

"Hello, Jose speaking."

So formal. He still answered the telephone as if he were in his office.

"It's me," said Brynne.

"What do you want, Brynne?"

His question was direct, and for a moment she was disconcerted. What did she want?

"I—I want to talk to you," said Brynne.

"I'm listening."

"I know it's a lot to ask, and if you're busy, it's all right—I just wanted to talk to you face-to-face. I—I thought about the things you said today, and I wanted to talk to you."

She felt foolish. She was probably the last person in the world he wanted to talk to in person or over the telephone.

"Where are you?" asked Jose.

"I'm at the hospital—but it's all right, we can talk another time . . ."

"I'll be there in half an hour," said Jose.

"Wait . . . ," Brynne hesitated, "I don't want to meet here. Could we meet in the coffee shop across the street . . . the one next to the parking lot?"

"I know the place," said Jose. "I'll meet you there."

He hung up before Brynne had a chance to reply.

Naomi

"What is all this stuff doing on your lawn, sugar?" asked Naomi.

In front of Camille's house, there were at least five suitcases with clothes hanging out of them scattered around. There were tire tracks on Camille's lawn. It looked like someone had driven laps on her lawn. What kind of mess was Camille involved in now? thought Naomi.

They had just dropped Laurel off at her house, and Naomi wondered what Laurel would say if she could see this particular scene.

"It's a long story," said Camille, "and I don't feel like getting into it right now."

Naomi and Camille walked up to the front door of her modern, bungalow-style house. Located in the fashionable section of Cleveland Heights, Camille's house was more modest than her neighbors'. It didn't matter that her neighbors on either side of her had houses that could best be described as Tudor-style mansions. Camille took pride in her three-bedroom, one-and-a-half-bathroom house.

Camille pushed the front door open, and Naomi followed. She was tired, and she was hungry. She hoped that Camille had some food in the refrigerator, and not those diet shakes she usually had.

"Make yourself comfortable," said Camille as she took off her shoes and walked toward the kitchen located adjacent to the living room.

Naomi followed her into the kitchen and watched as Camille poured some water into a kettle. The kitchen was Camille's favorite room in the house. Light and airy, the floors made of brightly colored Mexican tiles, which gave the room a festive atmosphere. There was a center island stove in the middle of the room, and her pots and pans hung on a contraption suspended from the ceiling. For someone who didn't do much cooking, Camille had an extensive kitchen.

"How about some tea?" asked Camille.

Tea sounded good, not as good as food, but it would do. First, however, Naomi needed some answers. Her granddaughter was in trouble, judging from what she saw on the front lawn, and if there was trouble, Naomi wanted to know about it. Someone had to save Camille from self-destruction, and if Laurel couldn't do it, well then, it was time for Naomi to get her own turn at bat.

"I want some answers, Camille. Your front lawn looks like you're getting ready for a garage sale. What on earth is going on?"

"I'm handling the situation," said Camille.

"If you don't mind my saying this," said Naomi, "any time someone dumps five suitcases on your front lawn and takes their car to do laps on it, I would say that the situation is handling you and not the other way around."

"Grandma Naomi, please," said Camille, "you're just as bad as Mama Laurel."

Naomi let that statement pass and said, "Camille, is the situation with you and that married man still going on?"

"Gram, I really and truly do not want to discuss it."

"Oh my Lord," said Gram Naomi, clapping her hand on her forehead dramatically. "What is it going to take to get you away from that man? He is absolutely no good for you!"

"For God's sake!" snapped Camille, already past her breaking point. "I agree with you! Just please, please, please let it go!"

Naomi looked at her granddaughter. As bad as she was, she had never raised her voice at her before. No matter what problems she had getting along with Laurel, Camille had always treated Naomi with respect.

Naomi shook her head. "There's no reason to shout at me, Camille," she said. "I'm not the one who dumped those cheap suitcases on your lawn. By the way, dear, you can tell a lot about a man by his luggage. His luggage is certainly substandard and I can only guess that he is too."

Camille started to cry. She didn't try to hide her tears as she usually did. Instead, she stood in her pretty kitchen crying like Brynne.

Naomi stood where she was and let her granddaughter cry. She knew that Camille didn't need her sympathy right now. Any sign of sympathy would only make matters worse. Naomi had often thought that of all her grandchildren, Camille was the most like her in temperament. She was tough and she didn't cry easily. The fact that she was here in her kitchen crying like a lost lamb only showed Naomi how desperate things had gotten for all of them, even Camille.

After a while, when the tears subsided, Naomi said, "How about if I make you some tea and we can talk about this situation?"

Camille shook her head. "I'm all right."

"Are you sure?" asked Naomi.

"Perfectly sure," replied Camille, wiping her eyes with the backs of her hands. "I'm just tired. I need to sleep."

Naomi watched as Camille walked up the stairs. Her back was as straight as that of any officer in the military. She was as tough as they come. One minute she was crying like her heart was breaking and the next minute she was as composed as a schoolteacher on a Monday morning.

But as tough as Camille was, Naomi knew that everybody had a breaking point, and from what Naomi had just witnessed, it seemed that Camille was not too far from hers.

Brynne

"Thanks for coming," Brynne said to her ex-husband. They were sitting in the coffee shop, and apart from an old man who was sleeping in the booth across from them, they were alone.

"What do you want to talk about?" Jose got directly to the point.

Brynne cleared her throat. "This is really difficult for me . . ." she began.

Jose sat down in the vacant chair next to her. "It doesn't have to be, Brynne. It doesn't have to be difficult at all. Just say whatever it is you want to say. I can handle it."

"I wanted to tell you how sorry I am that I hurt you. I never, never wanted that to happen."

"Brynne, you've said those words before. Trust me, you don't need to repeat them," said Jose.

"After today, I thought it was important that you understand that you still mean a lot to me. It's hard for me to see you around the family because I'm trying to get over you. I still love you, Jose—but we're divorced. We both are moving on. It didn't work for us, but not because I didn't love you. God knows that I do. It's just hard . . ."

"It's hard for me too, Brynne. To see you here, watch your pain, not to be able to hold you—to have you shut me out of your life, it's tough."

"This is what happens when a marriage ends, Jose," said Brynne. "People move on. They get on with their lives. I need to get on with my life and so do you."

"It looks like you've done a pretty good job getting on without me."

His words were harsh, but Brynne knew that they were coming from a painful place.

Brynne cleared her throat. "When you moved out of the house it took everything in my power not to run after you and tell you to come back."

"Why the hell didn't you, Brynne?" Jose's voice betrayed his feelings. "Why didn't you?"

"Because things weren't right with us, Jose, and they hadn't been right for a long time. You controlled everything about me. Somewhere along the line the me you fell in love with wasn't enough for you. My weight was a problem. My friends were a problem. Even the church I went to . . . Everything . . ."

Jose sighed. "I only wanted what was best for you. For us."

"No," said Brynne. "You only wanted what was good for you, and, for a time, that was enough for me. Then it wasn't."

"That's not fair, Brynne. You leaned on me. You asked me for direction. Then you got mad when you didn't like the answers."

"No," said Brynne. "I didn't ask you for direction; I asked you for advice. That's the difference. I wanted advice, but, in the end, it was my decision. But you didn't understand that."

"Why are you bringing this up now, Brynne? I already know that you weren't happy in the marriage. I wasn't happy either, but I never gave up. Till the end, I was willing to work."

"But I wasn't," said Brynne. "I was tired, Jose. I just wanted to be me. Not somebody's wife, somebody's sister, somebody's lawyer. I just wanted to be me. I lost me during our marriage, and I just wanted to get that back."

"Well, it looks like you got your wish—I'm out of your life."

"I'm sorry I hurt you."

"So you keep saying . . ."

"I know that you're angry at me."

"Damn right I'm angry," said Jose as he pushed back his chair. "You got me down here to tell me this? I've heard it all before."

"But have you listened?" asked Brynne. "I know you heard it, but did you listen? Did you understand?"

"All I understand is that you threw away our marriage."

"We both did that," replied Brynne. "I am not the only one to take the blame on this one. We both took the other person for granted. I'm guilty too. . . ."

Jose stood up. "Well, that's mighty nice of you. . . ."

"Don't leave me, Jose," said Brynne. "I know you're angry with me, but please don't leave me until you hear what I have to say. Please."

For a moment Jose did nothing. Then he slowly sat down.

"Thank you," said Brynne. "I just want you to know that you were the best friend I ever had, and I know that I didn't treat you right. I know I walked out of the marriage without giving much of an explanation, but the truth is that I still loved you, and I was afraid that if we talked, you'd somehow talk me out of leaving, and in the end I'd lose myself again. I just couldn't take that chance, Jose. I've always played by everyone else's rules—from Mama Laurel to you. I just became the person everyone expected me to be, but then sometimes I'd lie awake at night and wonder, who am I? I wanted to find out the answer to that question, Jose, and if I'd stayed married, I never would have found out. Can't you understand that?"

Jose reached across the table. "Give me your hand."

Brynne reached out and grasped his hand.

"I hear you, Brynne," he said. "I might not like what you're saying, but I hear you, and I am trying to understand. That's the best I can do right now."

She raised his hand to her lips and kissed it lightly. Then she allowed herself to be wrapped in silence, as she sat hand-in-hand with Jose. They would face this night together, and no matter what happened in the morning, Brynne knew that this man, her friend, would be there to help her get through this night.

"Come on, *querida*," said Jose. "Let's get back to the hospital."

Fourteen

Camille

Camille awoke to the smells of eggs and fried bacon. Grandma Naomi was at it again. Naomi worried that her granddaughters, who got compliments for their shapes from everyone else, didn't eat regularly, and while they shared the same area code, she was going to do her best to give them the benefit of her southern cooking. From experience, Camille knew that there were probably some grits, home fries, and homemade biscuits going on, as well as the bacon and eggs. Camille's mouth watered as she thought of the breakfast waiting for her. Grandma Naomi could pluck your last nerve, but she did know how to feed you, yes, Lord.

On any other day Camille would have avoided the fattening, artery-clogging, blood-pressure-raising food that she knew was waiting for her, but today Camille decided that she needed some real food. No low-calorie frozen breakfasts. No yogurt. No diet tea. She wanted something to stick to her ribs and if she had to put in some extra time on the treadmill, then that was life.

Camille got out of bed and put on her robe. She had not slept well. Her night had been filled with dreams of Roxanne, Harold, and of course, Olivia. The telephone had kept ringing throughout the night and because she thought that it might be someone with news about Olivia she had answered it. Each time she answered she heard Harold's voice. Each time she heard his voice she'd hung up.

She had checked her nine messages from the previous night and as she suspected, they were all from him, each more desperate than the last. In some, he was declaring his love for her. In others, he was cursing her. In one particularly curious message, Harold had talked about hurting her boyfriend. It took her some time to realize that he was referring to Omar. That brought a smile to her lips. As if she would go out with a high-school teacher, no matter how fine he was. Camille had expensive tastes that no high-school teacher salary could accommodate. Still, Camille realized that she was going to have to call that teacher to tell him to watch his back. Although she was sure that Harold was more talk than action, one never was completely certain that Harold was harmless. He had gotten into some brawls before where he had gotten his behind soundly kicked, but although Omar looked like he could defend himself, Harold was acting crazy. She hoped she could find Omar's number.

Camille got out of bed and walked barefoot to her kitchen. Her grandmother, who was by the stove putting pepper in the home fries, looked over at her and said, "I was wondering when you'd get up. We have to get over there to the hospital and see how your sister is."

"Gram, it's not even seven o'clock yet."

"I've been up since five o'clock this morning. I always get up at five."

"Well, I'm delighted for you," commented Camille, eyeing the home fries and the bacon, "but I like to sleep."

"Humph," said Naomi, who put an unhealthy amount of salt on the home fries. "That's just one of your problems."

"Don't start," said Camille. "It's too early in the morning for sermons."

"It's never too early for sermons," commented Naomi. "Pour yourself some juice and come enjoy this breakfast I've been cooking for you. By the way, there's some man in a fancy car outside who has been eyeing this house since early morning."

"What!" Camille stopped walking toward the refrigerator and turned to face her grandmother.

"He's been out there at least since I got up. Every time I looked out the window he was there."

"Gram Naomi, for God's sake!" said Camille. "Why didn't you wake me or something? This guy could be a thief, or a pervert or something."

"He might be a thief and a pervert, but I believe you know him," replied Naomi, heaping a mound of eggs on Camille's plate. "I think it's that married man checking up on you."

Camille walked over to the kitchen window and looked outside to make sure that her grandmother's well-known paranoia wasn't running wild. Her heart sank when she saw Harold's car parked across the street from her house.

"Do you want me to call the police?" asked Gram Naomi.

"No," said Camille, easing her feet into some shoes. "I can handle this myself."

"Looks like your chickens have come home to roost, Miss Camille."

"Looks that way," agreed Camille as she walked to the hallway closet and put on her coat. She was furious but she was trying hard not to let Gram Naomi see this. It would only give her more to talk about.

Camille put on her coat and went outside. She walked quickly down the front driveway and then across the street. Soon she stood in front of Harold's car and waited while he rolled down his front window.

"Have you lost your mind?" The words jumped out of Camille's mouth, even before the window was completely down. "Have you lost your natural mind? What are you doing here?"

"You wouldn't answer my calls," said Harold as though this explained everything.

"Harold, my sister is in the hospital. Fighting for her life. Your wife came to my job yesterday to pay me a visit. Your damn suitcases are on my lawn. My assignments at work are piling up and although my boss is nice, I think her patience is wearing thin. Do you understand? I cannot deal with you right now."

Harold reached through the window and tried to touch her arm. Camille quickly moved out of his reach.

"Let me help you, Camille," he said. "Let me be here for you. Don't shut me out."

"Harold, go back to your wife."

The tenderness she saw in his face dissolved almost instantly into anger. "Your boyfriend giving you comfort, Camille?"

"Get real, Harold," replied Camille. "I don't have time for this right now."

"It's that bald, black mother—"

Camille walked away. She had heard enough. Harold had finally lost his grip on reality. She wasn't sure whether it was the decision of his wife to give him the boot, or whether there was a full moon out there somewhere, but Harold had completely lost his mind.

As she walked away she could hear his curses ringing in her ear but they didn't matter. She was over him. Finally. After all this time. It was over. She felt as if someone lifted a burden off her shoulders, and her step became light. A gust of wind blew her coat open and she laughed because she felt, for the first time in a long time, free.

Mama Laurel

Old age is a hell of a thing. Mama Laurel walked down the hospital corridor as quickly as she could. Everything was going wrong this morning. Her alarm clock didn't go off until six-thirty, although she had set it for a full hour earlier. Then she had slipped in the shower and hit her hip on the faucet on her way down. Although the fall took the wind out of her and banged her up pretty well, she didn't have time to worry about it. Once she got up and found that she could still move her legs, she decided to keep going. She needed to find out what was going on with Olivia. She had called her room but there was no answer. Either Brynne had gone home, or she had spent the night like a coward somewhere other than where she needed to be: in Olivia's room.

Mama Laurel walked down the hallway in the ICU department, which was now all too familiar to her. She wanted to get to the waiting room before Naomi got there. At the thought of Naomi, Mama Laurel's lips twisted in disgust as if she had just sucked on a particularly bitter fruit. She had not wanted Naomi to spend the night with Camille. Camille's mind was already poisoned enough against Mama Laurel without adding Naomi's low opinion of her into the mix. She would rather have put up with that disagreeable woman than let Naomi spread her bad mouth to her grandchildren.

There was another reason why Mama Laurel didn't want Naomi to spend the night with Camille and she hadn't realized it until late last night when she lay in her bed trying to avoid dreaming about her dead daughter, which she always did in times of trouble. She was jealous of the relationship Camille had with Naomi. They understood each other. Naomi could always get through to Camille even when no one else could. They shared secrets. They shared a similar outlook on life. And no matter what Camille did, Naomi wouldn't judge her too harshly. Mama Laurel knew that Camille would go to Naomi first if she were in trouble, and that thought just brought hot spit to Mama Laurel's mouth. After everything Mama Laurel had done for Camille. Had done for all of her ungrateful granddaughters. Raised them. Clothed them. Fed them. Tried to help them with their problems. Gave them advice. Watched out for them. After everything, Camille had the nerve to be close to Naomi.

What had Naomi done for Camille? What had she done for any of her grandchildren except to throw money at them? It used to burn Mama Laurel up just thinking of how after spending all the time with the girls helping them during school, taking care of them day by day, Naomi would breeze in and reap the benefits. Trips to Martha's Vineyard, Aspen, New York, the Berkshires. Naomi spent the fun times with the girls. But when it came to the responsibility of raising young black women in a world that didn't expect too much from them, that was left to Mama Laurel.

"Life ain't fair, Laurel, and the sooner you realize that, then the better off you'll be." A voice from her past spoke to her loud and clear. It was the voice of her mother, Olive. Olivia was named for her. *Just goes to show you,* thought Mama Laurel, *that names don't mean a damn thing.* Her mother and Olivia couldn't have been more dissimilar if they tried.

Olive Mary Mingus Redwood was a woman who had fought with life every day she was on this earth, and every day had won the fight. She had run away from an unhappy mother and an angry father. Left the West Indies at the age of seventeen and never looked back. When pressed, Olive let it be known that she came from a family of substance. Her father was an educator and her mother didn't have to work. But Olive spent a childhood in the shadow of two people who didn't like each other very much and who spent most of their time ignoring her.

Olive had met and married Mosiah Redwood within two months of arriving in New York City. Mosiah was also from the West Indies, but he was far from established. All he had were his dreams of one day being a successful man, so successful that he could send for his family back home. His family had put together everything they had to pay his passage to America so that Mosiah would escape the cycle of poverty his family was trapped in. Mosiah had achieved enough success in the steel mills of Cleveland to help at least twenty members of his family to emigrate to the United States. But by the time Mosiah had the means to help his family, the two most important people he wanted to help, his mother and his father, were long dead.

Mosiah and Olive had moved to Cleveland because of the promise of industry. Mosiah worked in the steel mills of Cleveland until he was almost seventy. If he was unhappy with his lot in life, he never let it be known. The only person he loved more than Olive was Laurel. Her daddy spent every cent he owned taking care of his wife and his daughter, and although his life could not have been how he imagined it would be during his journey to the promised land, as the folk in the West Indies referred to America, he never complained and there was seldom a time that Mama Laurel saw him without a smile on his face.

Olive, however, was a person who didn't smile unless she had a good reason to spread her lips. Nothing pleased her. Until Antoinette was born, Mama Laurel had grave doubts about her mother's capacity to love anyone, including herself. In time, many years after her mother's death, Mama Laurel was able to understand how hard times can make a soft person hard. For Olive, the one thing that had kept her going in the face of a hard life—with parents who never cared much for her; a husband who, although he loved her, put work ahead of everything else including her; a daughter she did not get along with; a life spent serving people as a maid or as some other helpful black person—was her capacity to fight. To tell anybody off who messed with her.

Olive never got over having a dark-skinned daughter. All of Olive's relatives were light skinned, and Mama Laurel had heard that quite a few were back in the West Indies passing for white. Many people thought that Olive with her fair skin, blond wheat-colored hair, and bright blue eyes was white. Olive never denied her African heritage but Mama Laurel knew that her mother was color-struck. Mama Laurel also knew that the only reason her mother married her father, whose dark skin earned him the nickname of "Midnight," was that she was seventeen, desperate, and he was kind. Mama Laurel had spent most of her childhood out of the sun because her mother would tell her that she was "black enough." She spent countless days pinching her round nose to try to get it a little straighter, at her mother's insistence. Only Mama Laurel's long, curly hair earned her any compliments from her mother. "You got good hair," Olive would say whenever she was trying to find a compliment to push Mama Laurel's way.

Now that Olive had been dead almost thirty years, Mama Laurel could look at her more kindly. Olive was a product of a culture that glorified light skin. Olive received benefits because of her light skin and her Caucasianlike features. That had made her feel special. She hadn't gotten that from either of her parents, so Olive held on to her skin color as a badge of honor and threw it in everyone's face who dared to look down at her. No matter how high yellow a person was, Olive's skin was always lighter. Whenever Laurel would tell her mother how hurt she was when other children made fun of her dark skin, her round nose, and her full lips, her mother would reply, "*Life ain't fair, Laurel.*" Amen to that, thought Mama Laurel as she opened the door to the waiting room in the ICU.

It surprised Mama Laurel that even after all of these years that her mother lay in her grave, her mother's disapproval still hurt. When Mama Laurel was young she had promised herself that if she had a daughter she would treat her differently from the way in which she was treated. She had been able to keep her promise. Mama Laurel's relationship with Antoinette was a good one. She encouraged her daughter, believed that the sun rose and set on her, and helped instill the feeling of limitless possibilities in her. The only thing she had ever disapproved of was Antoinette's choice of a husband. Mama Laurel always felt that no matter how much money his family had, Sherrod Darling was not the right husband for Antoinette. He was too much of a dreamer. Antoinette needed a man, not a boy who spent his life dreaming about what he would achieve one day. Even though Mama Laurel disapproved of the match, she kept her thoughts to herself. She did not want to be like other mothers who drove their children away from their arms because of their disapproval of the choices their children had made. Mama Laurel did not want to be like her own mother who had never approved of anything Mama Laurel did, no matter how insignificant or how great.

But Mama Laurel wondered if her granddaughters viewed her the same way she viewed her mother. She was critical with them, and although God knows that they deserved all the criticism she heaped on them, thought Mama Laurel, she did not want her voice of disapproval to be the dominant voice that they heard. She did not want to be the cause of hurt to her grandchildren and yet, Mama Laurel knew, just as her mother's disapproval was a discordant melody that flowed through her life, her words to her granddaughters had probably shaped them and contributed to their being the people who they were.

She wouldn't take the blame for her granddaughters' mistakes, but Mama Laurel knew just as surely as she was walking in that hallway that her harsh words, even though they were said in the spirit of love, had probably done more harm than good, and she was ashamed. She didn't share Olive's hot spite, or her bitterness, but Mama Laurel knew that if she continued lecturing her granddaughters about what was wrong with their lives, one day they would avoid her as she had avoided her own mother. And perhaps one day they would feel the relief she had felt when she realized that she would never again have to hear her mother's words of disapproval.

Mama Laurel opened the door to the ICU waiting room. Brynne was sitting in a chair across the room from the door. She was alone and at this time of the morning, just past eight o'clock, Mama Laurel was not surprised. Her head was bent over a magazine, which she was flipping through casually. She looked up when Mama Laurel entered the room.

"Hey, Mama," Brynne called out a greeting, with a smile. "You just missed Jose."

"Oh?" Mama Laurel's spirits rose. Could her granddaughter finally have come to her senses?

"Stop giving me that look," said Brynne, lightly. "He was here as a friend. That's all. There's no hope for reconciliation, so just get those thoughts out of your head."

"You don't know what I'm thinking," said Mama Laurel, annoyed that her granddaughter could so clearly read her thoughts. Reconciliation would be the best thing for Brynne. She still loved Jose, and God knows that Jose still loved her. Foolish young people. Didn't they know that love was hard enough to come by without throwing it away?

"It's your life," Mama Laurel continued. "I'm too old to be messing in any grown folks' business."

Brynne laughed. "If only that were true."

Mama Laurel could see that despite her laughter, she was tired. Mama Laurel remembered the joy she felt when she saw her first grandchild. She remembered how she loved giving Brynne baths when she was just a baby, and how she loved the way Brynne smelled. That clean baby and powder smell. It didn't seem so long ago that she would rock Brynne to sleep in her arms. Mama Laurel knew she made a nuisance of herself, visiting Antoinette and Sherrod every time she had the chance, but the birth of her first grandchild was a joyous experience for her, and she was determined that despite the geographical distance between them, she would be a big part of her grandchild's life.

"I'm not going to give a response to that comment, even though God knows it deserves one," Mama Laurel said, walking over to her granddaughter. "How's Olivia?"

"Nothing's changed."

Mama Laurel sat down on the nearest chair. It bothered her that she was so out of breath after a relatively short walk. *I need to go and see my doctor,* she thought, *just as soon as I make sure that Olivia is all right.*

"I sure wish they would do something for her," said Mama Laurel. "It seems like the longer she is like this, the worse her chances are to get better."

Brynne replied, "We just have to keep on praying and hoping, Mama. That's the best we can do for her now."

There were two other women in the waiting room. One was sleeping in her chair and the other was immersed in a novel. Mama Laurel wished that right now she could lose herself in a book, in the world of make-believe, a place where things were all sorted out by the time you got to the last page.

"I sure hope Camille gets here soon," said Mama Laurel. "She should be here and not at home entertaining Naomi. Family should be together at a time like this. I just didn't raise that girl right."

"She'll be here soon," said Brynne, her tone mild. "Besides, Gram Naomi is family, remember?"

Mama Laurel sighed. "Don't I try to forget, but that woman can just get on your last nerve!"

Mama Laurel knew she sounded petty and she hoped that the Lord would forgive her, but it annoyed her the way Camille would always drop everything for Naomi. She certainly never held Mama Laurel in that high regard.

"Like you just said, Mama, family is supposed to pull together at a time like this. Talking bad about Camille and Gram Naomi doesn't strike me as fitting anyone's definition of 'pulling together.'"

Mama Laurel looked at her granddaughter and gave her a tired smile. "Since when did you get to be so sensible?"

Brynne walked over to where her grandmother sat and kissed her cheek. Mama Laurel looked up at her beloved grandchild and felt a momentary sadness that Antoinette had not lived to see the wonderful woman her firstborn had grown up to be. True, Brynne was confused, and prone to be overly sensitive, but with her quiet strength, her stubborn optimism, and her compassion, she had turned into a woman whom Mama Laurel not only loved dearly, but was proud of.

"Brynne, I don't tell you this as much as I ought to, but I love you, baby."

Brynne knelt down in front of her grandmother and wrapped her arms around her, tight. "I love you too, Mama."

Fifteen

Camille

He was following her. No matter where she drove, Harold was just a few car lengths behind her. She had tried to ignore him but the whole thing was getting more and more ridiculous. After making the suggestion that Camille call the police, which was quickly disregarded, Gram Naomi kept her tongue silent on the whole matter. But the look of disgust on Gram Naomi's face spoke volumes.

Camille had dropped Gram Naomi off at the hospital. She had a ten o'clock meeting with her supervisor about the possibility of some new hires, and she hadn't begun to prepare for that yet. Her supervisor had suggested that Camille take some time off to deal with "the situation" as her supervisor referred to Olivia's hospital stay, but Camille wanted to prepare for her meeting. She didn't want to sit around at the hospital. Nothing was happening anyway. When her family needed Camille they knew how to find her. That, as far as Camille was concerned, was the one thing in life that was absolutely certain. If her family needed her they would track her down.

After leaving the hospital, Camille had driven to work. At one point, Harold's car was directly behind hers. He was baiting her. Showing her that she couldn't leave him, not until he was good and ready. Harold had always been possessive and at one time Camille had thought that his possessiveness was cute. It was nice to have someone care about where you went and what you did. But after a while, his need to know her exact whereabouts at all times started to get on her nerves. Apart from the hypocrisy of it—after all, he was living with his wife—Camille was wary of the unspoken threat of violence. He never directly said anything, but Camille could remember that there were times when he used to grab her arm tightly when he wanted to get a point across. There was another time when he pushed her against a wall in anger. The apologies were always instantaneous and profuse. And Camille would wonder if the gleam of triumph she saw in his eyes when he did these things was part of her vivid imagination.

Camille, like the rest of the close-knit community, had heard the stories that Harold beat Roxanne, but he had denied the stories emphatically. For her part, Roxanne never acknowledged that any of these stories were true, nor did she deny anything. Camille had dismissed the talk of Harold being a wife beater. People loved to gossip. Look how much stuff people talked about her, although a lot of what was said did have the ring of truth about it. Still, Camille knew that people liked to make up stories about other folks. That kept them from dealing with their own issues.

Camille stopped her car at the stoplight at the intersection of Carnegie and Eighteenth Streets. She was three blocks away from her job and she was relieved. She wanted to get out of her car, go to work, and put everything else, including this fool driving behind her as if he had no sense and nothing better to do with his time, out of her mind. She felt the first bump before she looked in her rearview mirror and saw Harold's car directly behind hers. The second and third bumps occurred in quick succession. He was ramming her car. She looked around quickly to see if she could maneuver to the right-hand lane. There was a parking lot just ahead. But she was trapped by the cars that surrounded her on all sides. The fourth bump made her head jerk backward.

She unhooked her seat belt and put the car in park. He had lost his mind. Completely lost his mind. As she opened her car door, she saw Harold running up the side of the road toward her. His face was contorted with rage and something else she could not define.

"You bitch!" He was screaming at her. "You no good tramp! Don't you ever walk away from me again!"

Camille slammed the car door shut. Her fingers were shaking as she pressed the automatic switch that locked all the doors. Harold was banging on her window with his fists and Camille could hear the horns blaring. She saw that another man had gotten out of his car and he was walking quickly toward Harold. Harold kept banging on the window, even as the man stopped beside him. She could hear the man telling her to leave her alone.

Camille started pressing down on the car horn. Didn't the car up front see what was happening? She was trapped. She couldn't go anywhere. Harold was cursing at the man now. More people were getting out of their cars to see what the commotion was about.

The light turned green and the car ahead moved forward. Camille put her foot down on the gas and drove ahead as fast as she could in rush-hour traffic. When she was about a block away she looked back and saw that Harold was still arguing with a group of people.

She drove until she reached the underground parking lot to her office building. The parking attendant waved to her but she didn't acknowledge him. Instead she drove directly to her parking space, her eyes searching the lot as if she were afraid that Harold would suddenly appear from behind one of the pillars in the garage like a villain in a B movie. The parking lot was private and Camille knew that Harold had no access, but still her heart hammered in her chest with fear. Harold had looked as if he wanted to kill her. He had looked as if he could kill her.

Camille's hands shook as she rummaged in her pocketbook looking for a telephone number. She hoped that she hadn't thrown it away. But then she remembered she had thrown Omar's number away right after she stood him up. She knew that she could get his phone number from her friend Lessie who had introduced them, but Lessie was away on a trip to Barbados.

Think, Camille, think. He's a music teacher. He works at a school right here in Cleveland. Think, Camille think. She closed her eyes for a second and tried to force her mind to go blank. She pushed past the fear she felt and past the anger. *Think!* When she opened her eyes, the answer came to her as if someone had handed her a gift. Sojourner Truth High School.

She had to call Omar. She didn't know how much Harold knew about him, but she had to let Omar know that he would definitely have to watch his back. It was clear that Harold was coming after her. And Camille was convinced that the way Harold was carrying on, he would probably try to go after Omar as well. She had to call Omar. But first, she had to stop shaking.

Naomi

Gram Naomi entered the hospital waiting room carrying a peace offering. On the way to the ICU, she'd stopped off at the cafeteria and bought a pecan roll. It was time to put aside her differences with Laurel. They would never like each other, that much was certain, but they shared a love for their grandchildren, and Naomi knew that her feud with Laurel only served to punish her granddaughters. She knew that a pecan roll wouldn't make up for all the bad blood between them, but it was a start. Besides, if Laurel didn't accept the peace offering, at least Naomi could claim that she had tried to do her part to heal the breach.

This morning when she rode to the hospital with Camille, she'd realized that Camille, like the rest of her granddaughters, was in trouble. Brynne looked as if she was about to have a nervous breakdown, Camille's life appeared to be in shambles, and only the Lord knew if Olivia would make it through. It was time, past time, for her and Laurel to bury the hatchet, for the sake of their grandbabies.

Gram Naomi cleared her throat. "Good morning, Laurel."

Laurel looked at her as if she had suddenly grown three heads, all in different colors.

"Gram Naomi," said Brynne, greeting her grandmother. "I'm glad you're here. I'm on my way to work. You can keep Mama Laurel company."

"Well," said Naomi, entering the room with the brown paper bag containing the pecan roll clutched at her side, "I intended to do just that."

Naomi walked over to Laurel and handed her the brown paper bag.

"Laurel," she said, "I know how you like pecan rolls. I got this one at the hospital cafeteria, so I don't know how good it is, but I thought you might want something to eat."

Laurel's shock was almost comical. Naomi thought with a sense of wicked glee that Laurel probably expected that the pecan roll was laced with arsenic.

"Well, er . . . ," Laurel stammered as she got the words out. "Thank you, Naomi. That's very nice of you."

"It certainly is," said Brynne, enthusiastically.

Naomi sat down on the chair Brynne had just vacated. "I hope you like it. How's Olivia?"

"She's the same," said Laurel. "But, at least she hasn't gotten worse."

"Amen," replied Naomi. "That's a blessing."

"I'm off to work," said Brynne. "But I'll be back soon—sooner if you need me."

"We'll hold down the fort," Naomi assured her. "Right, Laurel?" Naomi turned and saw that Laurel's mouth was filled with the pecan roll, but she nodded her head in agreement.

"Then that's settled," said Brynne. "I'm off."

After Brynne left, Naomi said to Laurel, "It looks like we're going to be here awhile."

"Uh-huh," replied Laurel. "Thank you for the pecan roll, Naomi. It might be hospital food, but it sure tasted good. I guess I was hungrier than I thought."

"Don't mention it," replied Naomi, surprised that she was so pleased that Laurel had accepted her overture.

"I'll buy you a coffee, later on this morning," said Laurel. "After all, one good turn deserves another."

Naomi looked at Laurel. Now it was her turn to be surprised. This didn't exactly qualify as a miracle, but it was darned close. Laurel was actually being civil, even nice to her. Who would have thought that a hospital pecan roll would accomplish this?

"That would be quite nice," replied Naomi. "Quite nice, indeed."

Camille

Camille held on to the telephone receiver as if it were a life preserver. It had taken a lot of persuasion to convince the receptionist to interrupt Omar's music class. "We don't disturb our teachers when they are in the middle of class," the receptionist informed her after listening to Camille's request to speak with Omar.

"Tell him that it's his sister Camille," she finally said in frustration. "Tell him it's an emergency."

"I didn't know Omar had a sister," said the receptionist. "You said your last name is Darling. Omar's last name is Abdus Salaam."

"I'm his half sister!" Camille yelled in the telephone. "Just go and get him, for God's sake!" After waiting several minutes Camille was just about to hang up when she heard an amused male voice.

"Hello, sis."

"Omar, I'm sorry about bothering you while you're at work, but this really is urgent. There's something you need to know." The words tumbled out. Before she knew it she was crying over the phone as she told him about Harold following her and ramming her car. She had always looked at people who cried easily, like her sister Brynne, as weak, and here she was crying every day, it seemed, since Olivia had tried to kill herself. What happened to being strong in times of crises? Camille wondered.

When she had finished talking, Omar asked her, "Where are you?"

"I'm at work."

He was patient. "Where do you work, Camille?"

"At the Department of Transportation. On Euclid and Ninth Streets. Twentieth floor."

"I'll be right over," he said. "And, Camille, don't leave your office until I get there. Promise me."

Camille was silent as she stared at the roses in the vase that Harold had sent her yesterday.

"Promise me, Camille," Omar repeated. "Promise me you won't leave until I get there."

"I promise."

Brynne

"Hail to the conquering heroine," said Phillip Canzilotta as he joined Brynne on the elevator. They were riding in the one that was reserved for the lawyers and their clients. The rest of the general public took the elevators located inconveniently at either ends of the building.

"Good morning to you too, Phil," replied Brynne. So the rest of the firm knew about her discussion with Winston Gray. She wasn't surprised. News traveled fast and bad news traveled faster.

"It is a good morning, indeed," said Phil, grinning. "The whole firm's talking about you. Congratulations, it couldn't have happened to a nicer person."

The elevator swayed on its way up to the fifty-second floor. These elevators were particularly temperamental, given to shaking, stopping between floors, and scraping against the walls, particularly on windy days.

"Well, I hope you can help me type up this conquering heroine's résumé."

"No one's going to fire a black woman attorney." Phil's words escaped his lips before he had a chance to stop them. At least he had the good sense to look embarrassed, thought Brynne as she watched his sea-blue eyes slide to the floor of the elevator.

"I hate to be the one to break this piece of news to you, Phil," said Brynne as the elevator doors opened, "but black women have been getting fired for a long time now."

"Hey," said Phil, "you know what I meant, Brynne. They would have a hell of a lawsuit on their hands if they got rid of you."

Brynne shook her head. She was used to being in this position. Being the honorary African-American. The honorary African-American at school, at work, at play. Folks tended to forget that she was one of "those people." With her cultured Ivy League accent, a nonthreatening manner, and a general aversion to discussing anything dealing with race, Brynne was considered "safe." So safe that folks were themselves around her. Instead of watching what they said, they felt free to discuss their opinions on black folk in general. Brynne supposed this could be viewed as a blessing and not a fault. She always knew where she stood. Even Phil, a person she liked and respected genuinely, a person whom she would never describe as a bigot, thought that her race insulated her from any kind of unfair treatment.

"Don't worry about it, Phil. Suing this great institution is the last thing on my mind."

Brynne stepped off the elevator without waiting for a response. As she walked down the hallway she became aware of the many pairs of eyes turned in her direction. Did they all expect her now to go postal? To get out a gun, or worse, a spear, and throw it through the hearts of these good people? She avoided looking at anyone as she made her way quickly to her office. As she reached her office door, Mary O'Reilly, Winston Gray's secretary, walked by her.

"Hi, Brynne." Mary smiled her easy smile and her eyes were sympathetic behind those black cat-frame glasses she always wore.

"Mary," said Brynne, smiling back.

"How's your sister?" asked Mary.

"Hanging on," said Brynne truthfully.

"Well, good for her!" said Mary. "And, Brynne—"

"Yes, Mary?"

"Good for you too!"

Brynne smiled at Mary. She was one tough woman, that Mary

O'Reilly. Brynne knew that most of the people at the firm were going to keep their distance from her until they saw how the whole thing sorted itself out. They might hail her as the conquering hero, but they weren't going to align themselves with her. If there was going to be a fight between the one African-American associate and the most powerful partner in the firm, it was no contest. Brynne didn't blame them.

Winston Gray was a formidable enemy, and if she hadn't been out of her head that day, she would never have had the nerve to talk to him the way she did. Whatever. She knew there were consequences. Can't be afraid to stand up if you're afraid to fall, Mama Laurel always said. Brynne was prepared for the fall. Winston Gray didn't like an eyebrow raised in his direction, let alone a thorough cussing out. Payback was coming, Brynne was absolutely certain.

"Brynne, I don't have to tell you because you're a smart lady, but watch your back."

"Thanks for the advice just the same," said Brynne, but before the sentence was completed, Mary O'Reilly was already in motion, heading down the hallway toward her desk.

Brynne's thoughts turned to last night and the time she had spent with Jose. They had hardly talked, and Brynne had spent most of the night sleeping in the uncomfortable chair. But the knowledge that he was there with her had comforted her. When she'd awakened in the morning, she'd watched him as he slept. How many times had she done that while she was married? *If only we could have turned back the clock to that precise moment when we started moving apart,* thought Brynne, but she knew that their drifting did not occur at a specific moment, but was a culmination of a lot of moments, both great and small, when each had taken the other person for granted.

Brynne sighed as she opened her office door. She had no one to blame for the current state of her life but herself. She had walked out of her marriage and she was now going to walk out on her job. She just had to hope that she was walking toward something that would give her the peace that had escaped her all of her life.

Camille

Camille's secretary, Jim, ushered Omar into Camille's office without comment. Although his eyes betrayed his curiosity, he said nothing. After Jim left, closing the door behind him, Omar sat down in one of the chairs in front of him.

He seemed agitated and Camille watched as he clenched and unclenched his fists before speaking.

"Did he hurt you?" he asked.

Camille shook her head. "No."

"Has he called you since this morning?"

Camille shook her head again.

Omar stood up and walked over to Camille's window. He looked outside for several minutes without saying anything. When he turned to face Camille she could see the pain shadowed in his eyes. He seemed to be making an attempt to choose his words carefully.

"Camille, I appreciate your concern for me, but right now you need to be concerned about yourself. I can handle Harold. Trust me on that one. But you need to get some kind of help because you know that he's going to come after you again. You need to go to the police and file charges against him."

"No."

"Camille, I know you love him—"

"I don't love him," Camille said calmly. "I never did. But I don't want the police involved. I can handle this by myself."

"How?" asked Omar. "How are you going to handle this on your own? The guy rammed your car. Don't you understand? Today it's your car, tomorrow it's going to be your body. Go to the police."

Camille knew that she would never go to the police. What would she say to them? Her married ex-lover was following her around town? They would probably all believe that she deserved it. What goes around, comes around and all that. She knew the rules of the game. No one did the kind of dirt she did, without paying a price for it. She'd slept with a married man. She'd hurt a lot of people in the process. Was it worth it? Hell, no. But she'd gone into the situation with both eyes wide open, so she was not going to complain about the outcome. Besides, who would care?

"Don't worry," said Camille. "I'll be all right."

"Camille, my aunt was killed by her husband. She thought she could handle it. That's what she said to us. Her husband shot her three times in the face."

His voice was quiet, but Camille could see him continue to clench and unclench his fists.

"Omar, I'm sorry about that. I truly am. But Harold would never hurt me." The words sounded stupid to her own ears and Camille wondered how they sounded to Omar.

Omar didn't press the point.

"Listen," he said, "let me give you a ride home. You're not going to get anything done here. I'll stay with you if you're afraid."

Camille didn't trust herself to drive at that point. Even though it had been over an hour since her last encounter with Harold, her hands were still shaking.

"Could you give me a ride to Cleveland Med?" asked Camille. "My sister's in the hospital."

"Your wish," said Omar, "is my command."

Mama Laurel

The waiting room at the intensive care unit was now filled to capacity. Every chair was taken and there were some folks sitting on the available floor space. Others were sitting or leaning on the two windowsills. To Mama Laurel's eyes, there were five groups of people, including herself and Naomi. But unlike all the other groups who were talking and interacting with each other, Naomi and Mama Laurel were silent. They sat side by side, but there had been no acknowledgment of each other for the last two hours.

The door opened and a young Indian doctor walked in.

"My name is Doctor Singh," he said. "I'm looking for the relatives of Olivia Darling."

Mama Laurel's mouth went dry. Something had happened to Olivia. Something bad. She stood up at the same time as Naomi. Naomi spoke first.

"I'm one of her grandmothers," she said.

"I'm the other one," said Mama Laurel.

"Doctor Trahan told me that I would find you all here. I'd like you to come to my office, please."

Mama Laurel wasn't going anywhere until she knew what had happened to her granddaughter. "What's going on? Has something happened to Olivia?"

"Your granddaughter is coming out of her coma," said Dr. Singh, "but there is something we need to talk about."

Oh my Lord, thought Mama Laurel, fearing the second worst thing, brain damage. "What's wrong with her?" she asked.

"If you would please follow me," said Dr. Singh, who by his tone was getting very impatient.

"Come on, Laurel," said Gram Naomi. "The quicker we get to his office, is the quicker we'll find out the answers to all of your questions."

Mama Laurel and Gram Naomi followed Dr. Singh out of the waiting room and down a long white hallway. He opened one of the closed doors marked DOCTOR'S OFFICE and motioned for them to sit down in the two chairs in front of his desk. There was another woman in the office, standing off to the side near the solitary window. Mama Laurel sat down on the closest chair and Naomi took the only remaining seat. Dr. Singh stood in front of his desk.

"How is Olivia?" asked Naomi.

"We don't know," said Dr. Singh. "She awakened about an hour ago—"

"An hour ago!" A shout of outrage escaped Mama Laurel's lips. Her granddaughter had come out of the coma an hour ago and they were just now getting around to telling her.

Dr. Singh ignored the outburst and continued talking. "We have been working with her, but it has been very difficult. Your granddaughter is not being as cooperative as we would have hoped. She refuses to answer most of our questions, although we're quite sure that she understands us."

"What about brain damage?" asked Naomi.

"Our preliminary tests don't show any brain damage. We have been attempting to examine her but even in her weakened state, it is quite apparent that she does not want us to help her. She isn't speaking to us, except to tell us to go away."

"I'm going to see her," said Mama Laurel, standing up. "She'll see me. She'll talk to me."

"No, she won't." The woman standing in the corner spoke up for the first time. Mama Laurel turned and looked in her direction. She was a short, thin woman with a head full of tightly coiled dreadlocks, which were dyed in a shade between auburn and brown. She wore horn-rimmed glasses balanced almost at the tip of her nose. Like Dr. Singh she was dressed in a white coat, but unlike Dr. Singh she had cowrie shells dangling from her gold earrings, and hanging around her neck and her wrists.

"Who are you?" asked Mama Laurel.

"My name is Doctor Easington, but please call me Shelly. I'm a psychiatrist. Both Doctor Trahan and Doctor Singh thought that I could perhaps help them in their treatment of your granddaughter. She has been through a lot. She doesn't want to see you. We've told her that her family is here and we've asked her if she wanted to see you. She shook her head. Emphatically, I might add."

"You've said that she's been through a lot. She probably doesn't know her right mind—she doesn't know what she means," said Mama Laurel.

"She became very upset at the mention of her family," said Shelly Easington. "We don't want any setbacks. All we're asking is that you give us some time to figure out not only what's going on with her physically, but what's going on with her emotionally, before you talk with her."

"How much time?" asked Naomi.

"Let's take it a day at a time," said Shelly, handing both Mama Laurel and Naomi her name cards. "Call me tomorrow at about ten o'clock. I should be in my office. I'll have more information then."

"I want to see her today," said Mama Laurel, not ready to give up.

"And we're telling you that's not wise. It's certainly not the best thing for Olivia, and I'm sure you want what's best for her," said Shelly, not backing down.

"Just give us a chance to help your granddaughter," said Dr. Singh. "Give us a chance to see exactly what's going on. Our fear is that seeing you might upset her and cause some sort of setback, either psychological or physical."

Naomi spoke up. "Maybe they're right, Laurel. We don't want to do anything that's going to hurt Olivia's chances of getting completely well."

Mama Laurel looked over at Naomi. She could see the same pain she was feeling reflected in Naomi's eyes.

"What if she changes her mind?" asked Mama Laurel. "What if she decides that she wants to see us and we're not here?"

"I'll call you," said Shelly, "and if I'm not around, I'll leave instructions for the doctor and the nurse on call to telephone you. I suggest you go home. You both look tired, if you don't mind me saying that, and there's nothing you can do for Olivia right now."

"We have to look at the bright side of things," said Dr. Singh.

"The bright side?" asked Mama Laurel as if that were a foreign subject for her.

"Yes," said Shelly. "The bright side. Your granddaughter did not succeed in killing herself. She is no longer in a coma. These are things to be thankful for."

She sounded as if she were giving Mama Laurel a lecture, and Mama Laurel knew that the way she was acting, it was no wonder that the doctor was lecturing her as if she were a problematic child.

"What about Trahan?" asked Mama Laurel, hoping that her ally would overrule the doctor's decision to go with Olivia's wishes.

"He's with Olivia right now," said Dr. Singh. "We'll have him call you when he's finished examining Olivia."

Dr. Singh started walking toward the front door. The conversation was over.

"Why don't you two stay here and talk it over? If you want to go back to the waiting room, it's your choice. But you aren't going to get any more information sitting there than you would if we call you at home," said Shelly. "The best thing you can do is go home, eat, get some rest, regroup."

Shelly and Dr. Singh left the room together.

"I think that we should go home," said Naomi. Her voice sounded weary.

"But you're the one that said that we need to be in the hospital. Just in case she needs us."

"She may need us," replied Naomi. "But she doesn't want us and I for one am not going to force myself on her."

"Is that what you think I'm doing?" asked Mama Laurel.

"I think that you love her and you're concerned, but if you try and see her and she gets upset, what good is that going to do for you or, more importantly, for Olivia?"

Mama Laurel was quiet while she thought about this. Naomi was right. There was nothing she could do for Olivia right now. She was out of the coma, that was the important thing to hold on to. Her prayers had been answered. Olivia had not succeeded in killing herself. It didn't feel right just to leave without seeing Olivia, but if that was what the doctors thought was best, then Mama Laurel would give in to their wishes, even if she didn't agree with them.

"Let's go call us a cab and we'll go home," said Mama Laurel.

"I don't have Camille's house keys," said Naomi. "Maybe you could drop me off at her job?"

Mama Laurel stood up and rested her weight on her walking cane.

"You can stay at my house until Camille gets off work. It'll be a lot more comfortable."

"Make sure you call a different cab company than the one you used yesterday," said Naomi. "I don't want to run into that rude cab driver again."

Sixteen

Brynne

Brynne had been working in a law firm long enough to know that when the senior partner who never visited your office suddenly showed up at your door unannounced, it was time, as Mama Laurel would say, to call on Jesus. She knew from experience that the partners preferred to bring bad news to you on your own stomping ground, instead of calling you in to their own offices. Brynne had not quite figured out the logic in this, except that there was no logic behind it, and as everything else in W&S was ruled by tradition, the "it's not working out" talk was usually done in the associate's office.

"May I come in?" said Alexander Thurmond, one of the firm's most senior partners, who was also known as the surgeon. He came by this appellation as a result of his knack for ripping one's heart out with a minimum of blood involved. He was a short, balding man whose calm demeanor belied a soul in serious need of redemption. Alexander actually enjoyed being the bearer of bad news, and he did his job well. In a hushed voice, he would tell the associate, paralegal, runner, or fellow partner that it was time to go. Legend had it that at times he even shed a few tears during the process, but by the time his little talk was over, the victims, while suspecting that their throat had just been slit, could do nothing but wait for the blood to flow. At this point, Alexander would exit the room with the assurance that he would do everything possible to ensure that the "transition" was smooth.

"Come in, Alexander," said Brynne, knowing that this moment was inevitable. She watched as Alexander entered her office and shut the door behind him. Another bad sign, thought Brynne.

"Brynne, we need to have a discussion," said Alexander. "A heart to heart."

After hearing these words, Brynne began to pray silently. Her prayer was simple: *please give me the courage to get through this.*

Alexander hesitated as if he were waiting for a response from Brynne. Then he continued speaking. "Brynne, I spoke to Winston Gray the other day and I must tell you that after listening to him I have some concerns."

Brynne remained silent, but she continued her prayer.

"Now, I understand that your sister is in the hospital and that you are under a great deal of stress, and that's why I spoke up in your defense to my other partners."

"My defense?" asked Brynne.

"Yes, the partnership held a meeting to discuss the situation between yourself and Winston Gray. Mr. Gray is very upset about it. According to him, you threatened him with bodily harm and you were insubordinate."

"I never threatened him with bodily harm," said Brynne calmly, "although I guess my response to him could have been characterized as insubordinate."

"Yes, well, I have to be candid with you, Brynne, Mr. Gray wanted us to terminate you. He felt that there simply is not room at W and S for this kind of behavior."

"What kind of behavior?" asked Brynne, keeping her voice calm and her stare steady.

"Any behavior that can be characterized as insubordinate."

Brynne stared at this short man who seemed to be swallowed up by the leather chair, and wondered how she let herself be intimidated by him, and others like him. He held no real power over her. True, he could fire her, but, surprise, surprise, she could always get another job. Maybe not as well paying or with as many perks as W&S, but maybe another job wouldn't come with Winston Grays and Alexander Thurmonds.

"Are you firing me, Alexander?" Brynne asked.

Alexander was clearly taken aback by her direct question. It was obvious that he was not used to this kind of reception to his speech.

"No—not exactly, Brynne. I fought hard for you because I know that you are a hard worker and a smart lady; however, you need to be aware that this sort of behavior cannot happen again. If it does, there will be nothing I or anybody else can do to help your situation. You will be out of W and S so fast that your butt will hit the pavement before you even realize it."

Brynne sat quietly for a moment, digesting this latest piece of information. She glanced around at her office. It was spacious by associate standards. It had two large windows, a view of Lake Erie and downtown Cleveland. She looked at her diplomas, which were framed and hanging on the walls of her office. Wellesley College. University of Pennslyvania Law School. She stared at the pictures on her desk, a picture of her mother and father taken over thirty years ago, of Mama Laurel with her and her sisters at her college graduation, of Gram Naomi standing in front of her house at Sag Harbor, of Mama Laurel's parents on their wedding day. She thought to herself, it wouldn't take too long to clean out her office.

Alexander's voice broke through her reverie. "I hope you realize that by not terminating your employment, the firm has done you a great favor. I have to tell you, other associates have not been so lucky."

Lucky. The word danced around Brynne's head. Lucky. If she stayed at the firm she would always be indebted to them for allowing her to remain in their company. True, they paid well. Top-dollar. But they didn't pay enough to make her stay in a job where her advancement was based upon the goodwill of people she did not like or respect. She cleared her throat and said to Alexander Thurmond, "It's not that I don't appreciate your efforts in my behalf, Alexander, but you need not do me any more favors. I will be submitting my resignation to the firm today."

"Resignation!" Alexander clearly was not expecting this. "Brynne, don't be too hasty—you're a senior associate with one client. You're going to have a difficult time finding employment in another firm."

"True," acknowledged Brynne, "but my decision remains the same. I will stay as long as it takes to get my files in order."

Alexander shook his head. "I think you're making a big mistake here, Brynne."

"Maybe so," said Brynne. "Is there anything else, Alexander?"

Alexander shook his head again. He looked troubled. Brynne was the fourth African-American associate to leave W&S in two years. After Brynne's departure, the firm would not have any more minorities on its roster. This was clearly not the result he had hoped for. He stood up and held his hand out for Brynne to shake it. "Good luck, Brynne."

Brynne did not shake his hand. "Thank you, Alexander," she replied.

Alexander dropped his hand to his side, as if defeated. He left her office silently.

Brynne stood up and walked over to the window and looked out at Lake Erie. She had long ago made peace with the gray lake. It was not the blue waters of the Atlantic, nor would it ever be. But the lake had its own beauty. She had looked out of these windows on countless occasions. Soon she would have to stare at the lake from another window. Time to get the résumé in order, she thought. A headhunter had telephoned her last week about an opportunity at a smaller, up-and-coming law firm. At that time she had politely dismissed the recruiter, but now she would have to look through her legal pads to find the recruiter's name and number. It was time to beat the pavement again. She thought of Reggie's offer of employment but discarded the thought just as quickly as it entered into her mind. She wasn't interested in working for Reggie, no matter how much money she could make. Reggie was a great friend, but he was driven and he was unreasonable. Not a good combination for a prospective employer. Brynne walked back over to her desk and started looking for the legal pad with the headhunter's telephone number.

Camille

Camille and Omar encountered Mama Laurel and Gram Naomi on their way out of the hospital in the front lobby. Camille had told Omar that she didn't need an escort to the ICU waiting room, but he had insisted that he follow her. She didn't think that Harold would try to find her in the hospital, but she had not thought that he would ram her car and chase her through traffic either. She was grateful for Omar's company. And she was grateful that he had remained silent on the ride to the hospital. He asked no questions and he seemed to understand instinctively that she did not want to engage in any conversation. The only comment he made was to inform her that he was going to see that she arrived safely at her destination in the hospital.

As soon as she saw her grandmothers, all her thoughts about

Harold and his recent craziness disappeared as she focused on their tired faces. Her first thought was that something had happened to Olivia, but she pushed that out of her mind. If something had happened to Olivia they would both have held court at the hospital until the cavalry in the form of Brynne and herself arrived. Still, her grandmothers' faces looked drawn with worry. There had to be a bad reason for that.

"What's going on?" asked Camille, preparing herself for the worst. After the day she was having, she was ready to hear anything. Almost anything.

Naomi spoke first. "Olivia's conscious now."

For one moment, everything stood still except Camille's heartbeat. She had never experienced this feeling, where the world around her seemed to fade away and all she could focus on were the words her grandmother had just spoken. *She's conscious now.*

Hallelujah, thought Camille, even though she was not religious. *Hallelujah. Thank God. Thank God. Hallelujah!*

"Have you seen her? How is she? Is she upset? Is there any permanent damage?" Camille had so many questions that she didn't take the time to take a breath between each one.

Naomi explained to Camille what they had just learned from Dr. Singh and Shelly, the Rastafarian psychiatrist. She spoke quietly, yet Camille felt as if she were shouting every word at her. When Naomi finished speaking, Camille still didn't understand.

"What do you mean she doesn't want to see us?" asked Camille.

"That's what she says," said Naomi. "And the doctors think that it's best that we respect her wishes."

"Mama Laurel," said Camille, "what do you think about this?"

"Doesn't matter what I think," said Mama Laurel, her voice small and tight. "We've got to trust that these doctors know what they're doing. At least she's conscious. That's a blessing."

Mama Laurel sounded as if she was trying to convince herself.

Gram Naomi cleared her throat. "Camille, where are your manners? You haven't introduced us to your friend standing over there."

Camille turned to see Omar, standing a few yards away from them, waiting patiently. He had walked away during the conversation.

"His name is Omar," said Camille. "He gave me a ride over here."

Camille knew that both her grandmothers must be in bad shape because apart from the mildly curious stares they gave Omar, there were no questions about him or his purpose in life. She knew that they were hurt, especially Mama Laurel, who Camille knew would look at Olivia's wish to be alone as a personal act of betrayal against her first and the family second.

Omar walked over and joined the group. Introductions were made and polite handshakes were exchanged.

"Where are you all headed?" asked Camille.

"We're going back to Laurel's house," replied Naomi. "There should be a cab waiting for us outside."

"Ladies, I have a car right across the street with room for three extra passengers. It isn't fancy, but it's bought and paid for, and more importantly, it'll provide you with the smoothest ride in Cleveland. How about if I give you a lift home? Camille can vouch for me, I'm a safe driver."

Gram Naomi spoke up without any hesitation. "That's a lovely idea, Omor. I've had one bad cab ride too many since I arrived. We can tell the cabbie we got a ride in the meantime."

Camille noticed that Omar didn't correct the mispronunciation of his name.

"We should pay the cab driver something for his trouble," said Mama Laurel as she walked beside Gram Naomi and Omar.

"What for?" scoffed Gram Naomi. "That's how business goes. Sometimes you get a fare and sometimes you end up empty."

"Well, I'm not like that," retorted Mama Laurel. "Camille, pay the man a ten-dollar bill for his trouble."

Camille followed her grandmothers and Omar out of the front door. Olivia was back. She knew that Olivia had a long way to go, but hopefully she was on the road to recovery. *Well,* thought Camille, *even if she isn't on the road to recovery, let's hope that the road is at least in her sight.*

$\mathscr{S}$ even $\mathfrak{f}$ een

Olivia

Olivia stared at the white hospital walls. She'd failed. No surprise there. She'd failed at everything else she'd tried to do. Why should failing to kill herself be a surprise? She couldn't keep a job, she couldn't protect herself from cousin Ray, and she couldn't take herself away from this world. Now she had to face her family. That was worse than failing. Facing people who would be hurt and angry all because of her actions. They would never understand the pain that drove her actions. They would just see her as being weak, which she was, but it was much more than that. It was weakness, hurt, anger, fear, living in a world in which she was always on the outside looking in, a world that had turned its back on her a long time ago, a world in which little girls were not protected from perverted men, a world where she did not belong—all of this had driven her to take those bright, red pills.

Her head was throbbing. The psychiatrist had been in to see her several times this morning. Other doctors had come also, poking and prodding, as if she were an animal. *Leave me the hell alone,* she wanted to tell them but she didn't have the strength or the inclination to use her voice, although at one point, she'd whispered, "Go away."

The young intern making his rounds with the attending physician had stared at her when she said that. He looked as if he'd seen a ghost. "Go away," she'd whispered again. Those were the only words she'd spoken since her refusal to see her family.

"I can't stay here." Olivia spoke those words aloud. Her throat hurt. *I can't stay here. Not in this hospital and not in this life. I can't stay here.*

Brynne

Brynne walked around Malcolm's bookstore, Black Pearls, looking at the various limited-edition books by Langston Hughes, Zora Neale Hurston, Claude McKay, and other illustrious black authors. The bookstore specialized in hard-to-find novels as well as more modern, mainstream authors. Malcolm was helping a customer find an anthology on black women writers of the Harlem Renaissance.

She thought about getting some books for Olivia, but she realized that she had no idea what kind of books Olivia would read. Unlike Camille and Brynne, who read everything they could find the time for, Olivia had never shared her sisters' love of novels. Although Brynne was the one relative that Olivia would confide in, Brynne understood that in many ways Olivia was a mystery to her, just as she was a mystery to the rest of the family.

Brynne listened to Malcolm as he talked excitedly about a subject that was obviously dear to him.

"Have you ever read any of Zora Neale Hurston's works?" he asked the customer. "You've got to read *Their Eyes Were Watching God,* man. That book changed my life—made me want to just keep on reading. I didn't know anyone could work with words the way Zora did. . . ."

Brynne felt the tension drain away from her as she listened to Malcolm speak. It had been a rough day, but it had ended well. Olivia was doing better. Camille had called Brynne at the office and left her a message that Olivia was awake but she didn't want to see the family. It had taken every ounce of self-discipline not to run to the hospital to see her sister, but in the end Brynne decided to respect her wishes. There would be time enough to see her. For now, Brynne had to settle for the feelings of gratitude and relief that came with the knowledge that Olivia, at least physically, was getting better.

Malcolm had called her at the office and suggested that they meet for dinner. Brynne had welcomed the invitation and they'd agreed to meet in his bookstore at six o'clock. It was now almost seven, but Malcolm was still helping his customers. Brynne watched as he used his knowledge about African-American literature as well as some heavy flirting to sell books to his customers, many of whom he seemed to know already.

When the last customer left the store, Malcolm walked over to Brynne and put his arm around her shoulder. "How's it going, Brynne?"

Brynne returned his smile. "My sister is getting better so for this moment, all is right with the world."

He kissed her cheek and said, "Let's get out of here. I know this great Ethiopian restaurant—ever had Ethiopian food?"

"No." Brynne shook her head.

"Your culinary senses are in for some big fun."

"Is that right?" Brynne asked.

"Absolutely," Malcolm replied.

Mama Laurel

Mama Laurel was enjoying her conversation with Naomi. They were having a spirited discussion about rap music. Naomi felt that it was an assault on her ears, but Mama Laurel felt that some of that rap music was just as good as the music Berry Gordy put out when Motown ruled. Omar added another dimension to the conversation by talking about the women-hating lyrics in some of the rap songs, and Camille was silent. Mama Laurel saw that something was bothering Camille, and she wondered what trouble Camille had now gotten herself into. *Well,* thought Mama Laurel, as she studied her granddaughter, *I'll find out before the night is through.*

"That was a delicious dinner, Mrs. Darling," Omar said to Gram Naomi, in an obvious attempt to steer the conversation into another direction. Gram Naomi was starting to get hot when Mama Laurel compared Public Enemy's Chuck D to Marvin Gaye.

Naomi had surprised Mama Laurel by insisting that she prepare dinner. She'd found some perch in Mama Laurel's refrigerator and she fried some, and made some baked potatoes and salad. The perch was a little too seasoned for Laurel's taste, but she'd kept that information to herself. This was the first time in years that Naomi had cooked for her, and Mama Laurel had to admit that the experience was not at all unpleasant, overseasoned perch and all. She just wished that Olivia and Brynne were here to enjoy this evening. It had been a while since she'd had such a good time. But Brynne was off some- where, they'd been trying to reach her by phone, and Olivia was still in the hospital.

Why didn't Olivia want to see the family? Hadn't she put them through enough grief? This was time for family to pull together. No matter what had happened to Olivia, and Mama Laurel knew that a lot of it was bad, the family was there for her. Even when Ray had hurt Olivia, Mama Laurel had acted quickly to get him out of their lives. She'd made it clear that Ray would never be welcome in her house again. True, Ray deserved more punishment than that, but Mama Laurel couldn't see putting Olivia through any more hell, and that's what would have happened if they'd prosecuted Ray. And who needed to air all that dirty stuff in public? It would just make her fam- ily a subject of gossip, and how would that help Olivia? Besides, in the end, Ray got what he deserved, dying like a dog, in the construction accident. Still, there were times, many times, when Mama Laurel won- dered if she'd done the right thing by Olivia—maybe she should have gone ahead and prosecuted Ray. *What difference does it make now?* Mama Laurel wondered. *All that stuff is in the past.*

"How about some more perch, Mrs. Redwood?" asked Omar.

Mama Laurel pushed the painful thoughts away.

"If I eat any more perch, you might as well put me in Lake Erie and let me float away," replied Mama Laurel.

Mama Laurel heard the sound of laughter and realized that this had come from Naomi. In all the time she had known Naomi she could not recall the sound of her laughter. Mama Laurel knew that there must have been a time when she had heard Naomi laugh in all the years she knew her, but it was strange, she had no recollection of this.

Naomi's laughter brought a light to her face and to her eyes. She was a beautiful woman and Mama Laurel was just now realizing it. With her perfectly oval and still unlined brown face, and equally brown eyes, high cheekbones, full lips, and silver-gray hair, she looked like a painting Mama Laurel had once seen long ago of a woman from the coast of West Africa.

Naomi caught Mama Laurel looking at her and almost immedi- ately the laughter died in her throat. "I guess you wonder how I could be laughing at a time like this, don't you, Laurel?"

Mama Laurel shook her head. "Why shouldn't you laugh?" she said, as the truth of her words set in and took hold of her. "Olivia is back with us and even though things aren't the way we would want them to be, it's still a time for celebration. So laugh all you want, Naomi. There's too few folk laughing in this family."

Naomi nodded in agreement. "You're talking the truth, Laurel."

Camille stood up from the table and began clearing away the dishes. Omar stood up to help Camille clear the table, but Camille motioned to him to sit down.

"No, you sit down with Mama Laurel and Gram Naomi," said Camille. "I can handle this."

Hmm, thought Mama Laurel as she looked at her granddaughter. She had never seen Camille act so solicitous to a man. Usually, it was the men who were breaking their foolish necks to be nice to Camille, even when she didn't pay them any mind. Mama Laurel turned and looked at Naomi and saw that she was looking at Camille with the same speculation Mama Laurel was feeling. Something was definitely going on here, or at least Mama Laurel hoped so. She didn't know much about this Omar but from what little she saw, she knew that he was an improvement over Harold.

Well, I won't push, thought Mama Laurel as her eyes darted back and forth between her granddaughter and Omar. *But it sure would be nice to see Camille with a decent man for a change, and not a bad-looking one at that.*

Brynne

"Tell me about your ex-husband," said Malcolm as they drove in Malcolm's car to the Ethiopian restaurant.

Brynne shifted uncomfortably in her seat. She'd been thinking a lot about Jose lately. Maybe the guilt that she had felt when she walked out of the marriage was catching up to her, or maybe she was finally facing the pain she had felt when the marriage ended. She'd run away from those feelings, buried them somewhere deep inside— so deep that she wasn't tempted to examine them. After the divorce, she'd cut her hair, traveled to places she'd never been with Jose, increased her caseload at work, just kept moving until when she stopped she was too tired, too exhausted to think, too exhausted to admit to herself that she missed her ex-husband.

Brynne cleared her throat. "What do you want to know?"

"What kind of man is he? Why'd you break up? Is he the reason I still see sadness in those eyes of yours?"

"Is that all?" Brynne said, trying to keep her voice light.

"Sometimes it helps to talk about things," Malcolm said, as he slowed the car down at a red stoplight.

Brynne remained silent as the lights changed to green and Malcolm made a left turn onto Superior Avenue.

"Come on, Brynne." His voice was soft. "It's time to let out some of that pain, some of that sadness."

"My ex-husband's name is Jose and he was—is a good man."

"Okay," said Malcolm. "Tell me something else about him. Why'd you break up with him?"

Brynne took a deep breath. "Lately I've been asking myself the same question. I can't seem to come up with a good enough reason for leaving my marriage."

"What was the reason you told him when you left?"

"I told him that I wanted something different. I wanted a marriage where I still got excited when my husband walked through the front door. I wanted a marriage where we did more than just exist in the same space. I wanted a marriage where my husband didn't try to control everything I did—who I talked to, what I wore, what I weighed. I just wanted him to be happy with me. Flaws and all."

Malcolm took one hand off of the steering wheel and held her hand. Tight. "Did you tell him what you wanted?"

"Several times. But whenever I wanted to try, he didn't and by the time he was ready to try, it was too late. I wanted something—someone different. I wanted a fresh start."

"And you still love him?"

"Yes," Brynne replied. "I still love him."

"And he loves you?"

"Yes."

"When my marriages ended, the love was long gone," said Malcolm. "Seemed like a good idea to leave. If I still loved either of my ex-wives when we broke up, I would have tried to make the marriage work."

"You sound like my grandmothers," said Brynne.

"That might be a good thing," Malcolm replied.

They drove the rest of the way to the restaurant in silence, each person wrapped in private thoughts.

Camille

Camille was surprised at the disappointment she felt when Omar announced that it was time to go. Disappointed. She had hardly spoken to him during the afternoon, but she liked having him around. Much more to the point, she enjoyed the way in which the attention of her grandmothers was deflected to someone other than herself. Omar had a way of engaging people in conversations so that before you knew it you were caught up in everything he had to say.

Camille was used to men who spent the majority of time talking about themselves, and usually the conversation wasn't that interesting. Listening to Omar's conversation with her grandmothers, Camille had learned new information about them. She learned that Gram Naomi used to sing in a blues band while she was in college. She also learned that Mama Laurel listened to rap music.

Camille watched as he used humor to deflect potentially explosive subjects, usually any subject that dealt with the family. There were one or two times when the conversation would veer too closely to dangerous topics and Omar would steer the conversation another way with the skill of one who had successfully navigated stormy waters for a long time. It was an admirable trait that Camille hoped that she would one day master.

"I've got to get going," said Omar. "I've got to pick up my son, Justin, from basketball practice."

"Oh," said Gram Naomi, sounding disappointed. "You're married."

"I'm not married," replied Omar, "I adopted Justin when he was a baby."

"Now, that's unusual," chimed in Mama Laurel, and Camille shot her a look that she hoped would silence her tongue. It didn't. "Not too many men out there adopting kids."

"Justin's mother was an addict. She was a close friend of mine a long time ago. We both thought that I could give him a better life and so far I'm doing everything in my power to do that."

"Omar, you don't have to answer all these questions," said Camille, embarrassed at the way her grandmothers were getting all in this man's business.

"Oh, I don't mind." Omar's answer was as easy as his manner. "They've been telling me all their business this afternoon."

Omar stood up from where he had been sitting on the couch between Mama Laurel and Gram Naomi.

"Camille, get him his coat," ordered Mama Laurel; then she turned and faced Omar. "I can't tell you when last I've spent such an enjoyable afternoon, especially under the circumstances."

"The pleasure is entirely mine." Omar grinned. "I can't tell you when last I've been in the company of three more beautiful and engaging women."

Camille walked over to where Omar was standing and handed him his coat.

"Camille, why don't you walk Omur to his car?" said Gram Naomi, who had kept on mispronouncing Omar's name all afternoon.

Camille knew that both of her grandmothers were matchmaking. This was a sure and certain sign that they were making their way back to normal. Even though the whole ordeal with Olivia continued to wear them down, especially Mama Laurel, it was good to see that while they were down, there were definitely not out. She hoped that they wouldn't be too disappointed when they realized that there was nothing between Omar and herself. He wasn't her type, not that she knew what her type was, she just knew that he wasn't it. Besides, after everything she had been through with Harold, she was definitely not jumping into the arms of another man any time soon, no matter how nice he was to her grandmothers, and no matter how good that solitary dimple in his left cheek looked to her.

"Okay, Gram," said Camille as she went back to the closet for her coat. "I'll get Omar's coat."

Omar kissed her grandmothers good-bye as if they were all old friends.

"Ladies, it has been a pleasure," his deep voice rumbled.

Camille walked outside with Omar, feeling the eyes of her grandmothers on her. She knew that they were looking at them through the window and the thought brought a smile to her lips even though she knew that they shouldn't hope for anything to happen between her and Omar. The distance from her grandmother's front door to the spot where Omar's car was parked in the driveway was not far, but for Camille it felt as if it had taken an extraordinarily long time to get to the car.

"Are you going to be all right?" Omar asked.

Camille nodded her head. "I'm a big girl. I can handle Harold."

"I think you ought to let somebody know what's going on. You need to go to the police and get a restraining order out against this clown."

"No," said Camille, "we've already talked about this. I don't want the police involved."

"What about your family?" Omar asked. "You should talk to them about this."

"I don't want them involved either," said Camille in a tone sharper than she intended. "They have enough troubles to deal with."

He stood there for a moment, hesitating, as if he didn't want to go.

"Thanks for today," said Camille. "You really cheered my grand-mothers up."

Omar smiled. "They're great ladies."

"Looks like you have a way with the ladies," said Camille, trying to turn the conversation in a lighter direction. She didn't like the way he was staring at her, as if she were some kind of wounded animal that needed protection.

"Do I?" asked Omar. "Have a way with the ladies?"

Camille did not want the conversation to turn in *that* direction.

"Good night," she said, before turning to go. He didn't respond; instead she heard him get into the car. She didn't hear him start the engine until she had reached her grandmother's front door.

Camille walked back inside Mama Laurel's house and closed the door behind her.

"I do hope," said Gram Naomi, "that we will be seeing that gentle-man again."

"He really is a nice man, Camille," said Mama Laurel. "I don't think anybody else could have gotten me to smile after what I've been through these past few days."

"Well, now that Olivia's doing better, I think you'll have a lot more to smile about," Camille said.

"I don't know why she wouldn't let us see her today," said Mama Laurel without bothering to cover her bitterness.

"Mama, Olivia needs our help," said Camille. "Being upset with her because she doesn't want to see us is not going to help her get better."

"I don't know what's going to help her get better," said Mama Laurel, "but I know that avoiding her family is not the answer."

For Camille, avoiding her family sounded like the perfect solution to a whole lot of problems, but she chose not to share those thoughts with her grandmothers.

Eighteen

Brynne

After dinner, Malcolm drove Brynne back to the parking lot behind his bookstore, where she'd left her car. Malcolm had wanted to go out to a nightclub after dinner, but Brynne wasn't in the mood for music, or for company. She wanted to be alone with her thoughts. The conversation about Jose had unnerved her. Throughout dinner she'd had a hard time concentrating on Malcolm's words. She'd kept thinking about Jose, wondering what he was doing, how he was coping.

"If I still loved either of my ex-wives when we broke up, I would have tried to make it work." Malcolm's words had shaken her. Her grandmothers had said the same thing to her, but tonight those words had reached her. What had she done? She'd left her marriage to find happiness, yet neither she nor her ex-husband was happy. She'd left behind a man she still loved, a man whom she had hurt very deeply. What had she done?

Malcolm stood in the parking lot, and opened the driver's-side door of Brynne's car. "I don't know if you had a good evening, but I enjoyed your company."

"I'm sorry," Brynne said as she got into the driver's seat of her car. "I've just got a lot of things on my mind."

"Like your ex-husband?"

"Yes," replied Brynne. "My ex-husband, my soon to be ex-job, and I'm still worried about my sister."

"Sounds like your plate is just about full," said Malcolm.

"You're right about that," said Brynne. "Thanks for dinner. It was delicious."

"Any time," said Malcolm. "Just remember, for a good time call . . ."

"I will, Malcolm," replied Brynne.

She turned the key in the ignition.

"Remember, Brynne—even bad decisions can be reversed."

Depends on the circumstance, thought Brynne. *Some bad decisions last forever.*

"Good night, Malcolm," she said, before closing the car door and driving away.

Mama Laurel

Mama Laurel's telephone rang and she rose to answer it. Camille had left for her home a short time ago, and Naomi and Mama Laurel were sitting at the dining-room table talking about that handsome young man, Omar. His mama had most certainly raised him correctly. Except for Jose, Mama Laurel hadn't encountered a man with such good manners in a long time.

She walked out of her dining room and picked up the telephone in the short hallway between the kitchen and the dining room.

"Hello," said Mama Laurel, wondering if Brynne was finally returning her call.

"Mrs. Redwood, this is Shelly Easington." It was the psychiatrist from the hospital.

"How's Olivia?" asked Mama Laurel. "Is she all right?"

"She's resting comfortably," replied Shelly, using doctorspeak. Every time you ask a doctor about a patient in the hospital, the response is always the same: "resting comfortably."

"When can we see her?" asked Mama Laurel.

"That's why I'm calling," said Shelly. "I'd like you and your family to come by my office tomorrow to discuss possible courses of treatment for Olivia."

"Can we see her tomorrow?" asked Mama Laurel, annoyed that Shelly had not given her an answer to her question.

"We'll see what tomorrow brings," was the unsatisfactory reply. "Can you all come by about two in the afternoon?"

"I'm available," said Mama Laurel. "I'll let the rest know."

"Great," said Shelly. "Call me if there's a problem. My office is on the fifth floor. Room A-fifty-one."

"We'll find it," said Mama Laurel.

"My home phone number is written on the back of the card I gave you. Call me at that number if you can't reach me at the hospital. I'll be at the hospital tonight; then I'm going home."

"Thank you," replied Mama Laurel, wondering what kind of doctor gives out her home phone number.

"Nice talking to you, Mrs. Redwood," said Shelly.

"If Olivia needs us at any time, we're all available," said Mama Laurel.

"I know that," replied Shelly. " And, Mrs. Redwood?"

"Yes?"

"Keep the faith!"

Nineteen

Brynne

Brynne listened to her telephone messages on her car phone as she drove down Carnegie Avenue heading for Mama Laurel's house. There was one from Camille filling her in on the latest developments with Olivia. There were three from Mama Laurel all asking where in heaven's name she was. There was one from her secretary asking her for an address of a new client. And there was one from somebody named Omar. Brynne pressed the star key on the telephone pad to listen to the message again.

"Hello, Brynne. My name is Omar Abdus Salaam. I got your name from your sister Camille. She told me that she had a sister named Brynne who worked at this law firm and I tracked you down. I hope I have the right person. Anyway, Camille is in trouble. I don't want to tell you any more than that. She needs you. Please call her and make sure she's okay. If you need my help, you can reach me at 6-4-5-1-0-0-7."

Omar? Camille never mentioned knowing anybody named Omar. According to what he said, her sister was in trouble. What kind of trouble could Camille be in? Brynne maneuvered her car carefully through traffic as she dialed Camille's number. The phone rang twice and Camille's answering machine clicked on.

"Hi, this is Camille. You know the routine. Leave a name and number. Peace."

"Camille, this is Brynne. I just got a phone call from a man named Omar who says that you're in trouble. I'm on my way over to your house, but call me on the car phone as soon as you get this message."

Brynne thought about calling her grandmothers, but quickly discarded the idea. She didn't know what was going on and there was no sense in alarming them. For all she knew, this could be a practical joke.

She dialed Camille's office. After a few rings, Brynne heard the voice of Camille's secretary, Jim.

"Camille Darling's office, may I help you?"

"Jim, this is Brynne. I didn't expect you to be working so late. I was trying to find Camille."

"Oh, hey, Brynne. Camille hasn't been here all day. I'm just about ready to leave. I had some files I had to put in order."

On any other occasion, Brynne would have engaged in chitchat with Jim. He was one of her favorite people, and he was always good for a laugh. But tonight Brynne got right to the point.

"Jim, is everything all right with Camille?"

There was a moment of silence as if Jim was thinking about the question before he answered. Then he said, "I'm not sure. Something's going on with her today. She came here this morning all upset, but she wouldn't talk to me about whatever was bothering her. I thought maybe something happened to Olivia, but when I spoke to her later during the day, she said that Olivia was doing better. I can tell you this, I think that Harold's mixed up in all this. He's been calling here every hour looking for her. Something is definitely up."

Harold. When was Camille going to learn to leave him alone?

"Jim, if you hear from her, tell her I'm on my way over to her house."

"Sure thing, Miss Brynne," replied Jim.

Brynne hung up after a quick good-bye, then dialed Mama Laurel's number when she got to the next red light.

The phone rang a few times before Mama Laurel answered.

"Mama, is Camille there?" asked Brynne, trying to keep the worry out of her voice.

"Brynne, where have you been?" Mama Laurel's voice rose in annoyance. "I've been calling you and leaving you messages."

"I went out to dinner," Brynne replied. "Is Camille there?"

"You went out to dinner! Didn't you get my messages? Why didn't you call me back sooner?"

"Mama Laurel, I just got your messages. Where is Camille?"

Mama Laurel continued speaking as if she hadn't heard Brynne.

"Lord, can you understand Olivia? Not wanting to see her own family! I mean, we've been sitting in that hospital every day, praying for her to come back to us, and what does she do when she wakes up? Turns her back on the family. Can you understand that? I surely can't."

Brynne took a deep breath and counted to ten. "Mama Laurel, do you know where Camille is?"

"Camille? What do you want with Camille?"

The light changed and Brynne drove her car up Cedar Hill Road, the entrance to Cleveland Heights. Flanking the winding road were large Tudor houses placed on the top of the hill. Brynne knew that these houses carried with them a spectacular view of downtown Cleveland, but she was convinced that a good rainstorm would bring them sliding down the hill, with the mud, trees, and the rest of the foliage.

"I need to give her something," Brynne lied, hoping that Mama Laurel wouldn't challenge her.

"She left here about an hour ago," said Mama Laurel. "She took my car with her. Said she was heading home. She was real quiet today. Not like her to be so quiet, but with everything going on with Olivia turning her back on us and God knows what else, I can't say that I blame her—"

Brynne got off the phone before Mama Laurel had a chance to discuss in more detail Olivia's refusal to see the family.

"Thanks for the info, Mama. Got to go! Bye."

Brynne eased her foot down on the gas pedal and prayed that the vigilant cops of Cleveland Heights would not catch her speeding. Something was wrong with Camille and she needed to find out what was going on.

Camille

Camille turned Mama Laurel's car into her driveway. Mama Laurel leased a Cadillac every two years, even though she hadn't driven regularly for the past five years. No foreign-made cars for Mama Laurel. She took her Caddy out for a spin every few weeks, and the care she lavished on a car she hardly used was apparent. It was spotless and drove like a dream.

Camille looked around her driveway before leaving the automobile. There was no sign of Harold or his car. She placed the car in park and cut off the engine. She knew she was being silly about this whole thing with Harold, but she was spooked. She had never seen him act the way he did this morning. She knew he had a bad temper, but she didn't think that he would ever try to hurt her physically. She had always dismissed the stories about him beating Roxanne, but today, looking at the fury in his eyes, Camille knew that he was capable of anything, even hitting a woman.

At the thought of Harold ramming her car, she felt the anger, which had been eating at her all day, start again. Her rage was fueled by her knowledge that she had been helpless to stop his actions, and the knowledge that for one terrible moment she had been afraid of him. She who feared nothing and no one had cowered in her car like a victim while he heaped abuse on her. The thought of her own actions enraged her almost as much as Harold's actions.

I should have gotten out of the car and cursed his ass out, she thought, as she rummaged in her bag, looking for her keys. Night had fallen over Cleveland and with it came a sky full of sparkling, white stars. When she was a little girl she used to think that her parents were stars in the sky. Even though she was angry with her mother for long since forgotten hurts, there was a part of her that still missed Antoinette. Lord knew that she still missed and longed for her father. Two stars in a faraway sky, that's how her grandmother had described her parents.

She found her keys and opened the door to her living room. Turning on the light, she was surprised to see that someone had filled the room with roses. Red, white, peach, yellow, both pale-hued and vivid roses. Harold. How the hell had he gotten the roses into her house?

"No need to thank me, baby."

She heard his voice from somewhere close and turned to find him standing behind her. For a moment she forgot her earlier fear of him as she stared in amazement into his pale green eyes. Harold's eyes were a source of constant compliments and curiosity for many; they stood in direct contrast to his dark brown skin. They were unusual, and in some people's opinions they only enhanced Harold's physical appearance. There were times when Harold's eyes had unnerved

Camille, not because of their color, but because of the coldness she saw when she looked into them.

"How did you get in here?" asked Camille, suddenly aware of how close he was to her. When he spoke she could feel his breath on her face. She took a step backward, into her living room.

Harold had been standing by the door, waiting for her to return. He closed the door, with a wide, easy smile on his face. "I got the keys, remember?"

She had given him the keys to her house when they first started seeing each other, but he had never used them before. She had forgotten about that until this moment. She watched in amazement as he smiled at her as if this were a prelude to seduction. He walked toward her with both of his arms outstretched.

He said, "Let's kiss and make up."

Camille took another step backward. "Harold, I want you to leave."

She said the words calmly, but she began to taste the same fear she had felt this morning when he was running after her through the streets of Cleveland.

"But I don't want to go, baby," he said softly, as Camille watched the coldness descend over his eyes like a curtain. He wasn't smiling anymore.

Camille fought the urge to turn around and run like hell. She kept her feet still. She was not running away from him again. If she started running from him, she would never stop.

"Harold, please leave."

He was directly in front of her now. His right hand touched her face and he started to caress her cheek with his index finger. "I don't want to go, baby."

"I want you to leave." Camille said the words slowly and deliberately, without raising her voice. "I want you to leave now."

"Whose car is that, baby?"

The question was mild enough, but it carried the weight of menace with it.

"Is it your new man's car, baby?"

Who was he talking about? thought Camille as Harold kept caressing her face. Was he talking about Omar?

"He called here," Harold continued. "Said he wanted to make sure that you're okay. Everyone's worried about you, baby. Your sister Brynne called and Jim called too. You doing him too, baby?"

Camille pushed his hand away from her face. "Get out now," she said, her anger now replacing her fear.

"You doing Mr. Secretary, Camille? He's real protective of you. Makes me wonder if he's had some of my Camille."

Camille turned around and started walking toward the kitchen. She was heading for the telephone to call the police. If she couldn't get him to listen, the police sure as hell would.

She felt him grab her from behind and throw her against the wall. Her breath seemed to leave her body when her back hit the wall.

"Don't walk away from me, bitch! Don't you ever walk away from me!"

She turned from the wall and ran toward the front door, but he caught her and held her from behind.

"I wonder just how many people have had what belongs to me, Camille," he said. His breath was hot against her ear, and she could smell alcohol and peppermints. "Don't you know you belong to me, Camille? Whatever you got, baby, belongs to me and not to any other man!"

He was yelling at her now. His arms were wrapped around her and he lifted her from behind. She felt her feet leave the floor, even as he squeezed the breath from her.

She tried to tell him to put her down. She tried to tell him that he was hurting her, to get out of her house. But she couldn't breathe. Instead she clawed frantically at his hands to get him to loosen his grip.

Suddenly, he put her down on the floor. She turned to face him and the last thing she saw before his fist hit her face were his cold green eyes.

The first blow sent her to the floor. She raised her hands in front of her to ward off the rest of the blows that she knew were coming, but her raised hands only seemed to spur him on. Even as he hit her she could hear him cursing at her. After the third time she felt his fists, she stopped counting. He hit her in her face, on her breasts, in her stomach, on her legs, on her arms. He continued to hit her, to kick her, scream at her until he got tired.

She didn't cry out. No matter how much pain she was in, she refused to cry out. Instead, she curled herself in a ball and held on to herself. After some time, he seemed to grow tired, and the blows lost their power and their momentum. She heard him move away, throwing the rose-filled vases on the floor, cursing at her about how much he loved her and how she drove him to do these things to her.

Some time later, the cursing stopped. The sounds of things being broken and torn apart ceased. An unnatural silence descended on the house. Camille remained on the floor with her eyes closed. She did not open them, even after she heard him leave her house.

Brynne

Brynne found Camille lying curled up in the middle of her rose-strewn living-room floor. Every piece of furniture in the room was turned over. The television lay smashed in the corner of the room. There were holes in the wall that looked as if someone had put a fist through it. As Brynne walked through the room toward Camille, she could hear the sound of broken glass beneath her feet. She bent over her sister and cradled her as best she could.

"Who did this to you, Camille?" she whispered as she looked at her sister's battered face. Both her eyes were blackened, and there was a long gash running along the right side of her face. Her lips were swollen and the top one, which was split, was covered with dried blood. Her clothes were torn and Brynne could see that her arms were covered with welts, as if someone had taken a belt and beaten her.

Camille held on to her sister. She opened her mouth to say something, but her voice seemed to fail her. She opened her mouth again. This time she was able to speak. "Harold."

"Come on, Camille," said Brynne, trying as gently as she could to raise her from the floor. "We've got to get you to a doctor."

"No." Although the word was whispered, there was no mistaking the determination in Camille's voice. "Let me be."

This was not the time to argue with Camille. Brynne held her and began to rock her back and forth. She felt Camille's body shake from the tears she refused to cry. She held on to her until the shaking subsided.

She wanted to tell Camille that it was going to be all right. *Everything's going to be okay.* Those were her usual words of solace, but they sounded hollow and false to her. Instead, she spoke to Camille, saying words of prayer, lullabies, poetry, anything that came to her mind that she thought could give her sister solace. Anything to help her deal with the pain she knew she must be feeling. She sang songs to Camille. Songs that her mother sang when she was afraid. The song that seemed to stop Camille's shaking was one of their mother's favorites. "This Little Light of Mine."

"This little light of mine . . . I'm gonna let it shine . . . This little light of mine . . . I'm gonna let it shine . . . let it shine . . . let it shine . . . let it shine."

This was the song her mother used to sing when Brynne couldn't sleep. Her mother had sung this song when she was sad, when she was happy, when life was throwing nothing but questions at her. Brynne knew that she didn't have her mother's strong voice, but she tried her best and her mother's song seemed to calm Camille down. Seemed to reach something inside her.

"Don't leave me, Brynne," said Camille. Her voice small and frightened. "Don't leave me."

Brynne felt her own tears start to rise, but she refused to allow herself the release of crying. She was not going to let Camille feel that she pitied her. She was not going to cry. After everything Camille had been through, her eyes were dry. Brynne's eyes would remain that way, until she was in the privacy of her own house. In a place where Camille could not hear her anguish. There was nothing wrong with a good cry, but Brynne had spent most of her life crying over people and situations that didn't deserve even the salt from her tears. Crying hadn't done anything for her, and it wasn't going to do anything for her sister. Camille needed her to be clear eyed and strong. And that was what she was going to be.

"Camille, I've got to get you to the hospital. Do you think you can handle the car ride, or do you want me to call an ambulance for you?"

Camille shook her head, her eyes fierce and stubborn.

"No," she said. "No hospital. I'm not going."

End of discussion. Case closed.

"Okay," said Brynne. "I'll take care of you, baby. I'll take care of you. Do you think you can make it upstairs? I'm going to put you to bed."

Camille nodded her head yes, and with Brynne's help she stood up. Together they walked up the staircase to Camille's bedroom. Brynne spoke words of encouragement each step of the way.

When they finally reached Camille's bedroom, Camille's feet started to give way beneath her. Brynne felt her stumble and she bent and lifted her sister as if she were a baby. Brynne carried her to her bed and laid her down carefully; then she went to work. She went into Camille's bathroom, held a washcloth under some warm water, and then went back into the bedroom.

She cleaned the blood from her sister's face and body, all the while singing "This little Light of Mine." She cleaned Camille's cuts with iodine, apologizing for the sting of the antiseptic on her broken skin. Camille lay in her bed with her eyes closed. "Don't leave me here alone, Brynne," she said. "Don't leave me alone like Mama used to do."

"I'm not going anywhere, Camille," said Brynne. "I promise."

After she was finished ministering to her sister's bruises, she took Camille's clothes off her and helped her get into one of her flannel nightgowns.

"I'm going downstairs," said Brynne. "But I won't be gone but a minute."

Camille nodded her head, but kept her eyes closed. "Don't be too long, Brynne. Please."

Brynne walked out of Camille's room and closed the door behind her. Then she went downstairs to the kitchen to find a telephone. Unlike the scene of destruction in the living room, the kitchen was immaculate. Brynne picked up the telephone and dialed with shaking fingers a number she knew by heart, the number to the one person that she knew would never turn his back on her, the one person who would always help her.

"Hello," said Jose.

Brynne got to the point. "Jose, I'm at Camille's house. I need to ask a favor of you."

"What do you need?"

"I need you to go to Mama Laurel's house and drive Mama Laurel and Gram Naomi over here as quickly as you can. Tell them that Camille's been hurt. Tell them that I'll explain everything once they get over here."

Jose didn't ask any questions. "I'm on my way," he said.

Brynne hung up the phone and dialed another number that she had written down on a piece of paper and stuck in her pocket.

A man answered after the first ring as if he were expecting her call. "Hello, Omar speaking."

Brynne took a deep breath before she began talking. "Omar, this is

Brynne. Camille's sister. You don't know me, but I want to thank you from the bottom of my heart for calling me."

"Is she all right?" he asked.

"No," said Brynne. "But she will be."

"Is there anything I can do?" he asked.

"No, but thanks for asking."

"Tell her if she needs anything . . . anything at all, call my number."

"I'll do that," said Brynne. "And thanks again."

As she hung up she could hear Camille calling for her from her bedroom.

"I'm coming, Camille," said Brynne. "I'll be right there."

Camille

Camille drifted in a place near sleep. She was still awake, but just barely. She could feel herself falling into a dark, seductive place where not even dreams could reach, and she longed for the oblivion. The pain her body felt was terrible, but it was nowhere as great as the shame she felt for putting herself in this position. For being with a man who could do this to her. She blamed herself for her stupidity. Her stupidity in not recognizing a beast even when it stood right in front of her bearing roses. She cursed herself for her arrogance. Her arrogance in thinking that even if Harold had hurt his wife, he would never hurt her. *What goes around, comes around.* Her relationship with Harold was built on somebody else's pain, and it was inevitable and just that she should feel some of that pain herself.

"This is my fault," she said to Brynne, although she kept her eyes closed because she didn't want to see the hurt in Brynne's eyes. She had gotten too used to seeing people be hurt as a result of her actions. She didn't want to see that anymore.

"Don't ever, ever say that!" Brynne's response was swift and fierce. "You didn't cause this to happen."

Sleep was a good alternative to pain. Her body was starting to shut down. She felt a drowsiness descend, and for a moment the sleep that was calling her finally won; then she was awake again.

"This is what I get for hurting folks, Brynne. It's a wonder I haven't gotten my ass kicked before this."

"Is that what you think of yourself?" asked Brynne. "Is that what you give yourself credit for? For hurting people?"

Camille opened her eyes now. She wanted to talk to Brynne. She wanted to say these things before sleep won the fight with consciousness. "I took another woman's husband just for the hell of it. I didn't love Harold. I'm not sure I even liked him. But I took him, just like I take everything else. Because I can do it."

It took more strength than she knew she had to say those words. She was tired. Her body was telling her to let go, release, descend to a state where she couldn't feel the effects of Harold's rage. But she wanted to say this to Brynne. She wanted Brynne to see her for what she really was. Brynne always looked at life through glasses made of fantasy and wishes. When everybody else judged Camille, Brynne would still find something, anything, to defend her with. And in the rare times that Brynne openly disapproved of Camille's behavior, Brynne would still offer some explanation for whatever it was that Camille had done to cause disappointment. *Look at me, Brynne,* Camille wanted to shout. *Look at me. The package might be pretty, but it still stinks, any way you look at it.*

"There is nothing that you can say, nothing that you can ever do, to make me believe less in you, to make me believe that you deserve anything but the best that life has to offer," said Brynne quietly.

Camille looked over at her sister. Brynne was sitting on the floor by her bed. Her face had that stubborn set to it that looked a lot like Mama Laurel's face when her mind was made up. But unlike Mama Laurel's face, there was a gentleness to Brynne's face. An openness that Camille feared would always cause her sister to be hurt by someone not worthy of her love, like herself.

"Then you're a fool," said Camille quietly.

"I may be a fool," replied Brynne, "but I'm a fool who loves her sister, and a fool who'll never stop loving her sister, no matter what happens."

The tears that Camille had refused to cry when Harold hit her now spilled freely down her face. She didn't know what she did to deserve having a sister like Brynne, but she thanked the same God she'd cursed earlier for allowing Harold to beat her. She cried until sleep finally won the battle.

Twenty

Naomi

Naomi stood in Camille's living room and surveyed the evidence of destruction all around her. She felt the bile in her throat rise and for a moment she thought that she was going to be sick. Waves of nausea washed over her and she cupped her right hand over her mouth. She breathed in and out in her hand until the nausea left her. Behind her, she could hear Laurel's breath coming out in soft gasps, as if she was fighting for air. Jose had not prepared them for this. Nothing could have prepared them for the sight of a room completely filled with broken things. Broken furniture. Broken glass. Curtain rods hanging from the wall like some weird projectory. Papers scattered on the floor, lying next to roses. Brynne had been attempting to straighten things up when they arrived, but it was evident that it would take more than Brynne's assistance to set things right again.

Jose stood in front of Naomi, beside Brynne. He was silent while she spoke, but he held her hand. Brynne's voice was steady while she spoke the words that Naomi still could not comprehend, no matter how many times she heard them. Harold was responsible for this. He had beaten Camille. According to Brynne, he had beaten the hell out of her. *How could this be happening?* The words kept repeating themselves in Naomi's head. *How could this be happening?*

"How is she?" asked Jose.

"She's not in good shape," replied Brynne.

"Then why isn't she in the hospital?" The words came out sharper than Naomi intended, but she was past caring about anything other than getting help for her granddaughter.

"She didn't want to go to the hospital," replied Brynne. "You know how stubborn she can get."

"Let me see her," said Mama Laurel, speaking for the first time since she entered Camille's house. "I want to see my granddaughter."

Naomi turned and looked at Laurel. She saw in Laurel's eyes the same pain, bewilderment, and anger that she felt. They were, for once, speaking the same language. United in a common cause: concern for their granddaughter. She had thought that Laurel would come into Camille's house dispensing blame and judgment as she usually did when confronted with difficult situations. Instead, Laurel had surprised her. Her focus was on Camille, and her anguish for the situation Camille had gotten herself into was unmistakable.

"Let her sleep for now," said Brynne. "There's nothing we can do right now. I've called Doctor Reed and he's on his way over here. After he examines her, I'll take you all to see her."

Naomi had met Dr. Ezekiel Reed a few years ago, and she had been impressed. He was an old friend of Laurel's, but Naomi had not let that get in the way of her admiration of him. He was one of the last of a dying breed, the family practitioner who thrived despite his advanced age and the advent of HMOs. He was also courteous, discreet, and had a great bedside manner.

"That's a good idea, Brynne," said Naomi.

Mama Laurel agreed. "Ezekiel will take good care of my baby."

Naomi had never heard Laurel refer to Camille using those terms. Terms of affection were usually reserved for Brynne or for Olivia.

"What about the police?" asked Jose.

"She doesn't want me to call them," answered Brynne.

"They need to get involved," said Naomi. "They need to arrest Harold before I kill him."

"Don't worry about Harold," said Brynne. "I'll take care of him. As for Camille, I'll work on her too. I'm sure I can get her to change her mind about the police, but until then, I'm going to respect her wishes, although I surely don't agree with them."

Brynne sounded and acted as if she were a different person. She was calm, which was the first difference, thought Gram Naomi. Usually, Brynne would have fallen apart. She had fallen apart for much less. And the way in which she carried herself. As if she was certain of the decisions she had made, even if the decisions would ultimately not be the wisest ones. She stood her ground.

Gram Naomi watched as Brynne gently extricated her hand from Jose's. "Let's try and get this place back into some order."

Made sense to Gram Naomi. Instead of sitting around, waiting for Dr. Reed, worrying and carrying on, they could use their energies for putting Camille's house back together. She just hoped that Camille would be able to get her life back together after this. *Lord, when troubles come, they don't come in single packages.* Gram Naomi thought of Olivia in the hospital, hiding from her family. Another granddaughter in trouble.

"Jose," said Mama Laurel, "please go in the kitchen and get me some trash bags to get rid of these roses. The sight of them is making me sick."

"I'll help you," said Brynne, following her ex-husband.

Naomi bent down and started gathering the roses in her arms. She, who loved flowers and all manner of plants, could not see the beauty in the pale pink roses she held in her hands. Instead, she only saw the thorns.

Mama Laurel

Mama Laurel waited outside Camille's bedroom door while her friend Ezekiel examined Camille. She had made a fuss when Brynne brought Ezekiel to her room, but they had all expected that. Camille didn't want to see any doctor, even one that used to bring her chocolates when he came courting her grandmother. That was another lifetime, thought Mama Laurel. When a respectable amount of time had passed after her husband's death, a few years, Ezekiel had made his intentions known. He wanted more than the lifelong friendship that Mama Laurel had given him. Year after year, Ezekiel had kept pressing his suit, but Mama Laurel was not interested.

Her life revolved around her daughter, and then, her daughter's children. She didn't have any time, or the desire, to have a man in her life. She valued his friendship, and apart from one night when they had both had too much to drink, and the pain of missing her husband had overcome her, they had kept their friendship platonic.

Ezekiel eventually gave up the pursuit of the stubbornly unattainable Laurel and married a woman from South America who had recently died.

Mama Laurel trusted Ezekiel with her life. She knew that he was the right person to take care of Camille. Although they didn't agree on the right way to treat Olivia—Ezekiel felt that Olivia should have been admitted to a sanitarium a long time ago—Mama Laurel knew that he only had the best interests of his patients at heart. He also had a genuine fondness for Camille. He would find a way to get around her objections and examine her. If there was any medical treatment that Camille needed, Ezekiel would make sure that Camille received it.

Naomi and Jose were downstairs cleaning up. They had done a thorough job in the past two hours. They had cleaned up all the roses, the broken glass, and furniture, and they were now trying to see what was salvageable and what had to be thrown away. Mama Laurel had cleaned up as much as she could, but her leg had started hurting her and Brynne had banished her to the kitchen where she waited until the doorbell announced Ezekiel's arrival.

Brynne brought him up to speed as they walked up the stairs on their way to Camille's room. Mama Laurel trailed behind with the hope that they would let her be there while Ezekiel examined Camille. Once they got to the room, Ezekiel had made it clear that he only wanted Brynne to accompany him.

"Why?" asked Mama Laurel, hating the whine that had crept into her voice.

"Because that's how I want it," said Ezekiel. "Laurel, you'll only get upset and that's not going to help the situation. Once I examine her, then we'll talk about the best time for you all to see her."

It was the second time that day that she had been denied access to one of her granddaughters by a member of the medical profession. She was about to stop the foolishness and follow them inside Camille's room—after all, this wasn't a hospital, there wasn't anything they could do to keep her out of the room, short of physically tying her down—but something in Brynne's eyes stopped her.

"Mama Laurel, if you care about Camille, you'll listen to Doctor Reed," said Brynne. Her eyes reflected a resolve that Mama Laurel was not familiar with. This was another Brynne. Someone whom she had not encountered before.

Brynne's words were an unmistakable challenge to Mama Laurel and she didn't like it one bit.

"Mama, I don't want to be rude but we don't have time to engage in this debate. Doctor Reed needs to take care of Camille. He doesn't have time to have a discussion with you."

"Laurel, why don't you go downstairs and wait?" said Ezekiel.

"I'm staying right here!" Mama Laurel shot back. "I'll wait out here in the hallway."

"Fine," said Brynne, opening the door to Camille's bedroom. "Do what you want, just let Doctor Reed do his job."

Jose had heard the commotion downstairs and had brought Mama Laurel a chair, where Mama Laurel sat for forty minutes before the door opened and Ezekiel emerged.

He looked tired, as if he had just gotten through physically exerting himself.

"How is she?" asked Mama Laurel.

Ezekiel shook his head. "I don't think that there's anything broken, thank God, but I've convinced her to go to the hospital tomorrow to get an X ray. She's got some pretty bad cuts and bruises, but we've cleaned them all up. But emotionally she's in bad shape, Laurel."

Mama Laurel listened. No broken bones. Cuts and bruises. Bad shape. She felt a tightening in her chest, but she willed herself to concentrate on Camille.

"She wants to see you, Laurel," said Ezekiel.

These were the words that Mama Laurel had waited to hear. She stood up and tried to shake the stiffness out of her legs. This getting old stuff got on her nerves. Aches and pains, and a body that was increasingly refusing to cooperate. Still, she knew that she should be grateful. A lot of her friends hadn't lived to see the age that Mama Laurel was now seeing.

"I gave her a sedative," said Ezekiel. "A mild one. Go easy on her, Laurel."

The words of caution stung. Mama Laurel felt ashamed. What kind of a person did Ezekiel think she was that she would be hard on Camille, after what she had been through today? The same person who spent her life telling everybody where they had gone wrong.

"Don't worry," said Mama Laurel, as the pain wrapped itself around her heart like a fist. She took as deep a breath as she could and then blew it out slowly through her nose. Mind over matter. She was not going to give in to the pain. Not when her grandchild needed her.

"Laurel, when is the last time you saw a doctor?" asked Ezekiel, his eyes round and concerned.

"I'm all right, Ezekiel," said Mama Laurel. "I'm just worried about Camille."

"She's been through hell," said Ezekiel, "but she has her family to help her through this."

"If she lets us help her," said Mama Laurel, suddenly not as eager to face her granddaughter. She was afraid of what she would see when she entered Camille's room.

"Oh, I think she'll let you help her," said Ezekiel. "You just have to show her how much you care for her. Let her see that, Laurel, and she'll let you in."

Mama Laurel wanted to wrap her arms around her old friend. The years had been kind to him, and she believed that he was a good advertisement for clean living. He didn't smoke, drink, eat pork or red meat. And he walked three miles a day, every day. Even when it snowed. He had helped more people than he could remember and he never turned a patient away. Even those who couldn't pay him. At seventy-six years of age, his carriage was as erect as a soldier's, and although his hair was now covered with gray, his face was almost unlined, if you didn't count the wrinkles at the corner of his eyes that came from an abundance of good humor and laughter.

"I should have married you when I had the chance," said Mama Laurel.

He kissed her on the cheek and replied. "It's not too late."

Then he walked down the stairs to give his report to Naomi and Jose.

Mama Laurel knocked on Camille's door and waited for a response before she walked in.

"Come in," Brynne called out. Mama Laurel opened the door and entered Camille's room. The door closed behind her. The room was dark except for the lamp at Camille's bedside. Brynne sat on her sister's bed holding one of her hands. She was talking to her, but she was speaking so low that Mama Laurel couldn't make out the words. Camille lay in bed with her eyes closed and her blanket pulled up to her chin. Her face was swollen and her eyes had two black rings around them.

Mama Laurel felt the ground give way beneath her and she prayed to God that she would not fall down. She needed to be strong for her granddaughter.

Camille opened her eyes and looked over at her grandmother. She said, "I'm sorry."

The strength that Mama Laurel had just prayed for helped her make it across the room to where her granddaughter lay. Brynne moved aside and Mama Laurel took her space on the bed. Her breath caught in her throat as she looked at her granddaughter, whose beautiful face looked like that of a battered prizefighter. She could not imagine the pain that Camille must be feeling, and Mama Laurel fought the urge to cry. She lost that battle quickly.

"Don't cry, Mama," said Camille, speaking with great difficulty through swollen lips. "I'm so sorry."

Mama Laurel shook her head. "You got nothing to be sorry about, baby. I'm the one that's sorry—so sorry that you ever had to go through this."

"My fault . . ." Camille's voice drifted off.

Mama Laurel sat carefully on Camille's bed and held her granddaughter's hand. "Don't let me hear you say that, Camille. This is not your fault—don't take on Harold's madness."

"Will you stay with me until I fall asleep?" asked Camille. "I don't want to be alone."

"I'll be right here, Camille," replied Mama Laurel and she remained sitting on her granddaughter's bed long after she fell asleep.

Twenty-one

Mama Laurel

The next morning Mama Laurel woke up in Camille's guest bed-room. She looked at the clock on the wall and saw that it was seven-thirty. She had intended on getting up at five o'clock to check on Camille. She got out of bed as quietly as she could. She did not want to wake up Naomi. If someone had told her a week ago that she would be sharing the same bed with Naomi, she would have called that person insane. But if someone had told her that one grand-daughter would try to kill herself and another would almost get her-self killed at the hands of a jealous boyfriend, she would not have believed that either.

She left the bedroom and walked down the hallway to Camille's bedroom. This time she didn't knock. Instead, she opened the door and peered in. Camille was still sleeping. Brynne was sleeping in a chair by the window. Mama Laurel closed the bedroom door. It was time to check on her other granddaughter.

Mama Laurel walked down the stairs past a snoring Jose, who was sleeping on the couch. It was the only piece of furniture that seemed to have escaped the full brunt of Harold's fury. Somehow, she knew that Jose would not have left during the night. He loved this family, al-most as much as he loved Brynne. She didn't understand why these two people, who so clearly belonged to each other, were still apart. But it was time to let Brynne work out her own business.

Mama Laurel picked up the telephone on the kitchen wall and dialed Shelly Easington's number.

"Hello." Shelly's voice still had sleep in it.

"Doctor Easington," said Mama Laurel, "this is Laurel Redwood. Sorry to call you so early, but I was just checking on my granddaughter. Any word on how she's doing?"

If Shelly was annoyed at the early morning phone call, she hid her annoyance well. Instead, she replied, "Good morning, Mrs. Redwood. I just got back from the hospital about an hour ago. Olivia was resting. Physically, she seems to be progressing nicely, according to Doctor Trahan and Doctor Singh."

"Has she asked to see us?"

"No, she hasn't, Mrs. Redwood. She has a lot to sort out before she sees you. She's just not ready. I'll see you at two o'clock."

With everything that had happened last night, Mama Laurel had almost forgotten about her appointment with Dr. Easington.

"Will your granddaughters be coming?" asked Shelly.

"I haven't asked them yet," said Mama Laurel.

"Well, if they can make it, that's great. If not, I'll be happy to talk to you and Mrs. Darling."

Mama Laurel heard a beeping sound on the telephone, which signaled another call coming in.

"I've got to go, Doctor Easington," said Mama Laurel, forgetting the doctor's request to call her Shelly.

"See you at two!" said Shelly.

Mama Laurel tapped the receiver to answer the other call. "Hello?"

She could hear someone breathing on the other end of the line.

"Hello?" she said again, annoyed. "Hello?"

The person would not respond. Harold. She knew that he was the person calling, just as surely as she knew that night followed day. She felt her heart start to race as she struggled to contain her rage.

She took a deep breath to calm herself, but her voice still shook when she spoke. "Harold, if you touch my granddaughter again, I will kill you. If you come near her. If you call her. If you even breathe in her direction, I will kill you. That is a promise."

He hung up in Mama Laurel's ear.

Camille

Camille opened her eyes with difficulty. Her head was pounding and it didn't help that the sun was shining directly in her eyes.

"How are you feeling?" asked Brynne, who was standing over the bed looking down at her. Brynne was fully dressed, with her hair combed and her makeup on. She was obviously ready to go face her day.

"I've felt better," said Camille, trying to make a joke out of something she would never be able to smile about. "But all things considered, I could be feeling a lot worse."

I could be dead, she thought.

Brynne sat down on her sister's bed. "You look a little better to me," she said.

"That's because you love me," said Camille.

"And don't you forget it," said Brynne. "Gram Naomi's down there fixing you a big breakfast. Are you up to it?"

Her head was splitting, and her stomach felt as someone had spent a great deal of time kicking it, which, in fact, was the case. Food was the last thing on her mind. "It sounds great."

"Camille, have you given any more thought to what we discussed last night, about going to the police?"

Camille shook her head, and the effort brought fresh pain. "No police, Brynne. I don't want them involved."

She didn't know what she was going to do. It was obvious that she couldn't handle Harold. But she didn't want any more spectators to her drama. It was bad enough that her family was involved. She had to figure out a way to finally get Harold out of her life. Last night when she had awoken to a dark room she had had a lot of time to think about her future. Going to Atlanta would keep Harold away from her. She would make sure that only her family knew where she was. She was running and she knew it, but at this point she didn't care. She just knew that she had to get out of Cleveland and away from Harold before he killed her. She didn't attempt to fool herself that this was an isolated incident that would never be repeated.

"Camille, honey, just think about it," said Brynne. "Will you at least do that?"

"Yes," Camille lied. "I will. Where are you off to so early in the morning?"

"I won't leave you if you don't want me to go," said Brynne.

"Girl, you're dressed and ready to go. I'll be fine."

"Mama Laurel and Gram Naomi will stay with you today," said Brynne. "They're going to the hospital this afternoon, but Jose will stay with you while they're gone."

Camille wanted to tell Brynne that she didn't need baby-sitters, but the truth was that she was glad for the company. And she was afraid that Harold would come back again. "Thanks, Brynne."

Brynne stood up. She was ready to go. She had that determined lawyer look she usually got when she was off to court to give some other lawyer hell.

"No need to thank me, sis," said Brynne. "Just take care of yourself. I called Jim and told him that you wouldn't be coming in for the rest of the week. I told him you weren't feeling well. I hope you don't mind me coming in here and taking over your life."

"Looks like you're doing a better job than me. Did Jim ask any questions?"

"No, but you should talk to him. He's worried."

"I'll call him later today."

Brynne bent over and kissed Camille on the cheek; then she was gone.

Olivia

Olivia stared at the short, brown-skinned woman with her intricate dreadlocks. Shelly Easington did not look like any other doctor she'd ever seen. Except for the regulation white coat, everything else about Shelly screamed nonconformist—from the bright purple nail polish to the multi-colored *kente* shirt, the long, flowing black skirt, and the chunky black boots. Shelly looked more like an African gypsy than a psychiatrist.

"Do you want to get better, Olivia?" Shelly asked again.

Olivia cleared her throat. This was the second time that Shelly had asked her this question.

"I don't know," Olivia finally responded when it was clear that Shelly Easington was not going to leave her alone until she got an answer to her question.

They'd been sitting in Olivia's new hospital room for about half an hour. She had been moved there from ICU. This room was smaller than the other one, with only one small window that faced the parking lot.

Shelly pushed her glasses further down her nose and peered over them at Olivia. "You don't know?"

"No, I don't know," Olivia snapped. The woman was getting on her nerves. She didn't want to be here with this Bob Marley–looking doctor prying into her life. She was tired of talking. She'd been talking to psychiatrists for years now, and what good had it done?

Shelly shifted in her seat as if she were trying to get comfortable. She placed the note pad and pen she was holding down on her lap.

"You don't like yourself very much, do you, Olivia?"

Olivia closed her eyes. *Leave me alone,* she silently pleaded with Shelly. *Leave me the hell alone. You can't help me. My family can't help me. Just stop trying.*

"Talk to me, Olivia," Shelly said.

"Why?" asked Olivia. The question came from deep within her, from somewhere filled with pain. A wound so old that Olivia had long since forgotten its origin. Deep pain that went past the rape, past the death of her parents, past the voices she heard in her head. "Why?"

She was broken. Although fragile to begin with, something inside her was carelessly shattered and now could not be put back together again, no matter how many well-meaning folk came into her life.

"I believe that you want to get help, Olivia."

Olivia sighed. "That's pushing optimism a little too far."

"I've been accused of worse," Shelly replied.

"Look, I know that you're here to help me, but trust me, I'm way past the point where anyone—even you—can help me. I believe that most folks would describe the place I'm at as a lost cause."

"And what makes you so special?"

"Excuse me?" Olivia wasn't sure she'd heard the psychiatrist correctly.

"What makes you so special, Olivia? Why are you so convinced that there's something about you that would prevent you from feeling better? Aren't you tired of living with your pain, your hurt? Aren't you tired of it?"

"Of course I am!" Olivia shouted.

"Then do something about it," said Shelly.

As if it were so easy, thought Olivia. *If I could have done something about this pain, I would have a long time ago. I can't protect myself from the hurt, just as I couldn't protect myself from Ray, from my parents dying, from anything that caused me pain.*

"Do something about it."

Olivia stared into Shelly's eyes. "I did do something about it. I tried to kill myself."

"Is that the only alternative to pain?"

Olivia nodded her head. "Yes."

"You've got that same stubborn look your grandmother Laurel has," Shelly commented. "When I look at you, I see a lot of her in you."

"We're nothing alike," said Olivia, her voice hard.

"She's a fighter, Olivia. Just like you. You could have slipped away, but you fought your way back."

"Is that what I did?"

"Yes, Olivia. That's what you did. You've survived. Even though you've been in pain, you've survived. Maybe it's time to go beyond survival. Maybe it's time to live, Olivia."

Olivia had never thought of herself as being a fighter. She'd never thought of herself as being strong.

"All my life," said Olivia. "All my life, I've been in pain. Even before my parents died. The only happiness I knew was the time I spent with my mother. And then she left me."

"What about life with your sisters?" Shelly asked.

"They tried to take care of me," said Olivia. "Especially Brynne. I looked up to them—still do. It's just that I know I'm a disappointment to them. The only person who wasn't disappointed in me was my mother. I thought Ray . . ."

"Go on," said Shelly when Olivia faltered. "Talk to me."

Olivia took a deep breath. "I thought when Ray first started paying attention to me, it was like my mother coming back to me. I thought that I had found someone who cared about me, who didn't think that I was strange. And then he started messing with me. . . ."

"Messing with you?"

"He raped me, Dr. Easington."

"Do you want to talk about it?"

"No." Olivia shook her head. "It's ancient history."

"Is it?"

"Yes," said Olivia.

"Seems to me that you still hurt."

"What can I do about that?" Olivia asked. "Ray's dead."

"But the pain continues, Olivia."

"Yes, it does."

"Do you talk with your family about this?" asked Shelly. "Do you talk to them about the rape?"

"It would only make them feel pain," said Olivia. "Why cause them any more hurt over a situation that they had no control over."

"What about Mama Laurel? Did you talk with her about your feelings?"

"She doesn't want to hear anything about the rape," said Olivia, tasting the anger in her throat. "Ray was family. Family doesn't turn on family. God, how many times has Mama Laurel repeated that particular saying? Family doesn't turn on family—but she turned on me."

"How did she turn on you, Olivia?"

"I don't want to talk about this," said Olivia. This woman had succeeded in agitating her. She didn't want to think about these things. She didn't want to talk. She just wanted to be left alone.

"Tell me, Olivia," Shelly's voice was gentle, but it was also firm.

"After the rape she didn't support me. She didn't want me to prosecute Ray. She chose protecting the family name over protecting me."

"Have you talked to her about this?" asked Shelly.

"What good would it do?" asked Olivia.

"I don't know what good it would do her," said Shelly, "but it might do a world of good to you. That's a lot of anger that you're carrying around inside."

"Anger. Pain. What the hell is the difference? That's my life, Doctor Easington."

"It doesn't have to be," said Shelly. "And by the way, please call me Shelly."

"What miracle cure do you have for me?" asked Olivia.

"Sorry." Shelly smiled. "I'm fresh out of miracle cures. But if you're willing to work, there might be a way to find your way to a life that doesn't hurt as much."

"Sounds like a miracle to me," said Olivia.

"Whatever you want to call it, the first step begins with telling your grandmother how you feel."

"Why? Nothing's going to change. She did what she felt she had to do. It's over."

"Not for you."

"No, not for me."

"Talk to your grandmother," said Shelly. "Tell her what you've told me."

"It won't change anything," said Olivia.

"Maybe. Maybe not," replied Shelly. "You've got nothing to lose."

"Nothing to lose," said Olivia. "You don't know my grandmother. She is one tough woman."

"You can be just as tough."

"She won't like what I'm going to say to her."

Shelly nodded her head. "You're probably right. But sometimes you have to say things to people, even things that they don't want to hear. It's all in the process called healing."

"Like I said," Olivia commented, "that's pushing optimism a little too far."

Brynne

Brynne got into her car and breathed a sigh of relief. It had taken entirely too long to get out of Camille's house. There was a lot to accomplish today and at ten o'clock she was already late. She had hoped to make it to Roxanne's house by nine. Roxanne lived in Pepper Pike, which was at least twenty minutes away from Camille's house, depending on traffic. She knew that Roxanne had stopped working once she became pregnant, at Harold's insistence. Harold had bragged to all concerned that his wife didn't have to work. Once she became pregnant, it seemed, Roxanne relinquished all rights to pursue her career of choice, a manager of one of the more popular restaurants in downtown Cleveland. Brynne didn't knock any woman who decided to put her career on the back burner once little bambinos came into the picture, but it seemed to her that the woman in question should have the right to participate in this decision.

Roxanne's employment was at the very bottom of Brynne's list of priorities, and as she carefully backed out of Camille's driveway, she banished all thoughts of Roxanne and her career hiatus to another place. She just hoped that Roxanne would be home, and her philandering, wife-beating husband would be someplace else.

If her family knew what she was doing they would have a stroke.

Mama Laurel herself would have stood in front of Brynne's car before she let Brynne go over to Harold's house. Jose had left earlier this morning and she was glad that she didn't have to face him. He might have suspected what she was up to and she didn't want to lie to him. As for Mama Laurel and Gram Naomi, they were too concerned with Olivia's and Camille's troubles to pay attention to Brynne. This gave her the time and space to do what she needed to do.

Brynne pulled out of the driveway and eased onto the main avenue. Turning on the radio, she listened to the news of the day. War. Violence. Political corruption. What else was new? Brynne picked up her car phone and dialed her secretary. "I'm not coming in today," she told her. "Tell whoever is looking for me that I'm unavailable." Then she hung up the phone feeling a little better, a little more confident. She was one of those lawyers who called in to her office at least three times a day even when she was on vacation. Now that she had cut that umbilical cord between herself and W&S, it was a liberating experience, at least until the paychecks stopped coming. *That place took up too much of my time anyway,* she thought as she turned onto Shaker Boulevard, heading toward Pepper Pike, land of the head-turning homes and the people who could afford to buy them.

She drove up Shaker Boulevard past houses whose plots of land grew larger and larger. These homes were set way back from the road and many of them were obscured by large hedges and great old oak trees designed to keep the have-nots, or the haven't-got-it-yets, or the plain-old nosy at a discreet distance. Roxanne and Harold lived on one of the streets just off Shaker. They were the only African-Americans in a two-mile radius, and Harold was proud of that. He had told this to Camille as if it would make his stock rise in price, but it had only subjected him to Camille's ridicule.

"What the hell is so great about being the only Negro around?" Camille had asked.

Exclusivity didn't mean a damn thing when you were in trouble and your neighbors decided not to open their door for you, which is what happened when Harold's car broke down and he wanted to use a neighbor's phone to call AAA. No one opened the door for him, even though they were all home, and Harold ended up leaving his expensive car on the road and walking home to call for help. Still, he would brag, to anyone who wanted to hear, just how exclusive his neighborhood was.

Brynne turned onto Clearwater Street, the street Roxanne and Harold lived on. She hoped that she remembered the house. She had been there once before, a long time ago, before Camille starting messing with Harold. Roxanne had hosted a Links party at her house and Brynne remembered that she had been duly impressed by the house, the grounds, the china, and Roxanne's expensive clothes, all in that order.

She turned into the third driveway on her right, remembering the white stucco mansion with the ivy crawling up around it. The ivy was gone and in its place the vines clung, barren and bare on the sides of the house. Brynne parked her car in the driveway right behind the red Lexus with the ROXY plates. Roxanne was home, thank God. Brynne prayed that Harold was someplace else. His car wasn't in the driveway, but the attached garage door was closed and it was possible that he had parked in the garage. Camille had told her last night that Harold said that Roxanne had kicked him out, but she had done this before and she had taken him back with open arms. Brynne hoped that the reconciliation hadn't taken place yet.

She turned off the ignition and exited her car, closing the door with a slam behind her. Walking quickly up the cobblestone walkway to the front door, Brynne noted that today was the first time in a while that the weather had started to get warm. The sun was shining and she guessed that the temperature had risen to somewhere near forty degrees. A heat wave for Cleveland in February.

She pressed the buzzer at the front door and heard the sound of chimes coming from the environs of the house. She stood there for a while and was about to press the buzzer again when the door opened and she found herself facing Roxanne. She was dressed in a pink terry-cloth robe and was holding a cup of coffee. Her hair was combed and her makeup was applied immaculately. Brynne knew that no matter what the circumstance, Roxanne was a woman who was always going to look her best. Brynne saw that despite the makeup, Roxanne's eyes were puffy and slightly bloodshot as if she had been crying. Her stomach protruded from her otherwise slender body.

"What do you want?" she asked.

"I'd like to talk to you, Roxanne," Brynne replied. "I'm sorry to bother you, but this is important. I would have called but I was in a hurry."

"You knew if you called I would hang up on you."

She had a point. Brynne took a deep breath and started speaking. "I need your help. And I think you need mine."

Roxanne surveyed her for a moment before speaking; then she said, "Good-bye, Brynne."

She stepped back and started to shut the door, but in that moment Brynne stuck her leg in the doorway and prevented the door from slamming shut.

"What are you doing?" asked Roxanne, looking at Brynne as if she had lost her senses.

Brynne was desperate. She saw her chance of winning Roxanne over, a long shot at best, fading quickly. "Roxanne, Harold beat the living hell out of my sister yesterday."

There was another moment of silence; then Roxanne looked at Brynne, her stare hard, and her eyes unblinking. "And I'm supposed to care?"

"Look, I know you don't care for Camille," said Brynne, making the understatement of the year, perhaps the decade. "But you ought to care about yourself. Roxanne, I know that he's been beating you, just like he beat Camille."

Roxanne didn't bother to deny it. "I don't see how that concerns you, Brynne."

"It didn't," said Brynne. "Not until yesterday when he hurt my sister. Now it does."

"I don't mean to sound unsympathetic," said Roxanne, "but why the hell should I care about the woman who broke up my marriage? Did she care when she humiliated me? Did she care that while she was sleeping with my husband, I was sick from carrying his child?"

"All of that is true," admitted Brynne. "And I don't expect you to care about Camille. I don't want you to care about Camille. That's not why I'm here. I'm here because I think that we can help each other."

Brynne sensed a weakening in Roxanne, even though her eyes were still hard and her hand was still on the door. Brynne thought she saw a flicker of interest, or maybe curiosity in those hard eyes.

"Just give me a minute," said Brynne. "Please."

Roxanne opened the door, and stepped to the side, allowing Brynne to come inside. "You've got one minute, Brynne. One minute. I'm only letting you in because I've always liked you. No matter what your sister did to me, you've always treated me with respect."

Thank you, Lord. Brynne breathed a silent prayer as she walked inside Roxanne's house. They stood in the foyer by the door. It was obvious that Roxanne wasn't going to allow her to go any farther into her sanctuary.

"Okay, Brynne. Talk."

"Where's Harold?" asked Brynne, thinking that she should have asked this question before she came inside the house. There was no telling what he was capable of. She had already seen the result of his rage in Camille's pummeled body.

"He's not here, and I'm not expecting him back. Ever. I kicked him out."

"Good for you," said Brynne, as she added silently, *I hope it's for good this time.*

"What do you want, Brynne?" said Roxanne. "The clock is ticking."

"I want you to help us bring charges against Harold."

Roxanne laughed again. This time her laughter reached her eyes. She was genuinely amused at this request. "You've got to be joking, Brynne. This is the father of my child."

"That's precisely why you need to bring charges against him. What if he tries to hurt your child?"

"He wouldn't do that!" Roxanne's laughter stopped immediately.

"Can you guarantee that? Are you willing to bet your child's life on that, because that's what you'd be doing. Betting your baby's life that he'll do right."

"He may be capable of many things," said Roxanne, "but he is not capable of hurting his own flesh and blood."

"Just his wife," said Brynne. "Roxanne, how many times has he beat you? How many times? He's hit you while you were carrying his baby, hasn't he?"

"I think you need to go," said Roxanne, her voice quiet, her eyes on the floor in front of her. "Yes, I think you should leave now."

"I'm going," said Brynne, realizing that she wasn't going to get through to Roxanne, not this morning. No matter what he did to her, Roxanne wasn't going to turn against her husband. Even a husband that had turned his back on her a long time ago. "But if you care about yourself and your baby, you'll bring charges against him."

"What do you care what I do?" asked Roxanne, her voice hot with spite. "You never gave a damn about what Harold did or didn't do to me until your sister got in trouble. Now you're here, offering me advice about my husband."

"That's true," said Brynne. "But no matter what my reasons are, we can help each other. We can put him away so that he won't hurt you, your baby, or my sister."

Roxanne walked past Brynne to the front door and opened it.

"Brynne, I'm sorry about what happened to Camille," she said softly. "No one deserves that, not even her. But I'm not going to put the father of my child in jail."

"You're taking him back, aren't you?"

"No, I'm not taking the bastard back," said Roxanne. "But I'm also not about to put him in jail."

"With or without your help, we're going after him," said Brynne. "I want you to understand that."

Roxanne shrugged her shoulders. "Do what you have to do, but I am not going to be a part of it. My name's been dragged through Cleveland mud long enough."

Brynne walked through the open door; then she turned around and faced Roxanne. "Good luck," she said.

"I don't need your pity, Brynne," replied Roxanne and she shut the door.

I'm not so sure of that, thought Brynne as she walked back down the cobblestone path to her car.

Mama Laurel

Mama Laurel sat in Shelly Easington's office and looked at the diplomas on her wall. Naomi sat in the chair beside her, knitting a bright red sweater that was almost finished. Naomi always had to do something with her hands, Mama Laurel thought. Nervous energy. Not that she blamed her. The morning had dragged and Mama Laurel thought she would go crazy while she waited for morning to turn into afternoon. The entire time that Mama Laurel and Naomi were at her house, Camille had been resting in bed. No one could convince her to go to the doctor and Mama Laurel didn't have the heart to fight with her after everything she had just gone through. So Mama Laurel and Naomi had taken turns staying in the room with her, feeding her, and just making sure that she was as comfortable as she could be.

Whenever Mama Laurel thought about what Harold had done to

her grandchild, the rage she was trying to push away came right back again. She knew that Brynne was right, that getting someone to take care of Harold was not going to solve anything, but it sure would make her feel a lot better. It would go a long way in helping to control the rage that was eating at her.

"I wonder where that doctor is?" asked Naomi, her hands moving in rhythm with the knitting needles.

"I wonder where Brynne is," Mama Laurel responded, knowing that she was fretting. Brynne was supposed to meet them at the doctor's office at two o'clock sharp, but it was two-fifteen and neither Brynne nor Shelly Easington was anywhere in sight. Under the circumstances, Camille had decided not to go to the hospital, although she had made noises about wanting to accompany Mama Laurel and Naomi to Shelly's office. But Mama Laurel wouldn't hear of it. "We can handle this, Camille. You need to stay home and rest."

"Brynne's got a lot on her mind right now," said Naomi. "I wouldn't be surprised if she doesn't make the appointment."

"I just hope that she's all right," said Mama Laurel. "With everything that's going on, I just pray that nothing happened to her."

"I'm sure Brynne is fine," said Gram Naomi. "She's just probably tied up in a meeting or something."

"I wish she were here," said Mama Laurel, still fretting.

Naomi put her knitting down in her lap and looked directly at Mama Laurel. "Why?" she asked. "Why should Brynne be here? We're here. Whatever the doctor tells us, we can tell Brynne."

"I just wish she were here, that's all," said Mama Laurel, knowing that she was sounding defiant and dependent at the same time but she didn't care. Harold was running around on the loose and although he had no reason to try to hurt Brynne, Mama Laurel was still nervous about her.

Brynne walked in just as Mama Laurel was about to call her office. She kissed both of her grandmothers on the cheek and sat down in an empty chair beside Mama Laurel.

"Where have you been?" asked Mama Laurel.

"At the police station," said Brynne, settling into her seat as if it were the most normal thing for her to come breezing in from a police precinct.

"What's going on?" asked Naomi, her voice sharp. "Harold causing more trouble?"

Brynne shook her head. "Not that I know of. I was talking to a friend of mine who's a lieutenant. I wanted to find out the procedure of filling out a criminal assault charge."

"What on earth for?" This time it was Mama Laurel whose voice rose.

"I want to be able to give Camille good advice about filling out a criminal complaint for assault."

"Has Camille agreed to do this?" asked Naomi.

Once again Brynne shook her head. "No. Not yet. But she will."

"As much as she's been through," said Mama Laurel. "I can't say that I blame her. Who would want to go dredging up that awful mess again?"

"What do you propose we do, Mama?" asked Brynne, keeping her voice calm. "Wait until he beats on her again? We did this with Ray, remember? Those results weren't so good."

Mama Laurel felt as if Brynne had just kicked her in the middle of the stomach. Not a day went by when she didn't blame herself for what Ray did to Olivia. But how would prosecuting him have helped Olivia? Hadn't her baby been through enough?

"Brynne, you're out of line," Gram Naomi said quietly. "I know that these are trying times, but your grandmother does not deserve that from you."

"I'm sorry, Mama Laurel," said Brynne. "Gram Naomi's right. I was entirely out of line."

Mama Laurel shook her head. She couldn't speak. Brynne had hurt her badly, but like folks say, "the truth hurts." She should have prosecuted Ray.

There was a knock on the door and Shelly Easington entered the small room. She didn't have her white coat on; instead she was dressed like a regular person. That is, thought Mama Laurel, if regular people wore long, flowing, multicolored skirts that came to their ankles, black boots that looked like they came straight from the army, white, cotton oxford shirts buttoned up to the neck, and had dreadlocks pinned at the top of the head.

"I'm sorry that I'm so late." Shelly sat down behind her desk. "It's just been hectic out there."

"How's Olivia?" Mama Laurel asked. "Is she ready to see us?"

"She discussed talking with you, but I'm not sure she's ready," replied Shelly.

Disappointment covered Mama Laurel like a shroud. "When can we see her?"

"We'll get to that," said Shelly, "but first we need to talk about Olivia and the best way to treat her. I'm sure you all recognize that Olivia has problems, serious problems. Olivia needs help and I think we can give it to her. I think we all can give it to her."

"Are you talking about the family?" asked Brynne.

"Absolutely," replied Shelly. "From what I see there is a lot of love in your family, and Olivia can definitely feed off that. But there is a lot of other stuff also that needs to be worked out. One of the things I'm proposing is a joint counseling session."

"What exactly does that mean?" asked Mama Laurel.

"Mama, please," said Brynne. "Let Doctor Easington talk first and then we can respond."

"Please," said Shelly, "call me Shelly. I think that family counseling is in order. I think the first sessions should not include Olivia; she needs her own intensive therapy. However, I think in time Olivia can join the sessions. I think that it might be a good idea that when Olivia is released, she go to a place where she can have space from the family and deal with her issues."

"Why can't she stay with us?" asked Mama Laurel.

"Mrs. Redwood, I'm sure that you want Olivia to get better, don't you?"

"Of course I do," said Mama Laurel.

"Well, then just hear me out before you reject what I have to say. Olivia needs help, but I also believe that if we work together with her, we can make some real progress. I'm not promising any miracles, but I do hope we can come together and try to see if we can do something different, something that will actually help your granddaughter deal with her problems."

Mama Laurel saw that everyone was looking at her as if they were waiting for her permission to go on with the matter at hand.

"Shelly, what are you proposing?" asked Mama Laurel. "I'm not saying that we'll go along with it, but we'll hear you out."

"Thank you," said Shelly. "There is a place, very near the hospital in fact, that I think would be perfect for Olivia. It's a halfway house about twenty miles outside of Cleveland. It's a lovely facility. It's got a great staff, and I think it would provide her with a safe place until she can handle things a little better."

"Will she be put on medication?" asked Brynne.

"Maybe," replied Shelly. "Nothing real heavy, just some mild tran-
quilizers, in case it's necessary. I would be able to treat her at least
three times a week, and I'd like to see you all once a week, to start.
Maybe as time goes on we can adjust that a bit."

"What do you think, Laurel?" asked Naomi. "I'm willing to try this
if you think it might do some good. I can always rearrange my schedule so I can stay on in Cleveland for a few more weeks."

"That would be helpful . . . ," Mama Laurel replied, "but I hate to
have you be away from your home for such a long time."

"Both Camille and Olivia are going to need a lot of care and attention these next few weeks. I think I can help out, that is, if you don't
have any objection," Gram Naomi continued.

"What do you say, Mama?" asked Brynne, and Mama Laurel realized that she had not responded to Naomi's question.

"You can stay here as long as you like," said Mama Laurel. "You're
their grandmother and they all love you."

"There." Shelly Easington smiled. "That's settled. I'm going to talk
with Olivia later on. She's already expressed a willingness to go to the
halfway house. I think she wants to get better just as much as you all
want her to, but she's scared and she's lost."

Mama Laurel's heart twisted thinking about Olivia. Scared and lost.
Mama Laurel had no doubt that this was true. She prayed that Shelly
would be able to do something for her granddaughter.

"I'd like to start with the group session day after tomorrow. I realize
that this is short notice, but I'm sure you are as anxious for this whole
process to get started as Olivia is."

"I'll let Camille know," said Mama Laurel. "I'm not sure that she's
up to it, but if she wants to come with us, she can. What about you,
Brynne?"

Mama Laurel looked at her oldest granddaughter and wondered
again what was going on with her. There was a serenity to her that
Mama Laurel had not seen before. Mama Laurel stood up, her leg
starting to hurt. She cleared her throat and began speaking. "Doctor
Easington, I mean, Shelly, I know that I've been a little difficult to
deal with but it's just that I'm so worried about Olivia."

That was the closest that she was genetically able to come to making an apology.

Shelly understood. "Don't explain. I can appreciate how difficult
things have been."

"You ain't said nothing but a word." Who used to say that? Antoinette.

How could I forget all the funny comments Antoinette used to say? Whenever she agreed with something, that was the phrase she said. I miss you, baby, Mama Laurel thought. *It doesn't get any easier, even when all these years have passed since I laid you in the ground. It doesn't get any easier at all.*

Brynne stood up. "Thanks for everything, Shelly."

"I haven't done anything yet," replied Shelly, with a wide smile that Mama Laurel found very becoming.

"Oh, but you will," said Brynne. "We've got faith in you. Isn't that right, Mama?"

"Yes, indeed," replied Mama Laurel, who was surprised to find that she meant every word she said.

"I second that," said Naomi. "I'm starting to feel more hopeful already."

Twenty-two

Camille

Camille walked down the stairs in her house and every bone in her body ached. She clenched her teeth as the pains shot through her legs with each step. Maybe she should have listened to her family and gone to the hospital. Something might be broken. But the thought of having to explain to some medical official that she had gotten the stuff beaten out of her by her crazy boyfriend had kept her in her house surrounded by the pain and the vivid memories of Harold's fist coming in her direction.

Jose got up from the couch and walked toward the stairs. He had been watching television and eating a sandwich.

"You've been here since last night?" Camille asked.

"No," Jose replied. "I left for a couple of hours this morning."

"Thanks, Jose."

"How do you feel about getting a lift from me? You look pretty uncomfortable," he said, looking up at her.

"I am pretty uncomfortable," replied Camille. "But I can manage these stairs. Besides, I look worse than I feel."

"That's good," said Jose, smiling as if to take the sting out of his words. "Because you look like hell."

"Thanks a lot," replied Camille, taking each step slowly and carefully, but still unable to avoid the pain that seared through her body like hot liquid. "Believe me, I've seen better-looking men, myself."

"Well, that's a relief," said Jose. "If you can still snap on me, I know that you are feeling better."

"Who were you expecting?" asked Camille when she finally and thankfully reached the bottom stair. "Mother Teresa?"

"No," said Jose as he bent down and lifted her in his arms. "Just my wonderful, difficult, magnificent, ex-sister-in-law. I was not disappointed."

"Jose, I'm not an invalid. I can walk."

"Camille, don't you ever keep that mouth of yours quiet? You're just like your sister. By the way, where were you heading?"

"Nowhere. Anywhere. I just wanted to get out of bed."

He walked over to the couch and placed her down carefully as if she were a fragile piece of glass that could shatter at any minute.

Camille looked around her living room and felt her heart sink. Although someone had done a good job in cleaning up, the room still held traces of Harold's rampage.

"It's going to be all right," said Jose as he sat next to her. "How about something to eat?"

Camille shook her head, her eyes straying around the room, assessing the damage. How could she have fallen so far and so fast?

"How about something to drink?" Jose asked.

Camille shook her head again.

"Camille, I'm not going to pretend that I know how you're feeling. I don't understand how any man could hurt a woman. But I do know that there are places that you can go to talk about this. To people who are trained to deal with this kind of situation."

She knew that he was well intentioned. He meant well. He always did. But there was no way that she wanted to go and talk to some stranger about what happened to her. Her goal was to get as well as she could physically and get out of Cleveland. She would go far away. So far that Harold could never reach her.

The telephone rang. It was perched on the arm of the sofa closest to Camille. She picked the receiver up.

"Hello?"

"Hey, baby girl." It was Harold.

She felt her mouth go dry and she could taste the fear, which was immediate. Her heart was pounding and she tried to get her voice to work. *Leave me alone,* she screamed in her head, but the words did not leave her mouth.

"We need to talk," he said. "Things got so crazy last night. I don't know what came over me. I don't understand it. I love you so much, baby. I just got so crazy. So crazy, baby. And I am so very, very, sorry."

Hang up! the voice inside her head screamed, but she sat frozen, unable to move. The sound of his voice was as strong as if someone had taken a rope and tied her to the couch. She moved her mouth, but nothing came out.

"Camille, are you there, baby?"

Jose took the phone from her.

"Who is this?" he demanded. "No, I don't need to tell you who the hell I am. All I need to tell you is not to call her again. Do you understand? Well, come on with it, Harold. But you should know that I hit back, my brother."

He slammed the telephone down.

"I'm sorry," Jose said to Camille.

Camille found her voice. "Nothing for you to apologize for. I should be the one apologizing for getting you into this mess."

"Don't worry, Camille. He won't be able to hurt you again."

I wish you could guarantee that, thought Camille as she looked at the earnest face of Jose.

"What are you watching?" asked Camille, wanting to change the subject. She didn't want to think about Harold. She didn't want to think about last night. She did not have the strength to focus on what had happened. Not now. She had to get better, physically better. That was her focus.

"One of those talk shows," replied Jose. "This show is on men who've lost the women they love."

"How appropriate," said Camille, before she could stop herself. "Sorry."

"Don't be. This show is appropriate. I can definitely identify with those folk."

"It's not hopeless," said Camille. "Brynne still loves you."

Jose shook his head. "She doesn't want me anymore. When I had a chance to make a difference, I didn't. Now it's too late."

"What happened between you and Brynne?" asked Camille. "I've heard Brynne's side. But what's your side—if you don't mind me asking?"

"I don't mind," said Jose. "I'm not sure what happened. We drifted apart like a lot of married couples. Work. Other responsibilities.

Taking your sister for granted was easy. I took what she wanted for granted. It was all about me during our relationship. I figured as long as I kept the bills paid I was doing okay. So, I disappointed her again and again. I pushed her away. When she started getting too far away, I tried to clamp down. Tried to hold her. Tight. But by then it was much too late. So, I lost the only woman I ever loved."

"You sound just like Brynne," said Camille. "Ready to give up at the first sign of trouble. If you want your wife back, you need to fight for her."

"Fight for her?" asked Jose as if that were some foreign concept.

"Yeah, take a stand. Tell her how you feel. Do whatever it takes to get her back."

"I wish I knew how to get her back," said Jose. "Got any ideas?"

"I have no idea, Jose, but I suggest you start by talking to her. I know that she still loves you and even though love surely ain't enough, it's a damn good start. If I were you, I'd start getting busy trying to get my woman back."

"You make it sound easy," said Jose.

The telephone rang again. This time Jose picked it up.

"Hello," he said, as if daring the caller to respond. He listened for a minute, then said, "Just a minute, I'll see if she's available."

Jose put his hand over the receiver and said, "There's someone named Omar on the phone. Want to talk to him?"

"Yes," said Camille, reaching for the phone. "Omar, are you all right?"

"How are you?" asked Omar.

"Fine," lied Camille. "Thanks for calling the cavalry."

"I just hope the cavalry got there in time," he replied, unwilling to match the light tone in her voice.

"They did," Camille lied again.

There was an awkward silence in which neither party seemed to know what to say.

Then Omar spoke. "If you need anything, anything at all, please let me know."

"Thanks, Omar," Camille said. "I've got to go, but I'll keep in touch."

"Promise me," he said. "Promise me, Camille, that you'll keep in touch."

"I promise."

He hung up with a quick good-bye.

Jose looked at her with one eyebrow raised in speculation. "Seems like a good brother. He's the guy that called Brynne, right?"

Camille answered, "Yes, he is a good brother, and yes, he's the one that called Brynne."

Jose looked as if he was about to say something but at that moment the doorbell rang.

"I swear, it's like Grand Central Station in here. If the phone isn't ringing, then it's the doorbell," said Jose as he got up and walked toward the front door. He looked through the peephole, then opened the door in one swift movement.

A tall man dressed in a green coat and matching green baseball hat stood at the doorway, holding a bouquet of roses. Once again, Camille's throat went dry. She remembered the roses yesterday strewn across her floor.

"Who are they from?" asked Camille. "Open the card."

Jose opened the card, read it, and handed it back to the man in the green coat. "Take them back. We don't want them."

The man in the green coat seemed confused. He was obviously not used to having his deliveries turned down. "I got two more bouquets in the truck," he said.

"Take them back," said Jose. His voice hard. He dug his hand in his pocket and took out some dollar bills. Thrusting the bills into the man's hands, Jose said, "I'm sorry you had to go to all this trouble, man, but we don't want the flowers."

"Jose, let me see the card," said Camille. She wanted to see for herself what the card said, to see why Jose was so quick to shove the card back in the man's hands. She wanted to know exactly what it was that caused the alarm to spring immediately into Jose's eyes.

Jose shook his head. "Camille, you don't need to see this."

"Jose, please," said Camille. "Let me see the card."

She watched as Jose took the card from the man in the green hat and walked over to her. He handed her the card, still shaking his head. "Camille, you don't need to see this. Trust me."

Camille took the card from his hand and saw that it was written in Harold's precise handwriting: *You can run, but you can't hide from my love, Harold.*

She did not want Jose to see her fear. She did not want him to see just how the card upset her. She forced her face to remain impassive, even as she thought to herself: *I have to get the hell away from here.* She handed Jose the card. "Thank you."

Jose pushed the card into his pocket and told the man in the green uniform that he was free to go on to his next delivery. He left quickly. Whatever trouble he had gone through in delivering the bouquets was apparently forgotten upon the sight of the dollar bills Jose gave him.

"What are you going to do?" Jose asked her, after shutting the door. "He's not going to let you go."

"I'll think of something," said Camille. "Don't worry about me."

From the look in Jose's dark eyes, Camille could see that Jose wasn't taking her advice.

Naomi

Naomi, Brynne, and Mama Laurel walked up Camille's driveway. Naomi felt as if someone had literally lifted a burden off her shoulders. Talking to that Shelly Easington had been therapeutic for her. Shelly seemed to be in control of the situation. She also seemed compassionate. Compassionate and in control. Two good qualities that would go a long way in helping Olivia. Naomi was sure of it. Now, they had to deal with Camille's situation. One thing was certain, thought Naomi, Camille was through with that man. At last. She was just sorry that it took what it did for Camille to open her eyes and see what it was she was dealing with.

As they got to Camille's front door, Brynne turned around and looked at something across the street. Naomi watched as Brynne's eyes widened, then grew hard. Naomi turned and followed Brynne's stare. She recognized the car across the street. Harold's.

"What is he doing here?" asked Brynne, her voice low, her face furious.

Mama Laurel turned and looked over to where Harold's car was. In the same spot that Naomi first saw it. Across the street, parked by a giant oak tree. "You know what he's doing here," said Mama Laurel. "He's not content to break her body; now he wants to break her spirit."

"Camille needs to file a complaint against him," said Naomi.

After everything that he had done to Camille, Harold still had enough nerve to sit outside her house. He ought to have been hiding somewhere. Ought to have been consumed with shame for what he did, afraid to show his face now that he had revealed himself for the monster that he was. Laurel was going to have to get over her aversion to what the neighbors would say. Her granddaughter's life counted for more than that. And Naomi didn't fool herself for one minute into thinking that anything less was at stake than Camille's life. The way that man attacked Camille left no doubt in Naomi's mind that Camille was lucky to walk away with her life. Naomi didn't know if Camille would be that lucky the next time, and Naomi had lived on this earth long enough to know that there was always a next time.

"I'm going to give him a piece of my mind," said Mama Laurel.

"Save your breath, Mama," said Brynne. "Nothing you or anybody else can say will have any effect on that lunatic. The only person he'll listen to is a judge. If things work out the way I hope, he'll be having that conversation with the judge sooner than he would ever expect."

"Let's go inside," said Naomi. She was getting tired of standing outside in the cold staring at the man who had changed her granddaughter's face into a mass of cuts and broken flesh. It made her feel weak, ineffectual, staring at Harold. Made her feel her age. If she had been younger and more foolish, maybe she would have tried to do something. Even if all she did was let loose on some of her favorite curses. But standing here, letting the anger surround her and threaten to consume her, made her think for the first time in her life that she had lived too long.

"I'm with you," said Mama Laurel. "The sight of that man is making my stomach turn."

Brynne used her keys to open Camille's front door. Naomi used to think that it was obsessive and downright strange on Laurel's part to insist that she and her granddaughters all have keys to one another's homes, but Naomi thanked the Lord that Brynne had Camille's house key last night. She didn't want to think about what would have happened if Brynne had not been able to get into Camille's house.

Laurel followed Brynne, and Naomi entered the living room last. Camille and Jose were sitting on the couch watching television. Although the swelling in Camille's face had lessened, her face still looked distorted. Her features were now all exaggerated, her nose had swollen to twice its normal size, and so had her lips. There was an ugly gash that split her lip, and her eyes were still encircled with black rings. There was a nasty bluish-looking bruise on her left cheek. She looked as if she had been to hell and back, or more appropriately, as if she had stared at the devil. And in fact, thought Naomi grimly, she had.

"Harold's outside," said Mama Laurel, skipping right past "Hello, how are you?"

Naomi watched as the blood seemed to drain away from Camille's face. She grimaced as if she had just felt pain, and Naomi's heart constricted with love and fear for her granddaughter.

Brynne walked over to where Camille was sitting and sat on the floor next to the couch. "How are you feeling?" she asked Camille.

"I've felt better," replied Camille.

"We need to call the police," said Gram Naomi.

"I'll go outside and talk to him," said Jose.

Camille shook her head. "No police. He'll go away. He's just trying to make a statement."

"What statement?" asked Naomi, trying to keep the exasperation she was feeling at bay. What was it going to take for Camille to realize that this man meant business? He was not going to stop until he got his way, or he hurt her again. "That he'll put you in a coffin the next time?"

Camille seemed to shrink within herself. She looked at her feet, and Naomi thought for a moment that Camille was going to cry. Naomi felt instantly ashamed. After everything Camille had been through, she was only making her feel worse. "I'm sorry, Camille," she said quietly. "I had no cause to talk to you like that."

"Everybody's nerves are on edge," said Mama Laurel in an attempt to calm things down.

Brynne asked her sister, "Would you at least consider calling the police?"

"No, Brynne. I'm sorry, but I can't. I just have to figure out a way to work this thing out on my own. I don't want the police involved."

"That's settled," said Mama Laurel, as the telephone started ringing.

"Don't answer it, Mama," said Camille. "Please."

"You can't live as a prisoner in your own home," said Brynne, holding her sister's hand. "Besides, we've got your back, sis."

The phone continued to ring.

"Well?" asked Mama Laurel. "Should I get the phone?"

Camille picked it up and said a tentative hello. Naomi watched as relief settled over Camille's face like an old friend. It was obviously not Harold.

Camille handed the phone to Mama Laurel. "It's Shelly Easington. Olivia wants to see you."

Naomi tried not to let familiar feelings of envy get at her. Laurel had raised Olivia and it was only natural that Olivia would ask for Laurel. She watched as Laurel carried on a short, animated conversation with Shelly Easington. From what she overheard, Laurel was heading back to the hospital to talk to Olivia.

"Glory be," said Mama Laurel as she hung up. "Jose, can you give me a ride to the hospital?"

"My pleasure, Mama."

"Naomi, I'm sure that she'll want to talk to you next," Mama Laurel said, almost apologetically. "But Shelly says that there are some things that Olivia wants to say to me that she doesn't feel comfortable talking about in front of the family."

"Give her my love," said Naomi, putting her feelings of disappointment away. She wanted to see Olivia.

"Mine too," said Brynne.

"Give her all of our love," said Camille.

"I will deliver all the messages," said Mama Laurel, who was now standing up and putting on her coat. She walked over to the door, where Jose was waiting. Jose opened the door and looked outside.

"Looks like Harold has gone away," he said.

"Let's hope it's for good this time," said Naomi, even though she knew that she was engaging in wishful thinking.

"I'll be at the hospital if you need me," said Mama Laurel as she rushed out the door, bundled up in her bright red coat.

After Jose and Mama Laurel left, Brynne stood up and said, "I don't know about the rest of you all, but I'm hungry. I'm going into Camille's kitchen and I'm not coming back until I've prepared something to eat."

"I'll help you," said Naomi, who had remained standing by the window, looking outside as Jose and Mama Laurel drove off in a hurry.

Brynne wouldn't hear of it. "Sit on that couch with Camille and keep her company. And that's an order, Gram Naomi."

Twenty-three

Olivia

O livia heard someone knocking on the door to her hospital room. "Come in," Olivia called out, expecting to see one of the several nurses that routinely checked up on her.

Mama Laurel opened the door and walked quickly into the room. Olivia had never seen fear in her grandmother's eyes, but she saw it clearly now. She watched as Mama Laurel walked over to her bed.

"Praise God," said Mama Laurel as she grasped Olivia's hand. "He brought you back to us."

"Please sit down, Mama," said Olivia. It was time to talk with her grandmother. A small burden had lifted from Olivia's heart when she'd talked with Shelly Easington. Shelly had helped to ease the feelings of guilt that weighed so heavily on her mind. Her talk with Shelly had given Olivia the strength to take the next step—to talk with Mama Laurel. Yes indeed, it was time to have this conversation with Mama Laurel. This conversation was long overdue.

Mama Laurel sat down in a chair next to the hospital bed.

Olivia took a deep breath. "Thanks for coming. I wasn't sure you were going to. . . ."

"Of course I would come to see you Olivia. I've been at the hospital most of the time you've been here. What kind of a thing is that to say to me?"

Olivia took another deep breath. This was going to be much harder than she'd thought. "I know how much I upset you, Mama. I just thought that by now maybe you'd be plain old sick of me and my drama."

"Olivia, you are my blood. I would never turn my back on you."

Blood. The same words Mama Laurel had used to describe Ray when she told Olivia not to prosecute him. Blood.

"What does that mean, Mama?" Olivia asked. "That whole thing about us being blood. What does that mean?"

"It means that family counts for something. In this world, that's all you can depend on—your family."

"Families let each other down all the time, Mama," Olivia said quietly.

Mama Laurel leaned back in her seat. "Go ahead, Olivia. Say what's on your mind. I know that you blame me for what Ray did to you. God knows I blame myself."

"I don't blame you for Ray raping me," said Olivia. "I blame you for not supporting me once you found out what he did."

The anguish in Mama Laurel's eyes found its way into her voice. "What else could I have done for you, Olivia? I took you to the doctor. I tried to get help for you. What else could I have done?"

"You could have listened to me, Mama. I wanted to testify against Ray. . . ."

"You were just a child," Mama Laurel whispered. "After everything Ray put you through, I couldn't let him put you through *that*. You don't understand, baby. People talk. Once folks found out about what Ray did to you, then they'd talk about you . . . nasty gossip . . . ruin your reputation."

"Whose reputation, Mama?" Olivia's voice rose. "Mine or yours?"

Olivia watched as tears rolled down Mama Laurel's cheeks.

"I thought I was doing the right thing. I thought that I was protecting you."

"Mama, I was raped. What words can anyone say to hurt me after that? You were more concerned with keeping secrets to protect your own reputation, but keeping secrets hurts, Mama. It hurt me."

Mama Laurel was crying now. "What good would it have done to bring shame to you, Olivia? Don't you know that's what would have happened? People would always talk about you. You'd always be tainted by what Ray did to you. I wanted to spare you from that."

"The shame should never have belonged to me, Mama Laurel. I didn't do anything to make Ray rape me. The shame belonged to him, but you never understood that."

"No, Olivia, you're wrong. It was my shame too. I brought Ray into the house."

"I needed you to stand by me, Mama. I needed you to allow me to testify against him. Do you know how many nights I lay awake wondering if Ray was doing to some other little girl what he did to me?"

"I'm sorry, Olivia."

"This is how I still feel, Mama. Abandoned. Dirty. Unwanted. Ray's death didn't change anything. Maybe it made things worse for me—because I wanted him to pay for what he did to me and he got off easy, if you ask me. He got off easy."

"God will take care of him," said Mama Laurel.

"That's true," said Olivia, "but God put me in your care, and you turned your back on me, Mama Laurel. When you told me that I shouldn't go to the police because blood doesn't turn against blood—what do you think you were doing to me? Didn't my blood count, Mama?"

"Yes," she whispered. "Your blood counts, Olivia."

"I don't want to hurt you, Mama. I just want you to understand what it is I feel—what it is I'm going through—and why I took those pills to escape my pain. You didn't cause me to take those pills. Even Ray—he didn't cause me to do what I did. He contributed to the pain, but it was my decision. I can't live with the pain anymore, Mama. I can't live with the lies. I was raped. It's not a dirty little secret that only the immediate family and my therapists know. It's something that's real to me. It's something that I will never forget. It is a part of who I am, and I am tired of hiding it, as if this were my fault. I didn't rape myself, Mama Laurel. Ray did."

"I'm so sorry, Olivia. I don't know how to say it any other way. I don't expect you to forgive me, but I want you to know how sorry I am. I didn't want the scandal that would come with prosecuting Ray—but not for the reason you think. I couldn't care less what so-called society folks think of me; they don't put bread on my table. What I couldn't bear was folks knowing that I couldn't protect you from something so horrible, so vile. I didn't want people to know that I failed. I'm sorry, baby."

Olivia lost track of how long they sat there in her small hospital room, wrapped in silence, each person dealing with her own pain. She felt Mama's hands on her arm. Her touch was light, tentative—as if she were afraid of Olivia's reaction.

"All I can ask is your forgiveness," said Mama Laurel, "for the wrong that I did to you."

"I'm not ready to forgive just yet," Olivia replied, "but I'm working on it. That's the best I can do for now."

Mama Laurel wiped the tears from her face. "Then I'll take whatever I can get, Olivia. I'm a woman of faith, and I have faith that one day you will forgive me, but until then, I'll take whatever I can get."

Camille

Camille stared at her image in the bathroom mirror, and tried to find herself in the face of the battered stranger that looked back at her. She tried to find the spirit of the woman who had existed a few days ago, a woman who would never run from a man, who would have fought back and not lay cowering on the floor, whose spirit refused to broken or questioned. Did that woman ever exist? Camille wondered. If she had existed, at what point did she go away and at what point was she replaced by this person whose unrecognizable features stared back at her in the bathroom mirror?

She had deliberately avoided looking at herself until this moment. She had bypassed the mirror, and turned her head quickly whenever she caught a glimpse, a reflection of the face of the monster that was staring back at her. This face was the stuff of children's nightmares. In an effort to cheer her up, Brynne had informed her that she looked much worse yesterday, and Brynne was sure that she would look much better tomorrow. The eternal optimist, Brynne. Brynne was right that the scars would heal. The swelling would go down. The bruises would eventually fade. But would the woman that she believed herself to be, would that woman ever return?

Did she want that woman back? After all, that was a woman who could sleep with someone else's husband, and not give that act a second thought. A man she didn't love. A man she was with first for the excitement, the feeling of power, being with someone she wasn't supposed to be with, someone who everybody said was off-limits. Her decision to be with Harold was a declaration of her independence.

Independence from society. From her family. From somebody else's concepts of good and bad. Or, so she thought, back then. In time, she began to realize that her relationship with Harold had less to do with independence and more to do with boredom. She was bored with her supposedly perfect life, her perfect job, looks, house, family. Harold provided her with what little excitement she found in her life and even then, the excitement did not last. Excitement quickly gave way to habit. It was easier to be with Harold than to go out there, with the rest of the women looking for Mr. Right, or at least Mr. Right for the Night. True, there was no shortage of men who tried to claim her attention, but Camille had no interest in them. And she didn't have the strength, or whatever quality it took, to fake the interest.

The only other man who had interested her in the last two years was Omar, and he was not her type and she was not going to waste time trying to make a fit with someone whom she knew she could never be with. A high-school music teacher with a son did not possess the principal quality that she wanted. Cash, and lots of it. She supposed that there were folks who would call her money hungry. Brynne had hinted as much but she loved Camille too much to come right out and say it.

There was nothing wrong with wanting to be with someone who could provide her with the better things in life. It wasn't as if she wasn't out here hustling to attain that dream: to be financially secure. She couldn't see being with someone who couldn't provide her with all the things she wanted. She knew that Omar was not a poor man. He was hard working. Middle class. Solid middle class. But Camille was aiming for the upper class. The class with a whole lot of money. Omar could not provide her with that.

Camille leaned over the bathroom sink, and a memory she had long suppressed came back to her. As a child she used to force herself to throw up after every meal she ate. She would stuff herself with as much food as she could. Ignoring her mother's comments about gluttony and weight control. She would eat until her stomach hurt. Her mother tried to help her lose weight, by not giving her cookies and sweets. But Camille would take her allowance and buy chocolate candies. Her favorites. She would eat the candies in the solitude of her room. Then she would go to the bathroom and throw up. No one in the family knew about this, except for Brynne, who kept her secret until Camille was sixteen.

At that time, Brynne told Camille that she would tell Mama Laurel if Camille didn't get help, or Camille didn't stop. Camille had forced herself to stop. Getting help would have meant getting Mama Laurel involved, and Mama Laurel already had a low opinion of her, and Camille didn't want to bring anything to her attention that would confirm Mama Laurel's feelings. Camille stopped the purging. By then she had discovered diet pills and exercise and she had become the slim woman her mother had always wanted her to be. Brynne had been proud of her, and she had kept the secret all these years.

She wanted to force herself to throw up. She wanted to hurt herself, to hurt the woman that allowed a man to kick her, bite her, scratch her, punch her—to hurt this woman so badly that she would never show her face again. She would retreat to wherever she came from. Camille leaned over the sink, closed her eyes, and put her index finger on her tongue. Release was coming.

"Camille, are you all right?" Brynne knocked on the bathroom door. "You've been in there a long time."

Camille opened her eyes and saw herself in the mirror. She saw a woman with a finger stuck in her mouth. A desperate, unhappy woman. She saw herself. She turned on the water and rinsed her face, the cold water stinging the cuts that had not yet healed completely.

"Camille, is everything okay?" Brynne called out, still knocking on the door.

Camille turned off the water and dried her face. The desire she had a moment ago to hurt herself, to purge, left her as suddenly as it had come.

"Open this door, Camille, or I'll break it down."

Camille walked over to the door and opened it. She saw Brynne's worry leave her face and relief replace the other emotion.

"I'm fine," said Camille, "and I'm hungry. Whatever it is you're cooking down there smells good."

"I cooked some stewed ginger chicken and rice. And don't you dare tell me anything about a diet, either."

"Don't worry," said Camille, closing the bathroom door behind her, "I am going to clean my plate."

"I baked a pie for dessert. You've got to eat that too."

"Works for me," said Camille, realizing that she was indeed very hungry.

"It's sweet potato. Your favorite."

"Have mercy!" said Camille, watching her sister's eyes grow with pleasure. Cooking was a matter of pride to Brynne. She hardly ever cooked, but when she did, whoever she cooked for was in for a culinary experience. "How did you know that sweet potato is my favorite pie?"

"There's not much that I don't know when it comes to folks that I love," replied Brynne.

Life was full of near misses. Camille had come close to falling over the brink. She had gone to the edge of that cliff, but her sister, Brynne, had once again pulled her back, just when she was about to fall right down into the abyss. She knew that her ordeal was far from over. Long after the cuts healed, she would still be wounded. Harold had stripped her pride away, and the shame she felt might never leave her. But for now, for this moment, Brynne had helped her get through this particular fire.

Twenty-four

Brynne

Dinner was over and the dishes were cleared away. It had been difficult for Brynne to watch her sister try to eat her dinner. From the effort that Camille was making, it was clear that she was still in a great deal of pain, so much so that the simple act of eating could not be accomplished without a struggle. Brynne watched as Camille's hands shook each time she raised the fork to her mouth. Sometimes the tremor in Camille's hands was barely noticeable. Other times, her hands shook so badly that whatever food she had managed to get on the fork would fall to the plate by the time the fork reached her mouth. Camille chewed her food slowly and deliberately, but Brynne could see that this was a difficult process.

Any conversation Brynne and Gram Naomi tried to engage in during dinner eventually gave way to an uncomfortable silence. At one point, Brynne almost offered to help feed Camille, but she knew that any offer of assistance would be refused, and cause more damage to Camille's pride than she had already suffered. Gram Naomi, who apparently reached the same conclusion that Brynne did, stared at her plate for the rest of the meal, and concentrated on eating and avoiding looking at Camille. Mama Laurel had called them twice from the hospital, checking up on Camille. She had decided to spend some more time with Olivia.

"Tell Mama Laurel that I'm fine," Camille had said, but anybody could see that she was far from fine, and in Brynne's eyes, it would be a long time before Camille would be fine again.

After dinner, Gram Naomi and Brynne cleared the table and washed the dishes. "What are we going to do about this?" Gram Naomi had whispered to Brynne in the kitchen. "We can't just sweep away what happened to Camille, like we did with Olivia," she continued.

"No, we can't," said Brynne. She had known all along the specific course of action she was going to take, but she knew that taking this action might place her directly against Camille's wishes. Gram Naomi raised the very point that Brynne had been thinking about.

"I am not going to repeat history," said Brynne, not aware that she had spoken those words out loud.

"What?" asked Gram Naomi.

"I'm going to call Roxanne and see if she'll help us if we decide to press charges against Harold."

"Are you crazy?" Gram Naomi whispered furiously. "That woman would never help you testify against her own husband, no matter how sorry the son of a bitch is. She's already told you she wouldn't help you, and why should she after what Camille did to her?"

"You're probably right, Gram," Brynne agreed. "What you say makes perfect sense, but I'm still going to try. All she can do is say no and she's already said that. We don't have anything to lose. Maybe if Camille sees that Roxanne will testify against Harold, she'll change her mind and go to the police."

"That's the craziest thing I've ever heard," said Gram Naomi, shaking her head.

"Maybe so, but I'm going to call Roxanne."

Brynne was surprised that she was calm when she dialed Roxanne's number. Gram Naomi did have a point. This was not only crazy, but it bordered on harassment. The woman had already told her once today to leave her alone.

Roxanne answered the phone on the second ring. Her voice sounded breathless, as if she had just finished a strenuous exercise session. "Hello?"

Brynne took a deep breath and began talking. "Roxanne, it's Brynne. I'm sorry to disturb you. But we need to talk—"

Roxanne interrupted her. "Oh, it's you!" Her voice sounded friendly. Too friendly. And artificial. "Thanks for bringing those plants by today! And that gardener you wanted me to call, why don't you call him for me? Even though it's winter, I sure could use the advice! Tell you the truth, my yard really needs a lot of help!"

What on earth was she talking about? thought Brynne, wondering if everyone she encountered in this life eventually lost their mind. What flowers?

"You tell that gardener that I really need his services as soon as possible!" said Roxanne, talking fast now. "You know my plants are like my own babies, and I'd do anything at all to protect my babies."

There was a saying that Mama Laurel would use often. "I might be slow," she would say. "But I'm always on time." Brynne realized what was going on.

"Roxanne," said Brynne, "is Harold there?"

"Oh, yes!" said Roxanne brightly. "I've heard good things about your gardener. I just hope that you didn't exaggerate about his services. Anyway, I can't talk anymore, I've got company."

"Roxanne, I'm calling the police and I'll be right over."

"Thanks," said Roxanne. She hung up the telephone.

Brynne dialed 911 and gave the police operator Roxanne's address. She explained the situation as quickly as she could to the operator and then hung up. She walked quickly out of the kitchen as her mind raced through all the things that were probably happening at Roxanne's house, all of them bad. She knew from Roxanne's reaction earlier during her visit that Harold had beaten her during the pregnancy. A woman's belly swollen with his child did not offer Roxanne any protection from Harold.

"What's wrong?" asked Gram Naomi, as Brynne rushed into the living room.

"I'm going over to Roxanne's house," said Brynne, without slowing her pace. "Harold's there."

"Let the police handle this," said Gram Naomi. "Don't get involved. You know what this man is capable of."

"I've already called the police," replied Brynne, putting on her coat. "And it's because I know what Harold is capable of that I'm going over there."

Camille got up from the couch. "I'm going with you."

"What!" Gram Naomi could barely get the words out of her mouth. "Camille, have you completely lost your natural black mind? After what that man did to you! I won't allow it! And, Brynne, it's bad enough that you're getting yourself involved in this, but how could you drag your sister into this mess?"

"Camille, stay here with Gram Naomi," said Brynne, on her way to the front door. "I'll be back as soon as I make sure everything's okay." Camille walked behind her. "I said, I'm coming with you."

Brynne turned and looked at her sister. Camille refused to back down. The same stubborn look that was as much a part of Mama Laurel as the mole on her left cheek now seemed equally at home with Camille.

"I don't have time to argue with you, Camille," said Brynne, losing her patience quickly.

"Who's arguing?" asked Camille. "I'm coming with you. I'm not letting you go there alone. If the situation were different, would you let me go alone?"

That clinched it for Brynne. "Get your coat and hurry!"

"I'm coming too!" said Gram Naomi. "I'll be damned if I let you two crazy women face that man alone!"

Camille

By the time they arrived at Roxanne and Harold's house, there were two police cars parked out front, and an ambulance. Brynne had driven like a demon from hell, and the normally twenty-five-minute drive from Cleveland Heights to Pepper Pike had taken a little over fifteen minutes.

"You all stay in the car," said Brynne. "I'll handle this."

Camille looked out of the car window, as Brynne walked up to two policemen standing by the open front door. She watched as Brynne spoke to them, and although she had no idea what Brynne said, she had no doubt that it would do the trick. For someone who spent a lot of time complaining that she didn't like the business of law, she did that business quite well and she was impressive at it. Camille watched as the officers stepped aside and Brynne walked inside Roxanne and Harold's house.

From the grim looks on the faces of the two officers, whatever had occurred inside that house was not good. One of the officers walked down to where Brynne's car was parked. He was a short, squat man in his late forties. His face was reddened from the cold.

"I told your sister that this car has to be moved to the sidewalk. It's blocking the ambulance," he said.

"What's going on?" asked Gram Naomi.

The officer shook his head. "Her husband beat the crap out of his wife. And she's pregnant, poor thing. I don't know what gets into people."

"Is she going to be all right?" asked Camille.

"She'll live," said the officer, looking at Camille with open curiosity.

Camille averted her gaze to avoid the officer's curious eyes. She knew that she looked as if she had gotten beat up, or had been in an accident.

"What about the baby?" asked Gram Naomi.

"That's the problem," said the officer, his attention diverted from Camille's battered face back to the present situation. "The mother's water broke, and it looks like the baby's coming."

"It's three months early," whispered Camille. She remembered how Harold had bragged to her about Roxanne's due date.

The officer tapped the car on the hood. "Let's get this car moved out of here. They're taking the mother to the hospital."

The mother. Camille had never thought of Roxanne in those terms before. As somebody's mother.

"Where are they taking her?" asked Gram Naomi.

"Pepper Pike Baptist," replied the officer. "That's the closest hospital. I just hope they make it there in time before that baby comes."

Camille climbed over the armrest and sat in the driver's seat. Easing the car into reverse, she backed out of the driveway and parked across the street; then she got out of the car.

"Where are you going?" asked Gram Naomi.

Camille whispered a prayer. *Please, God,* she asked. *I don't know if you listen to the prayers of sinners, but please let Roxanne and the baby be okay.*

Camille stood by the front gate and watched as two paramedics carried Roxanne out on a stretcher. Roxanne was covered with a blanket up to her chin, and although Camille could hardly see Roxanne's face, she could hear her screams clearly. Brynne followed behind the paramedics and Camille could see that she was crying. Camille watched as the paramedics carried the stretcher into the back of the ambulance. Brynne climbed in after them and then the door to the ambulance was shut.

The sound of sirens wailed through the air, and the ambulance was on its way. Then Camille watched as Harold was led outside the house by two other officers. One of them was a black woman, and she was shaking her head from side to side in disgust. The other officer, a young white man with bright red hair and a face full of freckles, was holding Harold's arm as he walked toward the police car. His face mirrored the disgust on his partner's face.

Harold was handcuffed and sobbing.

"I didn't do it," he kept repeating. "I didn't do it."

The woman officer opened the back door to the police car, and her partner helped him get inside the car.

"I didn't do it." The words floated across the frigid air.

By now a crowd of the curious and the concerned had gathered in the street by Harold's house. Pepper Pike was one of the exclusive suburbs that had distinguished itself by not having any sidewalks. Camille ignored the presence of the onlookers and kept her gaze on Harold. As the police car pulled out of the driveway slowly, Harold looked out of the window at her. There was no feeling of triumph for Camille. Seeing the defeat and the fear in Harold's eyes as he looked at her did not give her a sense of vindication, or a sense of retribution. The feeling she felt was the same as that of everyone else who had looked at him as he was being led away by the police, disgust.

Camille hoped that Roxanne would have the courage to do what Camille was now determined to do. To press charges against him, so that no other woman would have to scream in pain the way Roxanne had screamed moments before. She watched until the police car carrying Harold away turned the corner and disappeared from view. Then she walked back to Brynne's car, where Gram Naomi was waiting for her.

Twenty-five

Brynne

Brynne sat in the ambulance and held Roxanne's hand. An oxygen mask was clamped over Roxanne's nose and mouth and her eyes were wide with either fear or pain, Brynne couldn't tell which. She leaned over and whispered in Roxanne's ear, "Have faith, Roxanne. Have faith."

Brynne wished again that Pastor Simmons were here. He always knew exactly what to say and how to give comfort. Everything that came out of Brynne's mouth was inadequate and sounded forced to her own ears.

Roxanne's eyes rolled upward and she grimaced in pain, squeezing Brynne's hand. This time, Brynne knew that the fear that Roxanne told her she was feeling just before they took her to the ambulance had given way to something much more basic and immediate—pain.

"Another contraction," said one of the paramedics, looking at a monitor that kept track of such things.

"Hang in there, Mrs. Bledsoe," said the paramedic. "We're almost at the hospital. We'll be there soon."

The other paramedic was examining Roxanne. He did not look happy. "This baby's coming," he kept muttering. "This baby's coming."

Roxanne lay on the stretcher, her body bucking with the contractions, which appeared to be coming every minute and a half, or so the paramedic keeping track said. Brynne looked down at Roxanne, and once again her heart twisted with anger and pity at the sight of Roxanne's face. Her left eye was blackened and swollen almost shut. Her mouth and her nose were bloody. Like Camille, she carried the scars of battle.

All the time they were examining Roxanne back at the house, she had kept asking about the baby. "Don't let me lose my baby," she had cried. "Please." The only other request she had made was that Brynne accompany her to the hospital. Brynne had been surprised by the request, but she knew that Roxanne was scared, and she was not going to turn her back on her.

"If I'm going to die," Roxanne told her during one of the times the contractions were not tearing at her body, "I don't want to die with strangers. Come to the hospital with me."

Brynne's heart flooded with pity. Roxanne was not an easy person to get to know or to like. Even before the whole Camille mess, Brynne had found her to be pretentious. Her claims to fame were her looks and that she had married well. And although Roxanne was known for her lavish parties, which were just as much the talk of upwardly mobile black Cleveland as her husband's philandering, Brynne never knew Roxanne to have many women friends. Roxanne had nobody to be with her. Just the sister of the woman who until recently had been sleeping with her husband.

"You're not going to die," said Brynne, "and you're not going to be alone in the hospital. I'll be there with you."

Harold had been in the next room being questioned by the police. The woman officer who stood with Brynne while the paramedics treated Roxanne told Brynne that Harold hadn't asked about his wife's condition or the baby's while he was being questioned. Instead, he went through various stories about how his wife ended up with a broken nose, a bloody face, and a battered body. First, he said that they were fooling around and it got too intense, whatever that meant. Then he said that Roxanne's injuries were self-inflicted. He told the police that Roxanne was trying to get back at him for leaving her. When he was asked about his bloody knuckles and torn shirt, he said that Roxanne attacked him. Finally, he kept repeating that he was innocent. He threatened to sue everyone in his house, even the paramedics who were working to save his child and treat his wife.

Brynne shook her head. Harold's time of reckoning would come soon enough. Roxanne squeezed Brynne's hand again. Hard.

"This baby's coming. This baby's coming!" the paramedic examining Roxanne snapped at the other paramedic as if the current state of affairs were his fault.

Roxanne pulled the oxygen mask off her face and let out a long scream. The paramedic pushed Brynne to the side abruptly. "Hang in there, Mrs. Bledsoe!" he bellowed.

But Brynne could see, as Roxanne rocked back and forth, her face contorted from the pain, that Roxanne was in a place where no one could reach her.

Mama Laurel

Mama Laurel sat on Camille's living-room sofa with Naomi. Camille was sitting on a pillow on the floor and Jose had gone to the hospital to be with Brynne.

"I'm pressing charges against Harold," said Camille, looking directly at Mama Laurel.

Mama Laurel replied, "I'll support any decision you make, Camille."

"Maybe if I had spoken up earlier, Roxanne wouldn't be in the hospital, fighting for her life and her baby's right now," said Camille.

"Lord, I just hope that she and her baby make it," said Gram Naomi.

"Whatever the outcome with Roxanne," said Camille, "whatever she decides to do, or not do, I'm going to the police station tomorrow and I'm going to file a criminal complaint of assault against Harold."

"I'll go with you," said Naomi.

Mama Laurel thought about the conversation she had just had with Olivia earlier at the hospital, about facing the truth no matter how painful. Well, decided Mama Laurel, it was time to put her money where her mouth was. "I'll go with you too, Camille."

Mama Laurel leaned back in the sofa and closed her eyes. Life was about to get more difficult. But maybe, just maybe, life would become a little bit better as a result.

Twenty-Six

Brynne

Brynne sat in the waiting room in the obstetrics ward with Jose. They sat with their shoulders touching and Jose was holding her hand. She had not questioned his appearance in the waiting room, shortly after she herself had arrived. Instead, she was just grateful for his support. Roxanne's baby was born three hours after they had arrived at the hospital. Brynne was not allowed in the room when Roxanne gave birth, but one of the nurses had come to the waiting room to tell her that the baby was born.

A little girl, said the nurse, which was good. The nurse had declared that the girl babies were born fighters and after everything the baby had been through, being a fighter was going to go a long way in helping that baby to survive. She was three months early and slightly over two pounds. That was all the nurse could tell her.

What a way to come into the world, Brynne told Jose. Having to fight just for your own existence. It didn't seem fair, right, or reasonable that a two-pound baby was handed this responsibility.

Nothing wrong with being tough, Jose had replied. Tough folk had the better odds when it came to surviving, and right now that was the fight that Roxanne and Harold's baby was facing—survival.

The doctor taking care of Roxanne came out to talk to Brynne and Jose. He told them that Roxanne was doing as well as could be expected, and that the baby had a very good chance of survival. That was the best he could offer and Brynne was happy to take it.

"The baby's in the neonatal ward," the doctor said to Brynne. "Mrs. Bledsoe would like to see you."

Brynne followed the doctor down the hallway, past two sets of automatic doors, turning down another short hallway. The lights in the hallway were muted, but the ward whose blue walls were painted with puffy white clouds from floor to ceiling looked downright cheerful. The entered the second door in the short hallway, where Roxanne lay in bed with her eyes closed.

She was dressed in a hospital gown, and there was an IV machine hooked to her arm.

"Mrs. Bledsoe," said the doctor, "I've brought you a friend."

Roxanne opened her eyes and looked at Brynne.

"I can see that," she said.

"I'll be around in a few minutes," said the doctor. "I'm going to check on your little one."

"Thank you," said Roxanne.

After the doctor left, Brynne walked over to Roxanne's bed.

"Thank you," Roxanne whispered.

Brynne shook her head. "I wish I could have done more."

"You saved my life and you saved my baby's life," said Roxanne. "There's nothing more you could have done for me. I'm grateful, Brynne."

"I did what was right," said Brynne. "Anyone else would have done the same." She was no hero here. The only reason she had come to Roxanne that morning was to help her sister. She hadn't been able to help her sister, and she had been too late to help Roxanne suffer the same pain that Camille felt.

Roxanne's lips curved into a soft smile. "No, Brynne, many people would have walked away."

Brynne did not know how to respond.

"I held my baby, Brynne," Roxanne continued. "Just for a second. But she's just beautiful, Brynne."

"Is there anyone you want me to call?" asked Brynne.

Roxanne shook her head. "The nurse has already called my mother. She and my sister are coming up from Columbus tomorrow. They should be here soon. When things get better with me and the baby, we're moving back to Columbus."

"Sounds like a good idea," said Brynne.

"Would you do me a favor, Brynne?" asked Roxanne. "Would you call Pastor Simmons? I want him to come and bless the baby."

"Sure," said Brynne. "Have you thought of what you're going to call her?"

"As a matter of fact," said Roxanne, "I have. Her name is going to be Faith Brynne. Do you like it?"

Brynne's face spread into a wide smile. "Are you kidding? I love it! No one's ever been named after me before."

"Well, she's named Faith for obvious reasons, and then I named her Brynne for the woman who saved her and her mother."

"I'm honored," said Brynne, and she was. Touched. Honored. Happy. Humbled. All those things, rolled up into one big smile.

"Can the police come to the hospital tomorrow so I can give a statement?"

"I'm sure they can," replied Brynne.

"Good," said Roxanne. "I'm pressing charges."

"It's the right thing to do," said Brynne.

Brynne spoke with Roxanne for a few more minutes; then she saw that Roxanne was getting tired. She left her with a promise to return the next day to visit with her. Neither of them mentioned Camille, and Brynne knew that whatever good feeling Roxanne felt toward her would never be extended to Camille. Too much water under the bridge. Brynne had no doubt that one day, maybe a long time from that night, but one day, Roxanne would forgive Camille, but she also knew that the hurt Camille caused her would never be forgotten.

Brynne walked back to where Jose was sitting. In his hands he had two bouquets of flowers.

"Who is the lucky woman?" asked Brynne.

"Women," replied Jose. "Roxanne gets one bouquet, and the woman that I love gets another."

Brynne sat down on the seat next to Jose. "The woman that you love?"

"Yes," said Jose, handing her the flowers. "The woman that I love."

"Jose, what are you saying?" asked Brynne, wanting to make sure she understood.

"I'm saying that I let you go without a fight—I can't change that, but I can fight for you. I can fight for us. I love you and I know that you love me. I want you to be my wife, but I know it's not what you want. You don't trust me. I know I have to earn your trust. Camille told me to fight for you, and I think I'm going to take her advice."

"Jose, I'm not ready for anything except friendship right now," said Brynne.

"Then I'll be the best friend you ever had, Brynne."

Brynne leaned over and kissed her ex-husband on the lips. She had wanted to do that for a long time, but she didn't have the nerve until now. She did not know what the future held for them. She didn't know if they could beat the odds and forget the past. But she was willing to try.

"I'm dating someone else," said Brynne.

Jose smiled at her. "Hopefully not for long."

Brynne grinned at her ex-husband. "Hello, friend."

Twenty-Seven

Brynne

"So where are you going to go?" Phil Canzilotta sat in Brynne's office and looked around at all the boxes of files to be transferred.

Brynne had already packed up all her personal belongings in the office, which didn't amount to much. A few family pictures, her diploma, her portable CD player, and some law books. It all fit in one box. It didn't seem real that she was leaving W&S. Up until the point when she had handed in her resignation letter, there was a part of her that felt that she would change her mind any minute. But any minute had not come; instead, her firm resolve to do something different with her life became stronger and stronger and, eventually, irresistible.

"I don't know what I'm going to do," said Brynne. "I've saved enough money to allow me a few months of doing nothing but thinking about the possibilities, and that's what I intend to do."

"What about working with Reggie?" asked Phil.

"I'd only be trading one master for another," replied Brynne. "I've decided at the age of thirty-six that it's time to find myself. Find out what Brynne wants, really wants out of life."

"Any ideas?"

"No," said Brynne with a laugh. Times had changed, that was for sure. "But when I find out, I'll let you know."

"Your grandmother is going to hit the roof," said Phil.

Brynne had to agree with that. "Both of my grandmothers are going to hit the roof; then they'll get over it. Eventually. I hope."

"Are you scared?" asked Phil.

"Absolutely," replied Brynne.

There was a knock on the door and Brynne cleared her throat and tried to sound authoritative. "Come in," she said.

The door opened and Winston Gray stuck his head in the door. This was unprecedented. Winston Gray never came to associates' offices. Hell, he never came to his partners' offices either. Brynne watched as Phil sat up in his chair, as if every part of his body were saluting Winston Gray.

"Mind if I come in?"

Brynne cleared her throat again. "Please come in," she said.

Phil got up quickly and said good-bye. Winston gave Phil a quick glance, but Brynne could see that Winston was preoccupied with other matters. Phil left the room without further comment.

Winston Gray walked in and seemed to suck the air right out of the office. He sat down, crossed his legs, and faced Brynne with an unblinking stare. He didn't beat around the bush. "I think you're making a mistake. I think you're making one hell of a mistake."

Brynne remained silent and concentrated on breathing.

"No matter what our differences are, Brynne, you're a good attorney. You're a smart attorney, and leaving W and S would be a stupid move. There are no other firms in this city, hell, in this state, that are as well respected as our firm. We are quite simply the best. Anywhere you go, and I mean anywhere, would be a step down. A significant step down, I might add."

You're preaching to the converted, thought Brynne. *All my life I've been grooming myself for everything W and S has to offer and it's going to be damn hard to give that up.* And that paycheck. Brynne didn't know who would cry the loudest once the paycheck was gone, Brynne or her accountant.

"I'd like you to take the time to make sure that you've thought this thing through, Brynne," said Winston.

"This is the right decision for me," said Brynne. "This is not the life I want to lead."

Winston shook his head. "Brynne, you're an asset to W and S. I would hate to think that my temper forced you out. I have a lousy temper. I lost friends and family because of it. Hell, I lost two wives. What I'm trying to say is that I'm sorry."

Brynne wondered if she had heard Winston correctly. He had just apologized to her. Winston, the man who made mere mortals tremble in his presence. Winston, the man who decided the fate of all concerned at W&S. Winston, the man who did not speak to her unless he had something belittling to say. Winston was apologizing to her.

"I accept your apology," said Brynne, "but no offense, Winston, I don't want to spend the next twenty years of my life in this law firm. I want something different, I just don't know exactly what it is that I want. Did you know that I was a pretty good sculptor once? Maybe it's time for me to find out just how good I really am."

Winston stood up. Brynne could tell from his eyes that he had accepted her decision, even if he didn't agree with it. "I'd like to see your work sometime."

He sounded as if he actually meant it.

"Thank you," said Brynne.

"Wherever you go, Brynne," he said, "you can count on me for an excellent recommendation."

Now doesn't that beat all? thought Brynne. *Just when you thought that you had a person all figured out, they do something to show you that you don't know a blessed thing when it comes to other folks.*

"Thanks," said Brynne. "I appreciate it."

"You can always come back to W and S if things don't work out," said Winston.

It was just on the tip of her tongue to tell him not to count on that, but Brynne held the comment back. Instead, she smiled like a woman with a secret and said, "You are too kind."

Camille

Camille sat in Pastor Simmons's office and tried to think of something appropriate to say. Nothing came immediately to mind, so she said, "I know that you're as surprised as hell to see me here."

Pastor Simmons sat behind his desk, cleared his throat, and smiled at her. "Well, I wouldn't put it quite that way, but yes, I am surprised and quite happy, I might add, to see you."

You can't be half as surprised as I am, thought Camille. She was not particularly religious. She believed in God, but that was the extent of things. Being in church made her nervous. After all the stuff she did, she half expected that a bolt of lightning would hit her the moment she walked through the church doors. Church was an obligation forced on her by her grandmother. It was not a place to which she willingly came.

But lately she had begun to have more questions with no particular answers. Camille knew that Brynne talked with the pastor a lot. She wasn't sure if Brynne got any answers, but she always came away feeling better after those talks. Camille thought she'd settle for just feeling good for a little bit, even if the pastor couldn't help her in any other way.

Earlier that morning she had gone down to the police station with Brynne. She had spoken to a very understanding policeman and she had sworn out a complaint of assault against Harold. Harold had been released on bail after his arrest for beating his wife. He had tried to call her once, but after that he had left her alone. Camille had no illusions that Harold would leave her in peace without a fight. He was merely lying low, licking his wounds, going around telling everyone that his wife was lying. Brynne had seen him last week in a restaurant with some woman. Maybe the woman hadn't heard about Harold and his wife-beating ways. Or, maybe she had heard, just like Camille did long ago, and had chosen to ignore the information. God help her, thought Camille.

"I'm not an evil person, Pastor," said Camille, as if to explain herself to him. She wanted him to know that. She wanted everyone to know that, including herself.

She had gone through life not giving a damn and she had still ended up hurt. The very state of mind she had wanted to avoid. Now, she did give a damn. About herself. About her family. And she wanted to set things right. To start over. To clean the slate. But she didn't know how.

Camille took a deep breath. "I've done some things," she said. "Things that I'm not proud of."

Pastor Simmons nodded his head, but reserved comment.

The tears came to her eyes before Camille could stop them.

"But I want to change, Pastor Simmons," she whispered. "Honestly, I do. I just don't know how the hell—sorry—to go about it."

Pastor Simmons got up and walked around his desk. He pulled up a chair next to hers and handed her a tissue.

Camille wiped her eyes and blew her nose. "Do you think people can change, Pastor Simmons?"

"I know they can, Camille," he said, looking into her eyes.

"How do they change?" ask Camille.

"They have faith," replied Pastor Simmons, as if that made sense.

Camille didn't understand what faith was, or how someone got it, and she explained that to the pastor.

"Well, now," drawled Pastor Simmons, as if he were getting ready to preach on a Sunday morning, "you dig down deep enough, I suspect you'll find that faith you're looking for."

"Pastor Simmons, you are confusing the hell—sorry—the heck out of me," said Camille.

"Tell you what," said the pastor. "You come to church on Sunday and I'll lay it all out for you."

Camille wiped her eyes again. "Is this your way of getting me to church next Sunday?"

Pastor Simmons smiled at her and said, "I see that your confusion is starting to clear."

Twenty-eight

Mama Laurel

Mama Laurel woke up with the sun shining directly in her face. She had fallen asleep in the chair in Olivia's hospital room. Sitting across from her, Naomi was knitting a sweater for Camille, and Olivia was reading a magazine. They had come early this morning to visit Olivia, who Mama Laurel was pleased to see was in good spirits. The psychiatrist, Shelly Easington, had cautioned Mama Laurel that Olivia still had serious problems to overcome, but for the first time in a long while, she saw a change in Olivia. It was as if she was finally ready to fight her demons, even if she was not certain about the outcome of the battle.

Mama Laurel felt a sharp spasm in her chest. Her heart again. Had she remembered to take her pills today? With all the excitement going on around her, she just might have forgotten. Dr. Reynolds, her doctor for the past forty years, had warned her about forgetting to take her medicine, but Dr. Reynolds thought that he had been put on this earth just to nag his patients into submitting to his view on things. *Sounds familiar,* thought Mama Laurel. *I've been accused of that and more.*

"It sure is hot in here," said Mama Laurel.

Olivia looked up from her magazine. "Are you hot, Mama? I can turn down the heat."

Mama Laurel nodded her head. She was suddenly out of breath. Old age, she thought. She felt the beads of perspiration on her forehead, and on her nose. Her new blue and gold silk blouse that she had just bought at Kaufman's clung to her damp skin. Maybe she should have taken those pills.

"Laurel, are you all right?" Naomi's voice sounded as if it had come from far away.

Mama Laurel looked at her and tried to nod, but instead she felt a wave of nausea overwhelm her. "I think I'm going to be sick," she said.

She stood up from the chair, and she was surprised by how weak her legs felt. She was dizzy and the heat surrounding her was overwhelming. The room was starting to spin slowly around her.

"I need to get my pills," she said out loud. Her handbag was on the windowsill.

"I'll get it, Laurel," said Naomi, standing up. "You sit down. You don't look so good."

Mama Laurel ignored her and walked slowly toward the windowsill. Her heart medicine was in there. She never left home without her pills, although she often forgot to take them. Once she took her medication she would go down to the cafeteria and have something to eat. That would make her feel a whole lot better.

Mama Laurel took another step toward the windowsill and then she fell to the floor, knocking over Olivia's untouched food tray. Olivia and Naomi rushed to her side.

"Mama!" Olivia called out in alarm.

"Don't move, Laurel," said Naomi. "I'm going to get a doctor."

Mama Laurel looked at the two faces staring at her. She was going to miss them, even Naomi. She had come to know her too late, it seemed. Lord, but she was going to miss her family, her precious girls, her granddaughters.

"I'm dying, Naomi," said Mama Laurel, her voice weak.

"Don't talk foolishness, Laurel," said Naomi, but Mama Laurel could see that she was scared. "I'm going to get the doctor!"

Olivia started crying. She held Mama Laurel's hand.

"Will you stay with me, Olivia?" Mama Laurel asked. "I need you. I'm not scared, but I need you to be with me."

Naomi knelt beside them. "Laurel, I've called the doctor. You just hang on."

The door opened and two doctors rushed in, followed by a nurse. "Please clear the room!" one of the doctors barked.

Mama Laurel grabbed Naomi's hand, ignoring the doctors.
"If anything happens to me, take care of my babies," said Mama
Laurel.
"Don't you worry," said Naomi. "I'll take care of them."

Olivia

Olivia sat in the waiting room in the coronary care unit at
Cleveland Med. She was tired of staying in her hospital room. Brynne,
Camille, and Gram Naomi were in the room waiting with her. Mama
Laurel had suffered a fainting spell. She was doing better, but she'd
given the whole family a scare. The doctors in the coronary unit were
examining her. There had been some concern that her heartbeat was
irregular. But, all things considered, it could have been a lot worse.
    Brynne shook her head. "I'm afraid to ask, but what next?"
    Gram Naomi chuckled. "I was beginning to wonder the same
thing. . . ."
    "Mama Laurel needs to start taking her heart medication regu-
larly," said Camille. "And I think we're going to be the ones who have
to make sure that she doesn't backslide."
    "What do you mean 'we'?" Brynne asked. "Last time I checked, you
were on your way to Atlanta."
    "I'll get to Atlanta some day," said Camille. "But I think I'm going
to stick around Cleveland a little while longer. Besides, what would
you all do without my daily drama?"
    Olivia looked at her sisters and felt something unfamiliar, but won-
derful. She felt connected. She felt as if she were a part of a circle, a
circle of warmth that included her. She looked at her sisters teasing
each other, and Gram Naomi, who was sitting in the corner shaking
her head at something outrageous Camille said. Harold had hurt
Camille, but he hadn't broken her. Olivia admired that. She'd let Ray
break her, but maybe she could rebuild what was broken. With help.
With a lot of help. With the help of her family.
    A nurse came into the waiting room.
    "Mrs. Redwood is resting. She'd like to see you. Her tests are fine,
but she is going to have to slow down a bit and take her medication.
The doctor will talk more to you about that."
    "That's great news," said Brynne.

"What would the world be like without Mama Laurel?" asked Camille.

Olivia found herself speaking up. "Let's hope we never find out."

Maybe forgiveness for Mama Laurel wasn't going to be too long coming. After all, what good was it to hold on to all that bad feeling? Mama Laurel couldn't change the past. But there might just be some hope for a different ending, no matter how bad the beginning might have been.

"I hate to ask you folks this," the nurse continued, "but is Mrs. Redwood always this difficult? She's in the hospital room giving orders—even to the doctors."

Olivia heard the laughter ring out in the waiting room and was surprised to find that her voice had joined with the others' laughter. Maybe, Olivia thought, just maybe.

newwies
stooped
1-800221-1713